BLOOD LIES

Also by Marianne Macdonald

BLOOD LIES

A Dido Hoare Mystery

Marianne Macdonald

THOMAS DUNNE BOOK
St. Martin's Minotaur ⚔ New York

THOMAS DUNNE BOOKS.
An imprint of St. Martin's Press.

www.minotaurbooks.com

ISBN 0-312-28305-9

First published in Great Britain by Hodder and Stoughton
A division of Hodder Headline

First U.S. Edition: August 2002

10 9 8 7 6 5 4 3 2 1

NOTES and ACKNOWLEDGMENTS

Residents of south-east Somerset might think they half recognise the setting of this book in the countryside between Wincanton and Wells. However, I would like to make it clear that (with the possible exception of the real-life Mr Spock, who was born in a village resembling Alford) all the characters like the events described are entirely fictitious. 'Alford' is a ford on the River Al where an ancient hamlet grew up around a manor house. 'Monksdanes' is a real name, though an entirely fictitious building; but like some actual great houses in England, it is a nineteenth century building on foundations going back through medieval and Viking times. There is a good deal about Alford that is as true as I can make it to contemporary life in the English countryside.

I would like to acknowledge Linda Grant's account of the illness from which Lawrence Waring suffers in her moving book, *Remind Me Who I Am, Again*. Thanks are also due for help, encouragement, information, suggestions, and proof-reading of all kinds to the usual suspects and more: Eric Korn, Sandra Macdonald, Merilyn Moos, Alex Wagstaff, and especially Andrew Korn, who is a good editor; and to my agent, Jacqueline Korn, and my editors at Hodder, Sara Hulse (to whom I owe thanks for working so hard on this book) and Carolyn Mays; also to certain TeaBuds who helped me over a setback.

CONTENTS

CONTENTS

'Now, my dears,' said old Mrs Rabbit one morning, 'you may go into the fields or down the lane, but don't go into Mr McGregor's garden; your father had an accident there . . .'

Beatrix Potter
The Tale of Peter Rabbit

CHAPTER ONE

Looking for the Dead End

I'm Dido Hoare. I am a self-employed dealer in antiquarian and good second-hand books, and I live in the flat over my shop in a side street in North London, although the place isn't big enough to swing a cat. The cat in question would be my ginger tabby, Mr Spock, and I can't really imagine that anyone would risk swinging a cat who is so sure of himself. The third and youngest resident is Ben. I'm a reasonably honest, hard-working person and I always mean to lead a quiet life, if only for his sake. And maybe some day, by popular demand, I'll learn to mind my own business. But I doubt it.

I was driving down to Somerset with Ben that Monday afternoon at the beginning of May. Lizzie – my old friend, Lizzie Waring – had rung me out of the blue a few days before, claiming that she just wanted to talk. Lizzie was my best friend when we were growing up next door to each other in Oxford, but I hadn't seen her for three years, not since I'd gone to her wedding; and when she had gone through the 'just-wanted-to-catch-up' stage and added, 'Dido, we mustn't lose touch like this: why don't you come down to Alford for a visit? You and the baby? There's lots of room, and I'd love to have you stay,' I'd jumped at her invitation. I had my own reasons, though I didn't admit that at the time.

We had crossed the grasslands of Salisbury Plain on the old

road to the south-west. Past Stonehenge, somewhere among all those little roadside village with old names, Wylye and Hindon, Chicklade and Mere and Zeals, my mobile phone burbled. Virtuously, I pulled into a convenient lay-by before I dug it out of my bag. The screen said that the call was coming from my father's telephone.

I took a deep breath. 'Hello, Barnabas. What are you doing at home? Are you all right?'

'Of course I am. However, nothing was happening at the shop. Ernie was reduced to dusting the books on the top shelves. So when the printers phoned to say that the catalogues won't be with us until tomorrow afternoon, I suggested that he might profitably go upstairs and do a little studying for his exams. Then I gave up and came home for a nap.'

I waited: something in his voice said there was a reason for this call.

'When I got here, I found the second post waiting. There is a letter from Diane.'

I said faintly, 'Diane?'

'Yes – *Diane*. Our old friend, Diane Harper. The friend who now lives in Harrogate. Your friend Lizzie's mother. Diane.' His voice faded, and I took the opportunity to glance at Ben in the child seat behind me. His eyelids fluttered but remained closed. Seventeen months old now, he was still astonished by everything in the world: motorways, buses, crows, fields . . . a hundred miles of excitement had exhausted him.

As usual, I broke first. 'Barnabas, what's going on? Did you tell her I'm going to stay with Lizzie?'

'No, oddly enough I hadn't thought to report your plans. I had assumed you and Lizzie capable of managing your own affairs. This appears to be an entirely independent approach. "Appeal", perhaps I should say, rather than "approach"?'

'Appeal?' I echoed feebly. 'Perhaps you could just read out what she says?'

Barnabas cleared his throat unnecessarily. *"Dear Barnabas"* blah

blah *"just wanted to ask whether you – or Dido at a pinch – could possibly help me out, as I'm growing anxious about Lizzie . . . can't put my finger on it, but when she phoned last weekend she sounded very odd, and I'm wondering whether there is some trouble with Mickey, or that dysfunctional family of his down there in the back of beyond, and of course as usual,"* blah, *"but I know there's something she's keeping from me, so I need someone I can trust to pop down and make sure she's all right. Otherwise, I'll have to go myself, although my doctor doesn't recommend the train journey, with my arthritis, but"* blah; Diane's sentence structure always leaves something to be desired.'

I said, 'Blah?' stalling for time, and then remembered, ' "Dido at a pinch"?'

'You must recall that Diane's cynicism regarding the younger generation is even greater than mine. But I too am starting to wonder whether your abrupt and uncharacteristically sensible decision to take the holiday which I have been urging on you daily since . . . well, February, has anything to do with what Diane detects?'

I said, quite accurately, that I had no idea what he was talking about. Then I wondered. Then I attacked. 'All she said was that she'd like my company for a while, so I don't see what the fuss is about – you know what a fuss-pot Auntie D always used to be. Of course I'll make sure Lizzie's all right. All right?'

I could almost hear my father's brain cells firing up. He said abruptly, 'Will you phone me as soon as you get there?'

'I'll ring at about nine this evening. By that time I may be able to tell you something, if there's anything to tell. You'll be at home this evening? If I'm really going to get down there by teatime, I want to get moving again.' I switched off but didn't pull out into the traffic.

The road atlas was lying open on the passenger seat beside me: we had to turn off the main road a few miles ahead, so this was a good place to sit for a while and wonder. I'd been a little evasive with Barnabas. Perhaps Lizzie had been evasive with me? I tried to remember our last conversation. I was starting to get a vague feeling I'd noticed something at the time . . . nothing in

3

particular, maybe just a tone of voice, an occasional awkward silence . . . Telephone conversations can be misleading: sometimes you need to see the other speaker face to face. And perhaps I hadn't been paying enough attention.

I was killing two birds with one stone.

It had been a bad winter, and Barnabas had been nagging me to get out of London for a change. As naggers go, my father wins prizes for his gritty persistence. Ever since his retirement from Oxford he has spent half his time helping me to run my bookshop, half his time researching English love poetry of the sixteenth century, and half his time keeping an eagle eye on my personal life, in which his intentions are benevolent though sometimes heavy. If that adds up to more than twenty-four hours a day — well, he's an energetic man, and very difficult to keep secrets from, especially when he gets a bee in his bonnet. I'd finally accepted it. I was going away not just to renew old ties but to relax and clear some cobwebs, get rid of the nightmare which came from something last winter I could do without thinking about all the time. Lizzie's invitation had seemed like a bit of luck. But now I wondered.

By four o'clock we were on a narrow secondary road skirting the market town of Castle Hinton, running between rows of small, tree-shadowed, ivy-grown stone houses: a landscape of limestone and dappled sunshine. Ben was still napping, blissfully relaxed, with his blond head lolling. I probably had a soppy maternal smirk on my face. Ben makes me happy.

When the road swung around the shoulder of the hill and the ground fell away steeply to the right, I pulled into a gated entrance to take a look. Black and white cows dotted the field below the road. At the foot of their steep pasture, railway tracks reached a station, split temporarily into the multiple lines of a freight yard, and then pulled themselves together and continued westward towards Yeovil and Exeter. I could see commuter cars parked by the station building in rows. The road flung itself down the hill, made a wide loop across the tracks west of the station, and then bent north again into the lush fields of a small river valley, with a line of hills across the northern horizon. Nothing moved under the afternoon sun except the grazing cows.

It all looked so quiet that for a moment I felt a pang of doubt – I'm a city girl, that's clear. Then I got hold of myself. I was here for Lizzie, but also for some of this country peace. Rest, recuperation, a mending of some edgy nervousness in myself.

'Cow!' a pleased voice announced.

'Cows,' I said automatically, and glanced behind me. Ben was suddenly wide awake again, bouncing forward against the straps of his seat.

'*Cow!*' he urged. I laughed, 'Later – soon!' and reached for the atlas, knowing by experience that the time had come when Ben needed to arrive somewhere quickly. Tucked into the book was the sheet of paper with notes I'd taken from Lizzie's telephoned instructions: *Railway station on right, turn left at pub, Woolpack. Fingerpost down but either of next two turnings OK too. About a mile, then past bus shelter, next left into side road, sign on corner says Dead End. Green in front of tin chapel . . .*

I explored the route with my eyes. I could make out a substantial building about a mile away which had to be the Woolpack. 'Five minutes,' I promised Ben. 'Nearly there.' And set us rolling downhill.

The Woolpack was a freshly painted white building on the main road with a big, empty car park. I turned beside it and was in another world: a narrow lane, ambling between ditches and edged by straggling hedgerows. Most of the fields beyond the farm gates were tangled with dandelions and long grass. A track opened to the left, rutted and overgrown, and I drove past it cautiously, half expecting to see a herd of cows or a farm tractor lumbering towards me. I was just starting to wonder where Alford was hiding when a second lane came in from the right and we swept together around a bend. Then suddenly I was driving past a big, red-brick house with ponies grazing in the field beside it, and then another, and beyond them was the grey stone of older buildings. I couldn't see a name-sign anywhere, but slowed to a crawl past a bus shelter. A fingerpost, as promised, identified the next road as 'Dead End'. I sounded my horn and turned in.

'Dead End' was lined with a mixture of old stone cottages, Victorian brick houses, and apple trees pink with blossom. *This is what you mean by a chocolate-box village*, I thought, and felt myself smile. We rolled past a roadside stand of lilacs, tall as saplings and thick with blossom. Some distance beyond them was an intrusion. I'd been curious about Lizzie's reference to a tin chapel, but there it was: a high-sided building with a stumpy tower, its walls covered with sheets of corrugated metal painted dark green, with a row of windows cut into the shape of Gothic arches, as though the builder had been having a laugh. The green in front of the chapel, where the lane circled an oval of rough grass, was surrounded by eight or ten cottages. Carefully, I edged my nearly new, deep-purple, multi-purpose vehicle (seven passengers with luggage, or a book dealer's everyday load of tat if the seats were folded) on to the narrow grass verge in front of a long stone building topped with a television satellite dish and a heavy growth of ivy. The vines had almost obscured the stone plaque above the door, which read: The Barton 1702.

I switched off the engine. There was nobody in sight. When I opened my door it was so quiet that I could hear the wind.

CHAPTER TWO

Seeing the Cows

I sat at the square pine kitchen table and watched Lizzie light another cigarette. She'd quit smoking five years ago, and if I'd been counting – and maybe I was – this was the third time she'd lit up, taken a drag, grimaced, and stubbed it out.

She had been preoccupied ever since our arrival, or at least after the first few minutes of greetings and hugs and cups of tea (or orange juice) in the kitchen, when I'd thought that everything was all right after all. I'd suggested unloading the van, but she swept that aside: Mickey would do it when he got home from work, and no, of course he wouldn't be too tired. Then she'd started to fidget around the Rayburn – a huge black iron cooker with a fire rumbling deep inside its belly – shifting casseroles in and out of various ovens and stirring the stock-pot that sat on a big back plate and not looking at me. Even *I* know that stock-pots are full of liquid and probably don't need that much stirring owing, as Barnabas would have commented if he had been there, to the effects of heat convection within the liquid. She hadn't stopped chattering about Ben, and asking questions about Barnabas's health that didn't need answers because we'd covered this ground days ago on the phone. Auntie D had been right to worry.

Lizzie had changed: she looked a good deal older than the person I had last seen leaving on her honeymoon. She was only just my senior, and she'd kept her weight down; but suddenly there were lines in the middle of her forehead and at the corners of her mouth, and grey threads in her smooth, well-shaped brown hair. She and Mickey Waring had married late, and maybe giving up a banking career in Bristol to move to a village and be a country housewife didn't really suit her. Maybe her mother was right and the marriage was in trouble. Or maybe it was some problem that I couldn't even imagine, because by no stretch of the imagination would anybody as bright as Lizzie Waring have invited me down for a bit of marriage guidance counselling.

I pulled myself together. 'Lizzie, what is it?'

She reached for the cigarettes and stopped herself. 'I'm just not sure I should have asked you to come, I don't know how I can explain—' She stopped, giving an impression of somebody stuck in fast-drying cement.

Ben said distinctly, 'Cows.'

Maybe if we wandered out into the sunshine she'd relax and this would get easier. I said, 'I promised him we could see some cows when we got here.'

She was looking at Ben with an expression that I couldn't interpret. 'He's interesting, isn't he . . .' She hesitated, visibly changed her mind about something, and went on, 'I do know where there are cows.'

Halfway back along the lane was a field with a barred gate. After his first look, Ben pressed back hard against my legs and stared. A semicircle of ten or a dozen large, lively, interested beasts were gathering. They stamped, lowered their heads, and examined us closely through the horizontal bars of their gate. I put my hands down softly on his shoulders and said, 'There: cows.'

'Actually,' Lizzie said behind me, 'they're bullocks. That's why they're acting this way. Dido, are they frightening him? Should we walk on?'

So this in fact was a gang of teenage bovine hooligans? One

of the lads bounced, stamped, lifted his tail, and let out what seemed a never-ending stream of yellow liquid. The warm animal smell deepened. When I bent over to look, I discovered that Ben's eyes and mouth had formed three big Os in his face, and the pressure on my legs let up as he took a step forward. 'I think he's just surprised,' I observed. 'They're a lot bigger than our cat. I must take him to the zoo to see elephants when we get home . . . *Lizzie, just tell me what's going on!*'

She held out a hand to Ben; solemnly he grasped it, and we all slid back on to the hard path at the side of the road and looked at each other cautiously.

'How did you know? I can't, that's the point. Dido, maybe I'm just imagining things.'

I brought out my big stick. 'I'd better warn you that your mother has written to Barnabas. Apparently when you last spoke on the phone she decided there was something you weren't telling her. She's delegated Barnabas and me to investigate and report back. She's threatening to come down here herself.' The look on Lizzie's face almost stopped me, but I hardened my heart and added, 'She thinks your marriage is breaking down. Is that what it is? And . . . what does she mean by Mickey's "dysfunctional family"?'

A flicker of sour amusement crossed Lizzie's face. After a moment, she sniggered, but when she spoke it seemed she was changing the subject. 'Let's go for a drink. The pub's open by now and it's only a few yards on. There's a nice garden; Ben will like it.'

Good idea. Neutral territory. I began to picture a heart-to-heart at a little table under an apple tree. She couldn't escape me by stirring pots while we were at a pub.

We reached the signpost, turned left, and almost immediately sidled through an opening in a waist-high stone wall and stepped into the garden of the Five Bells. Beyond its asphalt car park was a stretch of lawn dotted with garden furniture, deserted at the moment, with a slide and a couple of swings at the side, under the hedge. Red and white umbrellas with a brewery logo advertised keg bitter against the honey-coloured stone of centuries-old walls. We chose a table and helped Ben clamber up onto a plastic chair; I settled beside him with one hand out, ready to prevent accidents.

'What will you have? And would Ben like some orange, or something?'

I said I'd have a vodka and tonic and that Ben could manage a little more juice, and we watched Lizzie pass through the low, black door under the pub sign. She was back almost immediately with a small tray, walking slowly, and I couldn't help noticing that she and I were drinking doubles. I helped Ben to pick up his tumbler and watched him drink. When I looked away, Lizzie was already putting down a half-empty glass.

She smiled faintly. 'I suppose I should have known. Mum always finds me out, and of course the first thing she'd think of . . . I knew I should have warned you there's a situation here.'

'You mentioned ages ago that Mickey's father has some kind of mental illness. Is that what she meant by "dysfunctional"?'

Lizzie shrugged. 'Probably. It's not illness, exactly, it's age. He forgets things. More and more. Anything, especially the most recent things. He even forgets his own name now. I found it disturbing at first, but you get used to it. Dido, they invited us to dinner up at the house this evening, but I wanted to talk to you first, so I said you and Ben would probably be tired, but the three of us would go to luncheon tomorrow.'

'Is that it?' I asked when I realised that she had stopped, because of course it wasn't. I waited. When she remained silent, I said, 'Start with why you left Bristol. That was last autumn, wasn't it? I got your change-of-address card, and even at the time it didn't make sense.'

She stared at her glass so hard that I half expected it to shatter. 'All right, there *is* a problem. At Monksdanes. Mickey and I decided to move down here last year because we saw that

Rose and Helen couldn't manage on their own any more. The Warings have lived there for ages. It's a beautiful old house, but huge.' She noticed my face. 'Sorry. You were introduced at our wedding, but it must be hazy by now. You'd better get them straight. Mickey's parents are called Rose and Lawrence. They're both in their seventies. Helen is the only daughter, divorced, living at home again, helping Rose.'

I did remember her. Very thin, a younger version of her mother. Quiet. I was trying to recall the father of the groom, but couldn't remember any unusually odd behaviour.

'So we rented out our own house and moved down. The commuting isn't too bad, and it meant we could keep an eye on things. We travelled in to Bristol together every day. Then the bank closed my branch down just after Christmas, and they couldn't offer me anything else, either at manager or assistant level, anywhere near here, so I took the compensation package, and . . . here I am.'

'You miss working?'

'Yes . . . though it's not a problem, not any more.'

'Then what is?'

'Two, maybe three, weeks ago, I noticed an atmosphere up at the house. It happened more or less overnight. I'd find Helen and Rose sitting with their heads together, but they'd stop talking when I came into the room; and then Mickey suddenly went all silent and absorbed, exactly the way he did when his firm had to call in the regulators – that's another story. Anyway, I asked what was going on and didn't get anywhere. Mickey told me not to worry, which *really* worried me; men can be so stupid! What I couldn't bear was his keeping things from me. Then Tris turned up. I suspected that Lawrence had . . . done something, and they were all trying to persuade Rose it was time for him to go into a nursing home –'

'Tris – wasn't he the brother who married you?'

Lizzie nodded. 'Sorry. The Reverend Tristram Waring, vicar in a parish up near Malvern, married, very proper and unbelie-

vably old-fashioned. The eldest son. Mickey is . . . I thought
Mickey was the youngest child.'

I blinked at her. 'You thought?'

At that moment, Ben decided to get down from the chair. He
shook off my hand, rolled on to his belly, and lowered himself
from the seat. It gave us both a chance to watch him instead of
staring at each other. He squatted and examined something
invisible in the grass.

'Mickey has a younger brother who's been in jail.'

I snorted before I could stop myself. I'd been in the presence
of the Waring family for just one day, but I clearly remembered a
very upright bunch: proper, as Lizzie had said, and old-fashioned. The sort of family who would find any jailbird relative
deeply embarrassing.

'Dido, Mickey'd never said a word to me about him!' She
stared at me so meaningfully that I thought I'd let her go on
when she was ready to. 'All right, I finally caught Helen on her
own and bullied her into telling me about him, but she was so
odd about it . . . Dido, don't laugh at me, but I thought this man
must have been committed – put in a mental hospital, something
like that. Because of Lawrence, I thought there was something
hereditary that they weren't telling me about. You see . . .'

She stopped, but I had already put two and two together.
'You're pregnant!'

She laughed and nodded. 'I couldn't think what to do. It's
only about ten weeks. I mean, it wouldn't have been too late.
Then I realised that what I needed was to talk to an old friend,
and I phoned you. I thought if you came and visited it would
help me to . . . not feel so isolated. Of course, it would have been
lovely any time, but right now . . . And then last night I pinned
Mickey down and told him that if he didn't tell me the truth I
was going to get an abortion.'

'And?'

'At least it's not what I thought! Dido, something nasty
happened here a few years back, about the time that Mickey and

I met. There was a burglary at Monksdanes. Ted — that's his name — he shot an intruder, who unfortunately died. What's just happened is that he wrote to say he's being released. He's coming home. He was living here when it happened, and Mickey assumes that he intends to stay — for a while, anyway. Personally, I don't think he'll be here for long, because, well, you don't know what villages are like, do you: there are no secrets, and people can be cruel! Mickey isn't saying much, but I know that Rose and Helen are worried that things may be awkward. Dido, I'm so glad you've come, because Mickey and I may need all the friends we can get. But when I woke up this morning, I started to wonder whether I'd been fair. I would have told you, really, if I'd just known in time, but then it seemed too late, and I'm really hoping you'll still stay as we planned, even if it is selfish of me. Lawrence can be a strain to cope with until you're used to him, and when this man turns up . . . And of course it isn't . . . it isn't your problem, it's mine. Oh, I don't know what I mean! . . . Will he be all right there?'

Ben had reached the foot of the children's slide and was starting to pull himself up the ladder. We both jumped, but she got there first. I was a little slow; I'd just noticed the hole in her story.

CHAPTER THREE

Seeing the World

I stood in the doorway of the inn, watching the world. The world had started to arrive in large numbers just after five thirty. By six the car park was three-quarters full and all the tables in the garden were taken. It was a warm, sunny evening and business was warming up indoors and out. I was loitering in this strategic position because, just ahead of me, a weedy young man who was being eccentric in a green corduroy jacket that his father could have worn back in the fifties was holding things up. He was busy collecting a drinks order large enough to satisfy half the village, steadying a tray which the man behind the sliding hatch was loading with beers, lime-green alcopops, crisps and some vicious-looking mixed drinks with a lot of cider in them. From the quantities, I guessed he was the emissary of the group of loud kids, some of them well under drinking age, who had just turned up in two Land-Rovers and moved all the free tables together at the edge of the lawn. I was watching them while I waited. It was going to be noisy later. Somebody was celebrating a birthday or something.

Inside the Five Bells at each end of a wood-panelled passage-way were the two bars. The door to the saloon stood open, and I could see that half the tables were already occupied by a slightly older clientèle, sitting in twos and threes. The staff down there were doling out drinks and some meals-in-a-basket, but a good deal of chat was holding things up. At the other end, the door marked 'Public Bar' and 'Men's Toilets' was closed, but whenever somebody went in clouds of cigarette smoke and raucous male voices billowed out.

A voice behind me said, 'Coming through,' and the boy in the jacket angled his laden tray around me and vanished into the late sunshine.

'Help you?' a voice enquired. Its owner was leaning his elbows on the counter, peering out at me through the hatch which was set a little too low for his comfort, though just fine for me – at five foot three I am not a vertically demanding person.

'You're busy,' I said pleasantly, doing some leaning of my own. 'Is it always like this on a Monday evening?'

He seemed to stiffen. 'Sometimes. What would you like?'

Had I said something out of line? It had only been intended as a meaningless, friendly comment. I gave him our repeat order, and he half nodded.

'You'll be Mrs Waring's friend from London, then.'

Was it my imagination, or had his vowels just flattened suddenly into a phony oo-arrr West-Country-yokel drawl?

'Everything all right, then?'

I told him that everything was just fine with me, and watched him pour out another pair of double vodkas and hook a couple of tonics out of the cold cabinet. The sign over the main door had said that the licensees were Mr and Mrs William Hunt, and I guessed that this thickening, fortyish man was the landlord.

'Well,' he said, 'you have a pleasant holiday with us, and that'll be six pounds seventy, tha-a-anks.'

I was sure now that he was putting on a comic-yokel act for my benefit, and that prices had suddenly gone up. He was already looking vaguely for his next customer as he handed me my change and turned towards the public bar.

I crossed to the low wall by the play area, where we had perched after Ben had discovered the joys of the baby swing. I watched him kicking his feet and getting an occasional nudge from Lizzie, just to keep things moving.

'He's starting to wind down,' I observed, delivering the drinks. 'This had better be our last.' Even apart from the fact that the vodka and fresh air were beginning to take effect.

Lizzie nodded. She seemed more relaxed, and I wondered suddenly whether that could be put down to alcohol as well as confession. Lizzie hadn't been drinking doubles when I knew her better.

'More,' Ben said, but his voice was subdued, and he yawned.

Lizzie gave him the shadow of a push, and raised her vodka-tonic to me. 'Cheers, Dido.' Her voice was almost drowned in a burst of shouting laughter from the party, and I thought she winced.

'Who are the mob, and why is this place so lively on a Monday evening?'

'I don't think I recognise any of them,' Lizzie said slowly. She glanced at me and then away. I'd been here for less than three hours, and the awkward pauses seemed to be multiplying mysteriously. *You're imagining things, Dido. Barnabas spooked you with that phone call. Stop it!* She was still talking, and her voice was getting more forceful. 'Probably just a pub-crawl. It's the weather.'

Being grown up, I agreed and drank up. Before we had finished reassuring Ben that there would be more swinging tomorrow (I was starting to understand that I'd have to make space in my neglected back yard for an elaborate climbing frame with swing option) four or five other vehicles had inserted themselves into the last spaces in the car park. Most of the newcomers headed for the cluster of party tables with shouts and incomprehensible jokes. I watched a grey-haired couple, con-servatively dressed, lock their old Vauxhall ostentatiously and give the kids a po-faced stare as they hurried towards the entrance. Just behind them, the arrival of a van with lettering that advertised TV satellite dishes and aerial installation roused the party to what sounded like a ragged cheer, but the driver ignored them, apart from an ironic glance, as he vanished through the door in the direction of the public bar. I lifted Ben out of the safety seat and settled him on my hip. Heavy. In no time at all he'd be bunking off school and going on pub-crawls too, and I wasn't sure how I'd cope with that. It would be a challenge. And it wasn't until we had rounded the corner and put a few buildings and a row of trees between ourselves and the pub garden that rural quiet more or less returned.

Back at the Barton, Lizzie pushed the door open and stopped short. I heard her mumble, 'Oh, damn . . .'

'What?'

She glanced at me. 'I've got into the habit of leaving the door unlocked if I'm just popping out for a few minutes. Mickey was going on at me a couple of days ago. I must try to remember.'

I shrugged. I was more interested in the manoeuvres involved in getting Ben fed, bathed and to sleep in a borrowed cot in a strange house, than in debating rural crime figures. Nice, I thought fleetingly, to live in a place where you could feel safe with an unlocked house, and exactly how should I set about the important business of finding out whether Lizzie's casseroles contained something appropriate for a baby, or, alternatively, how to boil an egg on a strange, oil-fired Rayburn cooker?

CHAPTER FOUR

Seeing the Stars

'Dido?'

I might have been asleep for a few minutes, because I couldn't remember anything that had happened since I'd rung Barnabas and tried to reassure him without telling him anything. I said quickly, 'I'm awake! This is lovely.' It was true. I dragged my eyes away from the hypnotic embers of the log fire on the inglenook hearth and looked up at Mickey Waring, who dangled my key-ring between forefinger and thumb and dropped it into my lap.

'I've locked your car and set the alarm. It should be all right there for tonight, but you might want to move it up to the house in the morning. Lizzie keeps hers up there. There's plenty of space in the driveway, and Mummy won't mind. I've put everything in your bedroom. Not a peep up there. So I'm already creeping about, trying not to wake a baby! Lizzie told you?' He smiled at me rather charmingly. I smiled back as charmingly as I could manage and admitted that she had.

Mickey Waring is probably the only adult male I've ever met who in real life calls his mother 'Mummy'. Admittedly, he had been educated at Eton, but perhaps he did it to annoy people. On the other hand, maybe he's read too much P.G. Wodehouse.

He was still exactly as I remembered him from the wedding: a thin, rather elegant blond man of medium height, with a pale face featuring a prominent Roman nose, and delicate hands. He was still wearing his business gear — a three-piece grey suit which I assumed was the uniform of senior staff in the investment firm where he was a partner. As a concession to his efforts in emptying my van, he had gone so far as to loosen his tie.

I pulled myself together and thanked him as he settled back in his armchair on the other side of the hearth, and added, 'Where's Lizzie?'

'Making cocoa. We usually have a drink before we go to bed.'

I cast a furtive glance at the carriage clock ticking on the little table between the curtained windows. Nine fifty. Country hours. 'What time do you leave in the morning?'

'I usually catch the seven forty-five and breakfast on the train. There's a direct line from the local station. It isn't too bad.'

Maybe not, but I certainly wouldn't have wanted to spend so much of my life commuting. It made me appreciate my own convenient, if cramped, living-working arrangements. I took a small breath. 'Lizzie says you moved down here because of your parents?'

When he didn't reply, I looked at him hard. His head was bent, and he was fingering the creases in his trousers.

Eventually he shrugged almost imperceptibly. 'I gather you're going up to the house for lunch tomorrow, so you'll see for yourself. About eight months ago we decided we couldn't leave my sister to cope with things any longer. My mother is getting frail, and my father — did Lizzie explain?'

I said that she had.

'We've always been a very close family,' he said heavily. 'If we had a family motto, I guess it would be, "Blood is thicker than water." '

I looked around the dimly lit room for inspiration: I wanted to establish some kind of common interest with this man whom I scarcely knew, and it seemed like a good moment to leave a subject that was obviously making him feel uncomfortable and try something else.

The Barton was a long, low cottage built of irregular local

fieldstone, with thick walls, recessed casement windows, and low doors set symmetrically into each end of its face. A single row of rooms with low, beamed ceilings and old flagstone floors ran the length of the building, opening into one another. On the far side of the kitchen, where we had been eating a little while ago, was a big cold larder and a flight of narrow old stairs twisting up through the thick walls to the floor above. A low door connected the kitchen on this side with the small, beamed dining room where we were now enjoying the open fire. This room in its turn was connected, via a cramped passageway between the front wall of the house and a huge chimney breast, with the little sitting room. Beyond that again, the last door opened into a wide entrance hall, with cupboards and a less picturesque but more practical modern staircase, up which Mickey had been carrying my bags. The rooms upstairs were shallower, because a narrow passage had been carved out of them to run along the back of the house, linking the rooms in which Ben and I were sleeping, the master bedroom, the bathroom and a shower room. Frankly, this string of rooms seemed an odd design.

I took my chance. 'Can you tell me something about this house? What *is* a "barton"?'

Mickey looked at me quickly, and I saw I'd found an enthusiasm. 'Old local word for a barn.' His voice grew animated. 'You must take a good look round in the morning – you'll see it was originally a working barn, with stalls down here for the animals and hay and fodder stores above. Don't miss the two little windows in the back wall: we think they must date from the original construction in the 1500s. At the beginning of the eighteenth century they divided it into four labourer's cottages, one room up and one down, with shared chimney breasts and open hearths for heating and cooking. Whole families must have lived in one room down here, and slept in the one above. Lizzie showed you the old bake oven? We reckon that the end cottage must have been the village bakery.'

'How long have you had it?'

'Oh, it's not exactly ours – it belongs to Monksdanes. Well, all the land around here did, at one time, though it's been sold off bit by bit. My grandfather turned the little cottages into two small houses in the thirties, and then my father did it over again about ten years ago, when he decided that the best return would come from letting it out as one large holiday cottage. That's when they put in the upstairs corridor and the indoor plumbing. When Lizzie and I decided to come down here it was empty and we moved in. I always loved this house, and . . . well, it gives me a chance to make sure the parents get their rent regularly.'

I said 'Oh,' focusing on this flood of information. His story explained something that had been bothering me: Lizzie always had good taste, but the furniture was wrong. If I'd owned an old cottage with flagstone floors, beamed ceilings and rough, plastered walls, I would have wanted the right furnishings. What filled these rooms was modern but not new: the cheap, cottagey stuff made of blond pine that you can pick up in any small-town department store. It was holiday cottage furniture. Lizzie and her husband were just camping here. My uneasiness returned.

That was the moment when I formed my well-meaning plan. I was going to stay for a couple of weeks, as arranged, and Lizzie and I would spend some quality time together. We would talk and talk, rebuild our childhood alliance, work through all her worries; and I would be here if she needed me when the jail-bird turned up. I'd begin the campaign in the morning, as soon as we were alone and I'd had enough sleep to think clearly. At the moment, the idea of bed made it hard for me to do anything but yawn squeakily.

Ten minutes later the three of us paused on the upstairs landing. Mickey gave me a quick smile and vanished down the hall towards the bathroom. Water started to run. Left alone, Lizzie and I exchanged complicit glances, and I edged open the first door, which led into a small bedroom where a brand-new drop-side cot sat in the middle of the floor – and now I understood the reason it was there. We exchanged maternal smiles. In the glow from a night light, I could see Ben clutching his favourite checked blue blanket to his cheek and smiling in his sleep.

'He's lovely, isn't he!' Lizzie whispered. We stepped back, and I pulled the door gently to.

Just inside the second door, we stopped.

'Dido, will this be all right?'

I assured her that it would. There was more space here than in my London bedroom, though I wasn't accustomed to sleeping in a narrow single bed and there was something a little naked about the room. An electric radiator hummed and clicked beside the window, its little red light winking, and the air was stuffy.

'Then I'll say goodnight, unless there's anything you need? Dido, I'll be up by seven in the morning, but you don't have to . . . Oh, wait a minute.' She crossed quickly to the window and yanked the thick red velour curtains across it. Then she was back, flicking the light switch. The ceiling light came on, a reddish glow from the elaborate shade in the form of a nineteenth-century lady with huge flounced skirts. I noticed that her sister was a lamp on the bedside table. 'Keep the curtains closed at night, especially when you're undressing. You can see right into these windows from the lane, and Helen says that there's a Peeping Tom around: no point giving him a cheap thrill.' She hesitated. 'Dido, I'm so glad you're here.' Then she touched my cheek with her lips and was gone.

I brushed my teeth at the hand basin in the corner, inspected my (bloodshot) eyes in the mirror over it, and went to dig an oversized T-shirt out of my bag for sleeping. My jeans, shirt and underwear got dumped in a heap on the other bed – I'd unpack and sort everything out in the morning. I turned off the light, inched my way across the floor by the glow from the corridor, pulled the curtains back, swung the casement open with a rustle of ivy, and leaned my elbows on the eighteen-inch-deep sill to look out.

For a moment I couldn't see a thing. No street lighting at all! Terrifying blackness. *City girl.*

The wind had dropped at sunset, but something still whispered. When my eyes had adjusted to darkness, I looked past the rear of the tin chapel and found a distant glow. Three or four miles to the south, the highway I had used that afternoon passed on its way to Devon. I was seeing the glow of headlights, hearing a distant breath of traffic on its way down to Honiton, or back towards London. I looked away. Beyond the invisible door at the other end of the chapel a faint, pale shadow marked the course of the lane. There was one lone square of light in a window: another person still awake in one of the invisible houses.

Finally, I looked up.

It's rare to see many stars in inner London: a few – the brightest, the biggest planets – struggle in the glare of street lights. Here, in a moonless sky, the larger stars burned like sharp white points, and the Milky Way swept in a band of brightness above my head, brilliant and cold. I leaned out, dizzy, and dreamed that I could feel the world turning.

A sound, almost nothing, roused me: a rhythmic squeak and a whisper of tyres on pavement. Somebody was riding a bicycle on the track around the green. Invisibly it passed the cottage, and the sound faded. My eyes were closing as I stumbled towards the narrow, unfamiliar bed.

CHAPTER FIVE

The Hole in the Picture

I drove up the lane slowly – especially after I'd found myself having to steer around the golden retriever lying in the middle of the road (not dead, just resting, with a tail that thumped approval of my courtesy) – and straight between the crumbling stone gateposts that marked the end of the public road and the beginning of the gravel driveway, which swept to the right. I swept with it and hit the brakes.

Lizzie bounced against her seat belt. 'What's wrong?'

'N-nothing,' I told her quickly. 'You didn't tell me Monksdanes was a' – I had been meaning to say 'mansion', but that wasn't right – 'a stately home!'

She giggled, and we sat there and looked.

Monksdanes was big enough: a Georgian manor house built of ham stone tinged with the colour of old lichen, three main storeys high topped by low attics which had probably housed servants. The facade was classically symmetrical, with elegant sash windows and a central door of weathered, silvery wood set into a small stone portico. At each end were identical Victorian single-storey extensions. The house faced a rough lawn at the top of a driveway which curved in an elegant circle in front of the door. It looked as though a cavalcade of horse-drawn carriages might pull up there at any moment.

I said, 'I didn't realise how *smart* the Warings were.' But even as the words left my mouth, I started to see little details that said otherwise. The house must have stood for two centuries, but the last few decades had been hard on it. The window panes were dirty, and one on an upper floor had been broken and mended with a piece of cardboard; the paint on the frames was weathered and flaked; there were damp stains behind the old iron down-pipes.

Lizzie looked at me as though I'd gone loopy and just said, 'Put the car . . . van — what do you call these things? — round the back. It's really better if you leave it here; a lot of cars turn around at the green, and it's a bit narrow: my car was scraped a couple of times before I took to parking it up here.'

I was driving the nearly new replacement for my late-lamented Citroën estate, which had gone up in flames outside the shop a couple of months before to the deep displeasure of my insurance company. I was trying to avoid any more confronta-tions with them, so I followed instructions and came to a halt at the back of the house near a slightly battered blue estate car and an old bicycle. We were parked on a gravelled square surrounded by a row of low stone outbuildings and the back wall of the house. From somewhere nearby came the noise of a petrol-driven lawnmower. By the time I had checked my glove compartment to make sure it held nothing I was going to need immediately, Lizzie and Ben were ambling towards the house, deep in conversation. I locked up and hurried after them through the back door into a stone-floored, cupboard-filled entrance hall, and on into a dark kitchen, where a blonde woman looked up from preparing a series of salad plates at the kitchen table.

'Dido, you remember Helen?'

I said that I did, while the daughter of the house smiled silently and held up a delicate hand to demonstrate that it was covered in juice from her tomato-slicing and therefore unfit for shaking. I would have recognised her without any introduction, if only for her resemblance to Mickey: the same white-blond hair, pale face and elegant gestures. She looked fiftyish, and had the kind of dry skin that develops networks of fine wrinkles in middle age. Tired eyes.

She looked at Ben, who smiled angelically. 'I've brought down our old high-chair,' she said. 'Lizzie, I've set the table in the morning room, and there's sherry on the sideboard, if you'd like to go through.'

She turned down our offer of help, so I followed Lizzie through another door and into a long corridor running the length of the house. We crossed it diagonally and slipped into a bright, square room where Mickey's mother awaited us. Again, the family resemblance was unmistakable: the blue eyes, the Roman nose, the fine hands.

She rose to greet us. 'Dido, how good of you to come. And the baby.' She looked down at Ben. 'Helen has found the children's old high-chair in one of the attics. Elizabeth, I'm afraid Lawrence won't be eating with us.' Her eyes flickered at Lizzie. 'He's not very well today.'

We said that was too bad and passed some time accepting cut-crystal schooners containing small measures of pale sherry. They had covered the round table with an impressive damask cloth and laid five place settings, so the absence of the invalid had obviously been a last-minute decision. Lizzie and I settled at the table, with Ben between us in the curious antique high-chair of blackened oak. Rose sat opposite.

Just before the silence became awkward, my hostess fixed me with her faded blue eyes. 'So, Dido, how long are you staying with us?'

I replied primly that it would be ten days or so, unless something came up at home, and then Helen arrived carrying a soup tureen. She slid it onto the sideboard and began to serve broth into wide soup plates. Lizzie passed round a plate of unbuttered brown bread, thinly sliced and cut into delicate triangles. I divided my attention between answering questions and watching Ben, who was having his first, anxious-making experience of the silver cutlery and fine porcelain of polite society.

Rose persisted. 'I hope you'll find enough to do here. Do you have any plans?'

I told her honestly that I intended to rest, that it had been a hard winter.

Helen interjected, 'Oh, I wouldn't want to live in London — it's *so* noisy.'

We agreed about London noise, then went on and covered the usual territory: Ben's age, his demands on my time, my antiquarian book business, its demands on my time, my father and his health and his demands on my time . . . Rose and Helen took turns tossing questions and comments at me lightly while I struggled with the feeling that I was being buried under a pile of feathers but tossed back a few light answers, suddenly aware that I hadn't had much practice with social small talk lately and that I wanted to yawn and mustn't.

'Maybe Dido could look at the books in the library,' Lizzie said suddenly. Her voice had risen, as though she thought that the others were a little deaf. 'She'd be able to tell you what they're worth. You've been talking all winter about having somebody in.'

Her intervention silenced us. In my own case, this was because one well-known rule of the book business is, 'When offered the chance to see a country house library, run don't walk to the spot.' Of course, the appendix reads, 'Don't get your hopes up.'

I murmured that naturally I'd be glad to give any help that I could, hoping that I wasn't letting myself in for doing a free insurance valuation. But when I looked across the table, I knew that was not what was going on.

Rose Waring dabbed delicately at her lips with her napkin, lowered her eyes to her empty soup plate, and seemed to be considering the suggestion. She sat very straight on the armless dining chair. It struck me that her eyes were a little less kind than her son's. I put her age at about seventy-five, and her mental sharpness as unquestionable. In some ways she reminded me of Barnabas in his smoothly impenetrable mood.

Helen, separated from Rose by the empty chair, was also

watching her mother. She was fidgeting; I half expected to overhear a maternal reprimand. She spoke first, unexpectedly. 'We . . . a dealer bought some of the books a few years ago, Lizzie. I think he took the best ones.'

When Rose remained silent, I intervened briskly. 'I'm always interested in looking at libraries, and I can probably tell you right away whether it'd be worth my going through it carefully. How many books would you say you have now?' I knew enough not to ask whether they were 'old'. People always assure you that they have 'old' books. To some, 1930s reprints of E. Phillips Oppenheim thrillers are pretty 'old' books.

Rose decided to answer. 'Hundreds. I haven't thought about them for a time. Well, perhaps, if you'd be interested. Helen, is there anything. . . ?'

'I made some salad,' Helen whispered. I couldn't imagine why she was so nervous. She slid to her feet and made a business of clearing the soup plates and bringing the second course from the kitchen. The salad plates consisted of a base of shredded iceberg lettuce topped by neatly quartered tomatoes, a hard-boiled egg each, also quartered, a boiled new potato served cold, pickled beetroot and some finely sliced cucumber. A little puddle of thin mayonnaise (or maybe traditional salad cream) had been dabbed artistically in the middle. 'I didn't know whether Ben is too young for salad, but I made up a small plate, and I've chopped everything up quite small . . .'

I pictured the effects of a small plate of salad and dressing being transferred piecemeal to the tablecloth and carpet and said quickly, 'Maybe just another piece of bread.'

'We have a little strawberry yoghourt for afters . . .'

'Just right,' I enthused. I stabbed my egg and wondered what was going on. Well, the best thing was for me to be charming. By the end of luncheon (small cups of instant coffee) I thought I'd made an impression, mostly by my shameless chattering about how wonderful motherhood is. Luckily, Ben was in a good mood. Overawed, probably, by his surroundings.

I turned down the offer of a second cup of coffee.

'I ought to look in on Father,' Helen said abruptly. 'Mother, if you'd like to lie down for half an hour, I'm sure that Dido and Lizzie . . .'

I took my chance and told them all that I'd be very happy just being shown around their beautiful house and making a first survey of the books, and after a visible hesitation Rose Waring inclined her head graciously. A minute later, therefore, Lizzie and Ben and I were alone in the entrance hall surveying a house which, as I was realising more and more clearly, was only a shadow of its old, grand self. The light from the window above the front door fell on a wide wooden staircase leading to the shadows of the upper floor, with a runner that was threadbare at the edge of each tread. There was no carpet at all on the tiled floor. Lizzie dug out a fistful of tagged keys from a drawer in the side table, the only piece of furniture.

'I can show you round the rooms on this floor, anyway,' she whispered. 'Most of them only get opened up when the family come for Christmas, but you can see that they used to be lovely. Upstairs is bedrooms, of course, and the children's rooms above. Oh, and a Victorian bathroom that ought to be in a museum.'

I found myself whispering back, 'Is she all right?'

'Rose? Oh, you mean Helen, don't you! That's clever of you. This place is too much for her, of course. She came back to recover from a nasty divorce and found that she'd landed all this. Mickey wants to get some help in: he's offered to pay, but the women think it would upset Father to have a stranger wandering around, so Helen won't admit there's a problem. Personally, I think she has a martyr complex. At least they've shut up the two top floors.'

I considered the bulk of the old house and couldn't help whispering, 'They're mad!'

Lizzie grimaced at me. 'I know. Well, shall we start?'

I retrieved Ben from his own explorations and we set off on the guided tour. It was a house of symmetrical design, with the central corridor giving access to rooms at the front and rear of the building, and ending at the doors into the two Victorian extensions. Lizzie unlocked the first door, and we stepped into a long, bright room beside the one where we had eaten lunch. A huge walnut dining table filled the middle, and a few smaller tables, chairs, and a large sideboard encircled it. A formal fireplace took up most of the end wall, with an icy little breeze blowing down its wide chimney, as it must have been doing for the past two centuries. I shivered and wondered whether I should have put my jacket on: I'd just discovered that the arctic temperatures and rheumatic damp of the traditional English country house have survived into the modern world.

We proceeded, with a slow unlocking and relocking of doors, through the silent rooms: the huge double reception room on the other side of the entrance hall, and the bright Victorian music room dominated by the bulk of a grand piano, its lid down, probably long silent. There were several smaller and less formal sitting rooms at the back of the house which were still in use. As we proceeded, I began to notice the places where the wallpaper had peeled away from damp plaster, and faded patches where a piece of furniture had once stood or a painting had hung. The family must have been selling off their more valuable pieces. I started to fantasise about moving my business to a quiet country mansion with space and elegance, and had to get hold of myself: Monksdanes was having a strange effect on my normal sluttish instincts.

After the third or fourth of these big, lovely rooms, Ben abruptly lost interest and tried an experimental wail, which brought me back to reality.

'He's tired,' Lizzie commented. She was learning fast.

'And bored. I'd better take him away. I can come back for a look at the books another time.'

Lizzie hesitated. 'You don't think he'd come with me, do you?'

I asked him, and knew that he would when he grasped

Lizzie's hand with the eagerness of somebody suddenly and unexpectedly finding salvation from a prowling lion. She thrust the oversized bunch of keys into my hand and said, 'It's that room at the far end of the house, the other extension. You'll find us out back in the gardens.'

I thought I'd just take a quick look. But it took me a little longer than I'd expected to persuade the key to turn in the stiff lock, and when the door finally opened the shutters were closed and the room was dark. It had been like this for a while: I could smell the damp and dust of an unaired room even before I'd crossed the threshold. My book dealer's heart sank.

Flipping the light switch had no effect. I crept to the nearest window and struggled with the latch on the shutters until I managed to force it up and pull them open.

This room was different. It was panelled in dark wood, with a modest fireplace set into one wall and a big Landseer engraving of deerhounds in a heavy frame above it. The other three walls were lined with solid-looking oak bookcases. A writing desk stood under the shuttered window at the end of the room, matching the pair of little tables on either side of the hearth. In the middle of the carpet was a circle of leather armchairs, with dusty lamp tables still holding big ashtrays and a couple of old magazines. Helen's housekeeping had apparently faltered in here, and a thick layer of dust softened every flat surface. But it was a room that had been designed for Victorian comfort – reading, talking, smoking cigars, drinking port. In my imagination, I people it with old gentlemen reading *Punch*.

I would have liked it even more if the shelves had been full, but one of my competitors had certainly been here first. There were still quite a few books leaning against one another in the depleted cases, but several shelves were completely empty and all of them had gaps. As I'd been warned.

My eye fell on the writing desk. On its leather-covered surface I could see a little pamphlet with a reproduction of a Mercator map on its cover. I can recognise another dealer's catalogue at twenty paces, even in semi-darkness. I made my way over and picked up the list of an old business acquaintance who operates from a country house not – though I hadn't realised it before – so many miles from here. The cover said: 'General Literature Winter 1993–4', and somebody had tucked a letter away inside. Shamelessly I peeked. *Dear Mr Waring, I am pleased to offer you the sum of £6,000 for my choice of one thousand volumes . . .*

It was just what Helen had said. I wondered whether this particular offer had been accepted and, if so, just what good stuff might have gone at the bargain rate of six pounds a volume. Well, all book dealers have blind spots, and it was still worth discovering what he might have missed. I didn't expect much, but the family needed the money, and looking is always fun.

Slowly I circled the room: early twentieth-century novels: worth checking for first editions, though mostly without dust jackets; gardening books: always interesting; local history, its shelf much depleted, but even so . . . There might still be two or three thousand books here, and there had to be something worth while.

Then, I realised, there was the carpet. I'm no expert, but the floor was covered by a big flowered rug, not worn. It was certainly an Aubusson pattern, with a cream centre, pale-green borders, pink roses. Was it authentic? It was dusty, like every-thing else in here, but if by any chance it was genuine, surely it would fetch quite a bit at auction? I walked around the arm-chairs, finding no obvious signs of wear in front of them. And someone had had the sense to protect the area in front of the hearth from sparks, because a big, coarse-looking olive-green rug, about eight feet by six, had been laid on top of it there. Then it occurred to me that it could have been put down to hide burn damage.

My intentions were casually altruistic when I walked over and flipped up the corner of the rug with my foot. What I saw made me catch my breath, take hold of the end of the rug, and pull it back.

A jagged section had been cut out of the Aubusson, roughly six feet wide and three or four deep. I couldn't believe this. The edges of the cut were irregular, as though somebody had slashed and hacked in a frenzy. It took me a full minute to realise what I was seeing, and then I peered gingerly at the floorboards. They were spotless.

The old man could have been standing in the doorway for several minutes before I noticed him: thinning, longish white hair, curiously dead eyes, a sagging, square face above a plump body in an old, tartan dressing-gown, with striped pyjama legs and carpet slippers below. He was standing very still, watching me.

'Do I know you?'

I got hold of myself and explained, 'My name is Dido Hoare. I'm Lizzie's friend. We were here for lunch, and I'm having a look at your library. I'm an antiquarian book dealer.'

He nodded. Then immediately he looked at the great hole I'd uncovered in his library carpet. He frowned slowly and looked up again. I thought I heard him mumble, 'Where have you put Peter Rabbit?' and then he asked more loudly, 'Who did you say you are?'

CHAPTER SIX

Sundowner

Lizzie thrust a glass into my hand and gave me a little pat on the shoulder. 'Are you all right?'

I tested the liquid in the usual way and discovered that it was almost pure vodka. 'I'd just realised what I was looking at, and suddenly your father-in-law was standing there. He kept asking who I was, and every time I told him, he asked again a minute later. Helen turned up eventually and took him away for a cup of tea. She must have seen what I'd been doing, but she didn't say anything, and I put the hearth-rug back, got rid of the keys, and came away.'

'What was it?'

'One corpse-sized hole in the carpet? Lizzie, that's where it happened! And then somebody hacked it away.'

'Maybe Rose or Helen did it afterwards,' Lizzie mumbled. 'They must have been upset. There was probably a lot of blood.'

I protested that you would have the whole carpet cleaned professionally, you wouldn't cut it up. Then suddenly I wasn't sure. Not with these Warings. Odd people.

'What?' Lizzie asked. 'Why do you have that look?'

I hesitated, listening for noises from Ben's room, although I suspected he'd be safely asleep for at least an hour longer. Socialising had worn him out. I glanced at Lizzie and saw her watching.

I gave up. 'When you told me about this, there was something that didn't make sense, a hole in the picture. You said that the Warings were expecting things to be awkward when Teddy comes.'

She nodded. 'That's what Mickey thought.'

'Why?'

She frowned.

'Was there something you didn't tell me? Why would anybody hold it against him that he shot a burglar? A lot of people would cheer. All right, it was awful.' I couldn't go on right away, because there was something personal that I hadn't told Lizzie yet. I found my voice again. 'What is the problem? Did anybody suggest that he did it deliberately?'

'It's not what I heard,' Lizzie said tightly. Suddenly, a crafty look flitted across her face. 'Maybe you could talk to Mickey about it? You're just the person to find out exactly what happened: you're not family, but you aren't an outsider, either. If he won't tell you the whole truth, you can nag him the way I can't.'

I was a little outraged. 'Why can't you?'

'Because I love him.'

To do her justice, she did blush; even so I could feel a nasty wave of realism sweeping over me. 'Because you're scared of what he'll say?'

I was glared at. 'I'm *not* scared of Mickey! Oh, I don't know! Maybe I am anxious about finding out. I'm not making sense, am I? D-i-i-ido!'

I raised my eyebrows and kept them up until she looked away. Then I said, 'You are really going to owe me!' and pretended I was fed up, although in fact I already knew there was nothing that could keep me from asking questions, because it was this whole business – just too weird.

I never learn.

'To begin with, it isn't Alzheimer's.' Mickey Waring's voice was flat with fatigue. I wasn't in such good shape myself. We were leaning against the stone wall in front of the cottage holding two of the big glasses of vodka and tonic that seemed to fuel this household, and watching the red blush where the sun had just set behind the houses along the green. 'It's a kind of senile dementia. There's been a series of tiny strokes that damaged the connections in his brain. I suppose it comes to the same thing. It's as though he were living from minute to minute. As soon as each one passes, it has never happened.'

'He kept asking whether he knew me, and as soon as I told him my name, he forgot it again. Your sister finally turned up. Mickey, what does "Peter Rabbit" mean to you?'

'Oh, Lord.'

I waited.

'Did he accuse you of stealing it?'

'He asked me where I'd put it. He seemed to think I was hiding something.'

'The children's book, you know? There was a copy in the family, a present from Beatrix Potter to my great-grandfather. Our families knew each other in the Lake District, before we moved south just after the turn of the century. I think it was a first edition, or something. It was an odd old thing. It must have been some kind of cheap edition – the pictures were just black and white.'

Black and white? For a moment I couldn't breathe.

'She'd written something in it for the children, with a couple of little pen sketches of Peter Rabbit. It was kept in a box, and we weren't allowed to touch it when we were little, but Mummy used to read it to us as a special treat. It was in the library here, but it went walkabout a few years back.'

I couldn't even look at him. I was thinking, *six thousand pounds for a first private edition of 'Peter Rabbit' with a personal message and 'little sketches' AND other books?* I felt like crying.

'Dido?'

'A local dealer bought some books from your parents a few years ago, isn't that right?'

'Oh, *Peter Rabbit* went missing later – a couple of months afterwards.'

I asked him whether he was sure. He laughed drily and said that the memory was very clear: Father had been livid and announced that they might as well sell everything in the house if they were going to be robbed blind all the time. Some of the furniture had already gone.

I breathed a sigh of relief. I was probably going to pay a visit to the book dealer in question before long, and accusing him of cheating the Warings would have been a sticky way to begin.

He rattled his ice cubes and said, 'I'm sorry Father frightened you.'

I said I hadn't been frightened, and instructed my brain to focus. 'At the time, I was interested in something I'd just found, as a matter of fact.' I was beginning to wish I hadn't started this. 'I was in the library because Lizzie had suggested that I might buy the rest of the books. I noticed the carpet. It looked like an Aubusson. I don't know much about carpets, but I thought . . .'

I ground to a halt again.

Mickey closed his eyes. 'You found the . . . damage.'

I said humbly that obviously I had been sticking my nose into something that was none of my business, but I was just trying to help.

'The carpet's worthless.'

'Yes.'

'So you thought . . .'

'I thought for a moment that it might have been a burning log that rolled out of the hearth. But then I thought you wouldn't react to that by –'

'Cutting out the burns.'

'No. You'd just clean it up as much as you could. I can't stop thinking about it.'

Mickey snorted. 'And you told Lizzie, naturally, which is why she suggested we come out here for a drink while she sets the table. Would you like another one, by the way?'

'Maybe,' I said. 'In a minute. The hole seemed sort of . . . body-sized.'

'Let's go back in,' he said abruptly, and moved away towards the open door behind us. 'It's getting cool, and I need another one even if you don't. I'll tell both of you. Remember, I wasn't here when it happened, so this is second-hand.'

We went into the kitchen, found the meal waiting, and sat down to it; and Lizzie said quietly, 'Mickey?'

'I can only tell you what Helen said. She rushed over from Norwich as soon as Mummy phoned her. Mummy told Tris and me to stay away. Teddy didn't want us at his trial, and of course we respected that.

'Look: Teddy heard noises in the middle of the night. He went downstairs and realised that somebody must have broken in. The library door was locked from the inside, so he went through the kitchen, picked up one of Father's shotguns from the gun cupboard at the back door, and went along the gravel path to the library windows because he knew that's how the intruder must have entered. When he saw broken glass, and an open window, instead of phoning the police the idiot decided to catch the robber in the act. He climbed in and slipped over to the light switch on the wall by the fireplace. Before he reached it, somebody – he couldn't see who – tried to grab the gun. They struggled and it went off. When he got the light on, he saw that he'd shot a woman. It was some poor, stupid girl who lived in the village and came in to clean. I suppose she thought that if she pocketed anything while she was supposed to be there, Mummy and Father would guess. She must have thought breaking in at night would make it look like an outsider. And then that awful accident . . . poor kid, I don't think she was more than about twenty.

'Father came downstairs when he heard the noise and found Teddy sitting on the floor in front of the fireplace with the body, crying. He called the police.'

Lizzie put her hand on her husband's.

I just asked, 'Exactly what happened then?'

'Teddy was charged with manslaughter. He pleaded guilty. In the circumstances – because she'd broken in and there'd been a struggle – he was only sentenced to eight years. He's being released now; he's coming home this week. I haven't seen him since last Christmas. I hope he's . . . all right.'

There was something I'd been wondering. 'Why didn't he get a suspended sentence? It was an accident, wasn't it? Or self-defence, even?'

Mickey seemed to pull back. He reminded me, again, of his mother.

'Shouldn't he have appealed against the sentence?'

'I don't know,' Mickey said after a moment. 'I really don't know.'

CHAPTER SEVEN

Counting Backwards

———⟫◆⟪———

Lizzie sat on the spare bed, cleverly avoiding my little heap of dirty clothes without even seeming to notice it. I perched on the other bed, which I was more than ready to occupy. I'd drawn the curtains and switched on the doll-lamp on the bedside table, and we stared at each other in its pinkish glow.

'Are you all right?'

'Yes. Just tired. You?'

I told her that I was fine, and that she mustn't overdo it because having babies is ridiculously exhausting. Almost as bad as raising them. The carriage clock down in the living room had just tinkled ten o'clock, but in Alford that felt like the middle of the night.

'Dido?'

I waited.

'Dido, what you said about Teddy's sentence: I wouldn't call eight years a harsh sentence. He did kill somebody.'

I wasn't going to argue with her about the gravity of killing a human being, accidentally or otherwise. I clasped my hands together and said, 'It seems to me I've heard of people getting much less than that for a killing that was unintentional and had . . . mitigating circumstances.'

'So what happened?'

I told her that I couldn't imagine.

'I think it needs explaining.'

'Maybe,' I said slowly, 'the judge was a particularly harsh one. Maybe it was because the victim was a woman. I don't know why that would make a difference, though, if she was burgling the place.'

'Then — you said this yourself — he could have appealed against the sentence.'

I shrugged again. We exchanged cautious looks. Hers had a quality of raised eyebrows about it.

She said suddenly, 'I'm going to find out the truth about this, you know. Teddy is family, and he'll be here any minute, and there's no point pretending I'm going to be able to avoid him, because the Warings stick together like glue. I still think there might be something wrong with him that nobody's saying.'

I had stopped wanting to yawn. 'Are you really sure you should do this?'

'Of course I am! Look: on Wednesdays I always drive Helen to the supermarket in Yeovil. If you and Ben come with us tomorrow, we'll have over an hour in the car with her, coming and going. By the time we're back we should have managed to find out exactly what happened. I realise that she was in Norwich when it happened, but she got here pretty quickly afterwards. I think she knows a lot of things they never told Mickey.'

I suddenly recalled that when we were small I used to think Lizzie was a bossy little girl.

'Dido?' she said insistently.

I looked at her and shrugged. 'I'm with you,' I promised, 'but I have a better idea. I think Helen's more likely to tell you family secrets if I'm not there.'

'But you'll be on your own all morning.'

'Ben and I will explore. I'll take him out in the push-chair, and we'll walk around. I'll talk to everybody I see. I'll tell them all what a lovely village this is, and they'll tell me how they wouldn't want to live in London because it's so crowded and dirty. Women always stop for a chat when you have a baby with you:

you'll find that out yourself. They must have talked about nothing else for months here, after it happened, and because I'm *not* family, they might drop hints. Afterwards, we'll compare notes. If somebody's lying, it may show up.'

Lizzie's face lit up. 'Dido,' she said, 'you're brilliant! I'll go now so you can get to sleep. We'll need to get moving early in the morning. Bless you!' She bounced to her feet and went out of the room, leaving me to crawl under the blankets and worry.

At the time, I didn't think I had a choice; but I did wonder what I was going to say to my father that he could pass on to Diane. A stray thought trickled into my head. Hadn't it occurred to anybody that the dead girl might have stolen *Peter Rabbit*? Not on the night she was killed, obviously, or it would have been with the corpse. Maybe the timing didn't fit, though. Did the timing fit? I tried to remember what Mickey had said, and fell asleep.

CHAPTER EIGHT

Mrs Molyneux

A voice spoke just behind me: 'I believe you might find this of some use.'

I whirled around as quickly as my limp posture allowed – I had sagged restfully against a convenient stone wall at the corner of what I had thought was the empty garden encircling the unexpectedly modern chalet bungalow opposite the bullocks' field. The speaker who had just popped up on the other side of the wall was a short, stout, watery-eyed, grey-haired old woman with the sagging face of a bloodhound. A pair of oversized spectacles sat crookedly on her nose, and she wore a kind of pinafore overall of mud-splattered blue cotton, and green rubber boots. The hand that thrust a folded map at me was hidden inside a large leather gardening glove. 'Ordnance Survey,' she said. 'Two and a half miles to the inch – or at least, I'm not sure, but this series was before they recast it in kilometres. I find the Common Market, I should say of course the EC, shouldn't I – or do they have different initials now? – overly keen on unnecessary change, although of course I holiday with friends in the north of Spain every January and have done for years. I am Jane Molyneux. I presume you're Lizzie Waring's London friend, Dido Hoare? An unusual name, Dido. There are very few people nowadays who read Virgil. Are you by any chance related to Robert Hoare, of Hove? I

45

knew him many years ago. And that will be your son, little Benjamin, in the push-chair. He seems to be asleep – the fresh air; London air is so polluted these days!'

'Fresh air and the excitement,' I said very seriously. 'Thank you, my father did have a classical education. I don't know of any Robert Hoare. What made you think I need a large-scale map?'

Mrs Molyneux cocked her head and raised an eyebrow at me. 'I realised who you were when I saw you across the road yesterday with Mrs Waring. Then this morning, just after I noticed Helen and Elizabeth driving off, you came down the lane. When I went to the postbox, you were heading off towards the northern end of the village, looking around you, and I assumed that you were out exploring while Mrs Waring and Mrs Hill do their Wednesday morning shopping in Yeovil. A good decision, by the way: Yeovil has been ruined by redevelopment, and there is very little to see now, apart from roads, car parks and the usual chain stores. I'm sorry if that sounds snobbish, I'm getting old. At any rate, I went inside and looked out my map as soon as I returned, and I was waiting for you to reappear. Did you find the ford? And the church? The Mill House is very picturesque, too.'

I confessed that I had missed two of those landmarks and not got as far as the church although I'd noticed the tower at the far end of the sprawling village.

She smiled triumphantly. 'Then, before your next excursion, I'd recommend you consult this to get your bearings. Alford grew up higgledy-piggledy over the centuries along tracks connecting the Fosse Way to the west with the pack road to the east. The system of roads and paths is *quite* complicated, as you would imagine. Just let me have the map back before you go home. Can I give you a cup of tea and a biscuit? I was about to take a break.' She looked at me serenely. 'I've been working on my herbaceous borders. They made a slow start this year, but now they're coming on amazingly. There is nothing quite as civilised, to my mind, as a mature herbaceous border. You will have guessed they're a passion of mine? The gate is just to your left. I'm sure the push-chair will fit through.'

It did, and now I was sitting by a little table in Mrs Molyneux's parlour, listening to the ticking of her clocks, Ben's breathing, and the running of water and boiling of a kettle in a nearby kitchen. In my hostess's absence, I examined the room, which was crammed with well-polished walnut furniture dating from between the wars, and a serious collection of Staffordshire china that was displayed on every flat surface. From the carpet on the parquet floor to the parchment shades on the chandelier and matching wall lights, the room breathed old-fashioned comfort. It reminded me of my parents' house in Oxford. Ben was continuing his exhausted late-morning snooze, so I relaxed and listened to the kettle's rising whistle, an abrupt silence, and the creak of wheels in the passageway.

'And how do you take your tea?' Mrs Molyneux was asking as she arrived behind a trolley burdened with silver and fine china. 'I hope you'll have an Eccles cake? They are *not* home-made, I'm afraid, but the bakery in town is excellent. And now tell me what you think of Alford?' She settled on the far side of the little table, picked up the tea-strainer, and looked at me expectantly.

I tried to gather my thoughts, but all I could think of on the spur of the moment was, 'Very interesting.'

She looked at me and twinkled. 'You are right, of course. Most people say, "How pretty, how quiet!" when they mean, "How picturesque but how dull!" '

'Have you always lived here?' I countered.

'Over forty years. Not *here*, of course. I was a school teacher in Bath when I met and married my late husband, the incumbent of this parish. We lived in the rectory, up beside the church, until he retired and we moved down here.'

I thought, Bull's-eye! and said, 'Then you're just the person I need. When I came out to explore this morning, the village seemed deserted. There was some gardener cutting the grass up at Monksdanes, but the only living being that I've spoken to since I walked Lizzie up there was a dog lying in the middle of the road. According to his tag, his name is Barney.'

Mrs Molyneux's eyes were frankly amused behind her glasses. 'Ah, Barney . . . But perhaps you expected to see gossiping village women? Happy herdsmen driving their contented cows to pasture? Yeomen trimming the hedges along the lane?'

I giggled and said, 'Well, more or less.'

Mrs Molyneux shook her head. 'Forty years ago. Since then, the land has all been bought or leased by just two large farms – Barney, by the way, belongs at the one on your right as you go up towards the big house – who largely use contract labour. Most of the cottages have been bought up and modernised by outsiders who have been here for only ten or fifteen years. They come for the peace and quiet, and drive off to work miles away, or commute by train like your friend's husband; the railway station is a little too convenient, a mixed blessing. Some of the wives do the same, and the children are at least ten or twelve miles away at school for most of the day. After the war, although this was before my time, there was still a scattering of small shops opposite the pub, and even a primary school up opposite the church; now there is nothing between the pub at this end and the post office stores, and people drive everywhere, of course. You will see a few pensioners like myself pottering about, naturally, but it happens that, early on Wednesdays, a bus goes south to Castle Hinton and another runs north to Wells, so most of us will have gone shopping. I'm sure this isn't what you expected.'

I took a long, happy breath, realised that I'd found the proverbial horse's mouth, and set about getting myself educated. I listened to a lecture on the domestic architecture of East Somerset, the gradual disappearance of thatched roofs, of which only two were left in the whole village, the vexed problem of in-filling although (as we mustn't forget!) that had started in Victorian times, and the blessings of the district council's planning regulations which, so far as Mrs Molyneux was concerned, were better late than never although they had not really been in time to preserve the character of the place, as witness the tin chapel which was overly intrusive considering that its dwindling congregation met only one Sunday in the month. I kept myself from saying that I thought it was a fantastic building, especially the windows, though not perhaps what you might expect to find in this place.

'More tea, Miss Hoare?'

I turned down her offer of a third cup and a second Eccles cake in favour of trying to edge the conversation towards personal matters.

'You must know the Warings quite well?' I suggested tentatively.

She looked at me serenely. 'I've known Rose and Lawrence for many years, of course, and their children while they were growing up. Mr Molyneux got to know Tristram especially, as you can imagine, and encouraged his vocation; but Rose was not interested in the ladies' groups I helped to run, though she did turn out to help at harvest festivals and the midsummer fair, I'll give her that. I taught the children in the Sunday school when they were quite young. Of course they all went away to boarding school.'

I said delicately, 'Did you know Teddy?'

Her silence warned me I'd moved too fast. There was nothing I could do except try to look innocent and wait. The silence lengthened.

'I did,' she said eventually, 'though not well. I also knew Joannie and her family.' For a moment she looked as though she wanted to say more.

I waited, trying to work out how to get past the moment. Eventually I decided that the best thing to do was continue looking innocent and go away until next time. Ben cooperated by stirring, and I could say that I'd better take him back. 'I can't thank you enough,' I added. 'I really enjoyed chatting about the village. And thanks for the map – I'll return it soon.'

'No rush,' Mrs Molyneux assured me. 'I haven't needed it for a while. You *must* visit the church, if you like such things. It's good Perpendicular, and the interior is pleasant, although the Victorian restorers were not especially light-handed.'

I promised her that the church would be the next goal of my explorations, and allowed her to usher us to the front door. I was considering tactics.

On the doorstep, I paused briefly. 'Lizzie tells me that Teddy is coming home.'

I heard her draw a sharp breath as I set off, wheeling the push-chair to the gate without looking back. I thought she would be glad to talk to me again.

'Who are "Joannie and her family"?' I asked Lizzie.

'I'm not sure. She said that?'

I was certain.

We were relaxing in the kitchen after unloading the car and carrying groceries into the larder. We had been talking as we got the packets of frozen food into the freezer, but left the rest of her purchases in their bags when a clatter drew us back to the kitchen. Ben had abandoned the big plastic box filled with his favourite toys, which was supposed to be keeping him amused, and had climbed into the cupboard in the bottom of the Welsh dresser in order to eject an assortment of pots. Lizzie said that she didn't mind. Somebody was being spoiled.

She pushed a mug of tea in my direction and frowned. 'We'll ask Helen about Joannie some time. I'll wait until she and I are on our own.'

'Good idea. It must be the name of the girl who was killed, of course. What did Helen tell you?'

'She doesn't know much. She was busy keeping an eye on Lawrence, who was showing signs of this thing that's happened to him. The doctor was worried that his health might break down altogether during the trial. She doesn't seem to know more than Mickey told us.'

I wasn't sure I believed that, and I wasn't sure Lizzie did, either. We exchanged cautious looks and then Ben found a stack of pot lids and pushed them out on to the rush matting. They made a good noise.

CHAPTER NINE

On and Off the Record

———>•◇•<———

Ben and I were under the dining table being cats – his choice –
when the phone rang. Lizzie picked it up next door. I could hear
the tone of her voice, if not her words, and was crawling out on
hands and knees when she appeared.

'Dido, something's come up. I volunteer once a week at the
library in town – they're short of staff and the Friends of the
Library help out. I arranged for somebody else to do my
Thursdays while you're here, but she had a wisdom tooth pulled
yesterday, and they're having a school visit. Damn it, I'm going to
phone them back and say that I can't!'

I reacted placidly.

'But I don't want to leave you on your own again today!'

This whirl of activity wasn't exactly what I'd imagined,
either, when I'd pictured us engaged in long, quiet, chatty,
country rambles. 'What kind of library is it?'

She looked puzzled and said it was a public branch library. I
asked her whether that meant that it had a children's section.

'Dido, of course! You and Ben can come in with me and I'll
show you the town. Only –' her face fell – 'they want me to
introduce sixty-two nine-year-olds to library membership, so I
don't know how much time I'll have before lunch.'

I grinned. 'Never mind. Ben: books! Lots and lots and lots of
books for children. Just you wait till you see those pictures!'

Lizzie said that between the Parson Roberts Junior School and the Hoare visitation the library might never be the same.

I replied that I was glad to see that our visit was starting to cheer her up.

Past the railway station, the route to the town centre diverged from the main road and flung itself steeply upwards. Castle Hinton had been a fortified hilltop settlement since the days when King Arthur's knights kept dropping in to the pub for a few pints, and its age showed in the narrow, crooked streets leading uphill and converging in a tiny market square with an elaborate war memorial in the middle, surrounded by a tangle of illegally parked cars. I ran the gauntlet with my overly large vehicle and, following Lizzie's directions, edged in beside a rough stone wall halfway down a narrow passage.

The public library occupied a building that had started life as an early Victorian two-roomed schoolhouse. At the door, Lizzie rolled her eyes and hissed, 'I have five minutes before the children are due. Come on!' She whizzed us through an entrance hall, waved distractedly at the woman behind the circulation desk, and steered us rapidly down an aisle and through a door marked 'Children's Library'. 'I'll speak to them out in the main room,' she said, 'and show them the reference books, and then we'll bring them through here to look at the dinosaur books – and Young Adults, which is what little girls read nowadays. If you and Ben want to grab some books and settle over there in the reading area . . .' She gestured towards a little circle of chairs around a piece of carpet. 'The picture books are . . .' She waved at a section of shelves beside it.

'We'll be fine,' I said. 'Go on!'

Ben and I grabbed a stack of picture books and settled into the one adult-sized armchair. Out in the main room I heard feet trampling; voices rose and then subsided abruptly as Lizzie's sounded above them. We began to leaf through a battered copy of *The Pirate Queen*, with special attention to the piratical cat.

Somewhere at about the time when the story was circling round to its conclusion, the door opened and the librarian, with the first batch of visitors, pushed into the room, which promptly became crowded. Two dozen eyes fixed on us. I decided to retreat with Ben and his books through a door I'd noticed just beyond the reading area.

We stood in a passage lit by a couple of small windows high in one wall, and lined with metal shelving which was solid with boxes, folders and stacks of old books. Interesting . . . Ben seemed willing to settle on the floor with the pirates for the moment; I watched him turn a page, then sidled over to what looked like a stack of obscure early twentieth-century fiction, but it had more or less been destroyed by hard use. I was obviously in a storeroom for damaged or unpopular stock. I threw another glance at Ben and wandered along until I found myself surrounded by stacks of local newspapers: the *Western Mail*, the *Somerset Recorder*. The issues up to 1980 were bound in boards; for seven or eight years after that they had been filed in big manila folders; but more recent copies had merely been stacked along the sagging shelves to gather dust. The librarian must be keeping them as a local record; I couldn't believe my luck.

At that point I had to remember the date of the Monksdanes shooting. Lizzie had said something – when was it that she and Mickey met? I made a wild guess at five or so years ago.

'He was sentenced to eight years,' I pointed out to Ben, 'and he's being released early. You'd have to serve about half of a prison sentence before they give you remission, don't you think? So if I start with the files from five years ago, that will be safest.'

Ben ignored the interruption and went on turning pages studiously. I dug into the piles of the *Recorder* for no more serious reason than that it was a tabloid, and more convenient to search through than the other one.

It was easier than I'd expected. My eye was caught by a big front-page photograph of Monksdanes below a headline that declared, TRAGEDY IN SOMERSET VILLAGE, with the subheading,

Body in the Library. It had happened in March 1994. I checked Ben again, noted frivolously that he seemed to be developing the scholarly habits of his grandfather, spread the newspapers out on the floor, and started to trace the story through succeeding issues. When I'd finished, I turned to the *Mail* and checked to see what facts if any it might add.

The police had arrived at Monksdanes and promptly arrested the waiting culprit. An inquest had been held the following week and the date of the trial set soon afterwards. Reports of the trial itself were padded out with a reprise of events, and included a smaller reproduction of that photo of the house, but the court proceedings had apparently been short and sweet. Teddy Waring's conviction was a foregone conclusion: as far as I could see, he had entered a formal plea of guilty and offered no mitigating evidence at all. I paused over a picture of the victim. Her name was Joan Holt and they had reproduced a holiday snap in which she was sitting on a sunny beach, squinting at the camera. She had lived in Alford with her widowed mother, worked at Monksdanes, and had absolutely no business being in the house in the middle of the night. She had been just twenty-one when she died. There was no suggestion that she had ever before done anything criminal; I wondered about that, but of course everybody has to start somewhere. The story was perfectly clear and agreed entirely with what Mickey had told us. No mysteries. Nothing.

'Read!' Ben commanded from behind me.

I took a handful of the old newspapers and went to join him. Fifteen minutes later, Lizzie came and found us on the floor with Ben on my lap, sucking his thumb; we were surrounded by printed matter – picture books to the right, newspapers to the left. She shut the door to the children's section firmly behind her as I looked up and asked, 'Finished?'

She groaned. 'Getting there. I had to have a breather. If only I hadn't given up smoking again last Sunday, I could sneak out for a cigarette. What are you doing here? This is storage.'

I pointed out that the storage included newspapers, and gestured. 'It seems straightforward. He shot her, the police came, Teddy was arrested. His father corroborated his story. At the trial, he pleaded guilty. Neither of the local papers could make anything much of it. It was just a sad, stupid accident. The only hint of anything strange is the sentence: I still think it was harsh. The judge made some remarks about "gross irresponsibility" and "the tragic curtailment of a young life however mistaken its path". And then – eight years. He didn't like Teddy much, but you can't tell why, not from anything I've seen. I wonder what Rose would say if we asked her what really went on?'

'She'd find the question ill-bred and pretend she hadn't heard you,' Lizzie said, and I knew she was right. 'It's no good?'

'I wouldn't say that,' I objected. 'We need to talk to the right person, and I have an idea about it. You remember I told you that Mrs Molyneux said she knew "Joannie and her family"?'

The anxious face of the librarian appeared around the edge of the door. 'Mrs Waring? Do you think . . '

Lizzie started to edge back towards the noise. 'They say Mrs Molyneux is the unofficial village historian. They mean she's a busybody who knows everything that goes on.'

I'd already worked that out, but it wasn't what I'd been thinking of.

'We ought to think how we can talk to Joannie's mother, or any other family members who are still around; Mrs Molyneux might help.'

Lizzie whirled around with the light of battle in her eyes. 'Dido . . .' The voices in the other room were rising. 'Dido, I'll be finished here in less than an hour. Will you be all right that long?'

'If Ben gets restless,' I told her thoughtfully, 'I'll just take him out for a walk and come back later. Right now, I'm going to make a few notes. Facts, if there are any. I wonder whether the reporter who covered the case would remember it, at least if we jogged his memory?'

'They go at twelve thirty,' her voice floated back to me from beyond the doorway. I started skimming the relevant reports again. Names. Places. Dates. There had to be something.

Fifteen minutes later I was bundling the newspapers up and shoving them back on to the shelf. I glanced at my wristwatch. Five to twelve. I had an errand to do, and with luck there'd be enough time. Ben and I tiptoed hand in hand past Lizzie, who was coping confidently with Question Time. When we emerged into the square I looked for somebody to ask directions; but my eye was caught by a familiar kind of blue sign on a darkened stone building across the square: I had found the police station all by myself. We ambled over, edged past a pavement display of fruit and vegetables in front of the greengrocer's, climbed two stone steps and entered the usual notice-filled waiting room with its row of wooden seating. I picked Ben up and settled him on my hip for added emphasis before I rang the visitor's bell.

After a while something stirred and a hatch beside the bell-push opened to reveal a policeman's face. 'Help you, miss?'

I smiled ingratiatingly and produced the first results of my newspaper reading: the name of the detective who had been in charge of the case. 'I need to speak to Detective Inspector Harry Atyeo. Is he still at this station?'

The face frowned slightly, suggesting that my luck had run out. 'No, miss, but I think I've heard the name. I'll find out where he's gone.'

I said I would wait, and we did. I was starting to look at my watch again when a door beside the hatch opened, and somebody emerged and focused on us. He was a fortyish, large man. Plump. Not in uniform.

'You wanted Inspector Atyeo? Can I help you? DS Cole.'

I shook my head, still hopefully. 'I need to speak to him personally about a case he handled a few years ago. Can you tell me where he is?'

'Retired, miss.'

My heart sank, but not my determination. 'Then can you give me his address? Does he live in Castle Hinton?'

I knew as I spoke that it wouldn't work; the sergeant looked slightly askance. 'I'm afraid I can't give that out.'

'But you do have it?'

'It would be in the files,' Cole said simply.

Of course it would. There would be pension records at least. I tore a blank leaf out of the notebook in which I had scribbled Atyeo's name along with the other facts about the case, and printed my own name, with the number of my mobile phone. I added the words: 'About shooting at Alford in 1994 – please contact me.'

'Will you please make sure he gets this?' I asked simply. 'I think he'd be interested.'

The sergeant looked at the paper and, beyond a sharp, short glance in my direction, betrayed no suggestion that it meant anything to him. 'I'll do my best,' he said. It sounded a little too casual to me.

Ben and I paused on the steps and looked across the square. A coach had appeared, and the visiting children were just starting to file on board. I reckoned I still had time for my next errand. Or two, come to think of it: we stopped to buy Ben a banana before we cut across the square again to the post office at the lower end. It was old-fashioned enough to contain two public phone booths, and one was furnished with last year's telephone directory. No Harold Atyeo was listed. We went to get Lizzie and find some lunch.

CHAPTER TEN

Out of Time

———⟫•◈•⟪———

I switched off my mobile phone. I'd just told my father that everything was fine, and that Diane shouldn't worry because Lizzie was about to give her some news, some tremendous news which would explain her recent distracted air. Now I sat on the wooden kitchen chair that I'd shifted over to the open window, wondering how long it would take Barnabas to find out the facts. If there were any. Just about the only fact I had in my pocket this evening was that I couldn't see where to go from here.

Yes I could. Maybe. I picked my mobile off the window sill and pressed the button to ring the phone in my own flat. Ernie Weekes, my friend, employee, sometime bodyguard and present flat-sitter, answered promptly.

'Hey, Dido! How's everything? You having a nice time?'

'Weird,' I said briefly, 'and don't you dare tell Barnabas I said that. I have something I'd like you to do next time you're downstairs. Will you look out that new Directory CD and see if you can find a telephone number for somebody called "H, for Harold, Atyeo"?' I spelled the name. 'I'll assume he still lives somewhere nearby, so try for Somerset area codes first. On the other hand, he's retired, so he might have moved to some resort on the south coast like Bournemouth. It's an off-chance, really, but the name isn't common, so you may be lucky. Phone my mobile if you get anything, will you? If I don't answer, leave a message. If you get a lot of possibilities, you'd better fax a list to the number here, because I need to find this man as quickly as I can.'

Ernie expressed a satisfactory determination to help, as he always does when he suspects that I am about to entertain him. I enquired about his health, Barnabas, Mr Spock and the business in that order and, satisfied by his answers, hung up to wait.

The clock ticked on the dresser. Ben had fallen asleep upstairs a little while ago, almost before I'd tiptoed from the bedroom. Lizzie had set off up the lane to check on the people at Monksdanes, and I'd been watching Alford's version of an evening rush hour from this window: five or six cars going up the lane, one boy on a bicycle who came from that direction and pedalled twice around the green without stopping before he went on, a man who drove up to one of the cottages on the right, parked in the lane, and vanished inside. A dog was barking somewhere. Light clouds had covered the sky an hour or so before; there would be no red sunset today. I yawned, waited for Lizzie to return, and listened to the clock.

A car with a taxi sign on its roof came into sight, circling the green. Lazily I watched a thickset man with a holdall get out and pay. He turned and was coming through the gate, up the path to the kitchen door, and I was thinking, *I'd better go and say he'll find Lizzie at the house*, when he opened the door without knocking. I heard the holdall hit the flagstones, and suddenly he was in the kitchen. I scrambled to my feet and hesitated.

'Lizzie?' He looked at me, then stepped forward quickly and leaned over, planting a kiss on my cheek. 'Lizzie, it's good to meet you at last.'

I stepped back instinctively and got tangled in the chair legs, yelping, 'I'm *not* Lizzie!'

He stepped back too, with a look of dismay. 'Oh lord! I'm sorry, I've only seen her photograph. I'm her brother-in-law. I'm sorry, seeing you sitting there I assumed you . . .'

I said flatly, 'I'm Dido Hoare, a friend. You're Teddy

Waring. We didn't know you were arriving today, and I don't think they were expecting you here. Lizzie's up at Monksdanes now.'

He hesitated, his eyes roaming around the kitchen. He said, 'I'll wait, if you don't mind. I wanted to speak to Mickey first, anyway. Are they all . . . all right?'

There were a lot of ways I could have answered that, but I simply told him that Mickey was due home from work in about half an hour. We stood and sized each other up. I couldn't see any resemblance to the Warings in this man's face. I said, 'I think I'll make a pot of tea.'

CHAPTER ELEVEN

Business Matters

———⟫◆⟪———

'Dido? *Dido!*'

I opened my eyes, focused on Lizzie's anxious face and propped myself up on an elbow. 'What's wrong?'

She continued to hover over the bed. 'I thought I heard crying, but when I came in you were asleep.'

I sat up and passed a hand over my eyes, knowing the nightmare had come back again. 'What time is it?'

'Seven thirty. Ben's awake: he's talking to himself. And there's a fax for you in the machine downstairs. Somebody must have sent it during the night.'

Unsurprised to hear that Ernie had been burning the midnight oil, I made a quick calculation. 'If Ben's only talking, then I probably have time for a quick bath, if that's all right. Has Mickey gone?'

'Just now. Dido . . . ?'

I smiled at her evasively, slid out from under the covers, and staggered towards the stairs. The fax machine was on a small desk in the dining room. I ripped the dangling page from its jaws and, feeling tired and sweaty, headed for the bathroom. Shut in, I filched some aromatherapy gel from a shelf and leaned over the tub while it filled with hot water and foam, looking at the results of Ernie's investigations: a computer printout with just three items and the scrawled note: *Dear Dido if these don't work I'll try again*

Ernie. The nearest Atyeo lived at an address in Frome, ten miles away. Yes!

I fell into the tub. My brain was showing signs of life.

It had been a strange evening. Alone in the house with a convicted killer, I had minded my manners – and yet why should his presence bother me? We sat in the kitchen, drank mugs of tea, looked at each other and chatted stiffly. I was wrong: I'd thought that Teddy was the odd man out, a cuckoo in the Waring nest, but I realised that the old man up at Monksdanes must once have looked like this strong, brown-haired man in his late thirties, with his square, bony face and his cheap jeans and sweatshirt. I had started to talk about Lizzie, about our growing up best friends in Oxford. He offered nothing in exchange. I tried to imagine life behind bars among drug-dealers, burglars and con-men, and couldn't, though probably his lack of polite small talk came from his years there. A car drew up outside at last; when Mickey entered, I mumbled something about Ben but went out into the lane and waited there for Lizzie to come walking down so that I could warn her who had turned up at last.

After an hour or so, the brothers had left the Barton together – under cover of darkness, as I couldn't help thinking. Lizzie and I had stayed, eating an emergency frozen pizza and finishing off a bottle of red wine. Eventually, she asked what on earth was wrong with me, and I told her. That I also had killed somebody. That it had happened last February when I'd found myself in the company of a seriously dangerous man. That I still dreamed of his face as he turned, raising his gun, and the hollow thump as I drove his own car straight over him. She opened a second bottle of wine and we talked about people we had known at school, prompting each other when we forgot a name. When we went to bed at midnight, Mickey still hadn't returned.

I finished my bath, shampooed myself, and decided to get us out of Alford for a few hours.

✻   ✻   ✻

Driving down the lane in the purple van, I found Ben and Lizzie waiting for me by the entrance to the chapel. I left the engine running, got out and settled Ben into the child seat.

Lizzie asked slowly, 'Did you see anybody up there?'

I told her that Monksdanes had been silent when I drove away.

She shrugged. 'Explain to me what we're going to do. Buy books?'

'Probably. I know the dealer who may have bought the Warings' books a few years ago. His name is Kevin Jenkins. I phoned him before breakfast and asked if I could come around. As far as he's concerned, I'm going to look at his stock. I probably should visit him anyway while I'm down here. But if he remembers the Monksdanes library, I can talk to him about the collection.'

'Why?' Lizzie asked, short and to the point.

'I'm uneasy about *Peter Rabbit*. I want to ask him whether he ever saw the book and what it was like.'

Lizzie frowned. 'Would it be very valuable?'

I avoided answering. Any first commercial edition of *The Tale of Peter Rabbit* is worth a couple of thousand pounds if it's in good nick; but monochrome illustrations meant this was the strictly limited edition, privately printed in the same year. I'd never even seen one. Beyond that, there were the notes and sketches that Mickey had mentioned. We were well into five figures. Twenty thousand? Forty?

'I can't get over the idea that it has some kind of connection with the shooting of a burglar at Monksdanes,' I said finally. 'Its theft seems too much of a coincidence. I'd like to ask the police whether they were told anything about the book at that time.'

Kevin runs his business from a large house in a Dorsetshire village. We drove through Castle Hinton, turned right, and made our way through rolling countryside by a web of hedge-lined secondary roads. Thanks to the road atlas, our cross-country journey was made without any problems apart from having to reverse two hundred feet to let a milk tanker past. We curved past a hilltop church whose bell was striking the hour of ten, coasted towards a scattered settlement in a small valley, and turned right into a driveway marked by a discreet painted sign reading BELLTOWER BOOKS. By five past ten we were walking through a door in the side of a converted stone barn into a huge space filled with metal bookshelves and their burden.

'You're going to look at all *these*?' Lizzie enquired in a whisper.

A nasal voice behind us cried, '*Dido Hoare!* Good to see you, Dido. What is this: busman's holiday?'

I turned to face Kevin, a lanky sixty-year-old with a crumpled, humorous face, and got down to it.

'Children's books,' I said. 'I want to build stock: there's a specialist fair in London soon and I've taken a stand. By the way, I don't know whether you've met Lizzie before?' He hadn't, as I knew perfectly well. I explained who she was.

His face expressed friendly interest, nothing more. 'Nice old place up beyond Castle Hinton, right? I remember it. I got a van load of assorted stock from there a few years ago. It was an old-fashioned reading library, not a collection, so they hadn't paid any attention to editions, and they'd thrown out a lot of the dust jackets. Nice books, though.'

I took a little breath. 'Did they show you their *Peter Rabbit*?'

A dreamy reminiscence crossed his face, and I knew that it had been good. 'I wanted to make them an offer, but they weren't selling.'

'Real first issue?' I prodded.

He nodded again. 'I checked it afterwards, just as a matter of interest, and it was right. Presentation copy to somebody in the family, with a note on a blank leaf and some pen sketches here and there.'

'That does sound very good,' I said soberly.

'I would probably have sent it straight off to auction in London,' Kevin said, 'but anyway they weren't selling.' The memory made him wistful. 'They haven't changed their minds, have they? If they do, you be sure you get it. Would you like some coffee?' He looked from me to Lizzie and back again.

I said, 'In about half an hour I'll be dying for it. Lizzie, if you can keep Ben amused for a bit, I'll make a start . . .'

An hour, two large cups of strong coffee, and some lively negotiations later, I shut the back doors of the van on two cartons of books. I waved goodbye to Kevin, standing in the doorway of his book barn, backed the van around a rose bush, and headed towards the road.

'That was nice,' Lizzie said. She was clutching an old Agatha Christie novel (second issue) that Kevin had given her when she told him she didn't recognise the title.

'Profitable too,' I told her. 'I don't mean what I've bought, though I'm going to be pleased with that. I mean *Peter Rabbit*. You heard what he said; I'd look for it to be worth at least twenty or thirty thousand.'

'Then where is it?' Lizzie wondered loudly.

Not having the answer, I remained silent.

We were approaching the turning at the Woolpack when Lizzie said suddenly, 'Let's not go home. Let's stop for a sandwich, shall we? I've never been in here.'

The clock on the dashboard said it was nearly twelve thirty, but Ben was still lively, so I shrugged, signalled and manoeuvred through the gate. Three cars and a couple of vans were lined up along the front. We joined them and looked around. It was an old building, freshly painted, with a folding board beside the door that offered 'Home-cooked Lunches 12–2', which seemed hopeful, despite the lack of customers. We made our way down a short corridor and poked our heads into a large, bright saloon bar with bunches of fresh flowers on the window sills. A couple of the tables were occupied, but the place was quiet and civilised. A man behind the bar looked up when I opened the door and nodded.

'We have a baby with us,' I said cautiously. 'Is that . . .'

The landlord smiled. 'Don't worry. Take the window table around at the side there. You'll find a menu on the blackboard – that is, if you're eating? I'll come round in a minute for your order.'

We made our way to a kind of side extension where we settled at a table that held a little glass vase full of fresh buds. The blackboard offered a selection of home-made pies, Wiltshire ham, Thai stir-fry and venison sausages that made us raise enquiring eyebrows at each other, and order hopefully when the landlord appeared.

'If you like real ale,' he said, 'I have some from a little brewery over towards Glastonbury. It's called Pigswill, but don't let that worry you. If the baby likes apple juice, there's some stuff I get from one of the farms.'

The food, when it appeared, lived up to expectations. So did the ale. 'There's just one thing I don't understand,' I said to the landlord as we paused contentedly beside the till half an hour later. 'Where are all your customers?'

He smiled oddly. 'Well, lunch is always slow and it's quieter than usual today. But you're right, it's been a bit of a disappointment to my wife and I. We came over from Gillingham six months ago, and we were refurbishing for two of those, but it hasn't worked out all that well.'

'Why ever not?' Lizzie asked sharply. 'Your food is nice, the beer was lovely . . .'

His laugh was short. 'If you were local,' he said, 'you'd know.'

I saw Lizzie open her mouth, presumably to correct his idea that we were just passing through, so I said quickly, 'Know what?'

He shrugged. 'When we took over, this place was falling apart, but the turnover was good. It was an old pub, neglected, same landlord for years. We wanted to do the place up and make it a decent family pub, serve meals – the wife is a good cook, isn't she? So we closed down just after the New Year and renovated, cleared out all the dark little cubby-holes where things went on –'

Lizzie blinked. 'Things?'

'Drugs. I found out after we took over that this place was where everybody came for heroin and speed. I don't even mean just a bit o' pot. Well, I wouldn't have that, so we cleared out the place in more ways than one. The regulars used to come from all over, places like Alford and Lovington and Champflower; and now they've gone. Don't get the locals any more, or anyway not that sort. It's starting to build up again slowly — I just hope we make it.'

I squeaked, '*Drugs? Here?*'

Lizzie echoed, '*Heroin?*'

The landlord just laughed at us. We wished him good luck, promised we'd come again, and headed out.

'You wouldn't think — out here in the country. Or would you?' I asked, strapping Ben in his seat, noticing that he was starting to flag at last, and at the same time thinking that I was being naïve: who ever said that drugs are confined to the dark alleys behind inner-city clubs?

But Lizzie had already turned to other things. 'What now?'

I said, 'Nothing. Nap time.'

But I was remembering how busy the Five Bells had been on Monday evening. Maybe the trade had simply moved down the lane.

CHAPTER TWELVE

Party Time

———————>•◇•<———————

'Dido, you *must* come! *Please!*'

I started to say, 'Ben —'

'I *know* it'll be late, but Helen says she can make up a bed for him in the next room. He's so good-tempered, he'll be fine. Dido, Mickey's coming home early, and I've accepted for all three of us, seven o'clock for seven thirty, and I need some back-up, you absolutely *have* to help me out here.' She stopped and laughed, trying to make a joke of it, but I'd heard the nervousness in her voice. And I didn't really want to miss what promised to be an interestingly awkward evening.

We had been summoned to dinner at Monksdanes to celebrate Teddy's homecoming. Black tie. I'd pointed out that it would be after Ben's bedtime. I'd objected that I hadn't even packed a party dress, much less a black tie, to which Lizzie replied smartly that I would have to borrow one of hers, and produced a dark-red crushed-velvet affair with a low neckline and long sleeves which not only fitted me, but, as she pointed out triumphantly, really suited my colouring. Then she looked at me and the dress with narrowed eyes and said, 'I'll lend you my pearl choker. And I'm going to make up your eyes properly. You'd look great if you'd just bother with a bit of liner and mascara.' Which seemed to settle the matter.

'Lizzie, if Ben's unhappy, I'm leaving and bringing him back to bed.'

'Done!' Lizzie agreed and began to wonder aloud what she could wear, while I carried the borrowed dress to my borrowed bedroom and took the opportunity to make a private phone call.

I was answered on the first ring: '*Dido Hoare, An –*'

I interrupted. 'It's me. Hello, Barnabas, is everything all right?'

'Naturally. I might ask you the same. I tried to ring you this morning.'

I told him that I had switched off my mobile for a few hours, and was replying now to the message he had left. 'Has the catalogue gone out? Is it all right?'

'Quite handsome,' Barnabas conceded. 'We are putting the last ones into envelopes, and Ernie will take the mailing across to the post office shortly to catch the last pick-up. How is Ben?'

I told him about everyone's health, explained that an unexpected brother-in-law had turned up and, after a moment's hesitation, added, ' . . . from jail. On parole or something.' He would find out sooner or later, and there was no point asking for trouble.

'Really?' My father's voice became stiff. 'What is the man like? How old? Dido, try to remember that you are strangely attracted to men of very dubious –'

I interrupted again. 'He killed a woman. Accidentally, with a shotgun. He looks and acts sane but creepy, and I am *not* attracted. Look, Barnabas, we're going up to the house for a family dinner soon and I have a lot to do, and I need Ernie to look up a book for me. Can I speak to him, please?'

There was a lengthy pause while Barnabas considered his tactics. After a moment I heard two muffled voices conferring, and then Ernie answered. He sounded subdued.

There was no point saying anything while I could assume that Barnabas was eavesdropping, so I moved to the reason for my call. 'Ernie, I need some information about a book. Do you have a pen? Author: Beatrix Potter. Title: *The Tale of Peter Rabbit*. First privately printed edition. The important thing is that except for the frontispiece the illustrations are black and white. Do a web search, all the usual sites. I want to know two things: first, is anybody offering a copy at the moment? They're pretty rare: I think only a couple of hundred were printed. Second, has anybody sold one of them, an association copy, at any time in the past five or six years, with author's notes and sketches? Check the auction records and the specialist children's book dealers. You can probably limit that to British ones at first, but check the major foreign auctioneers as well as the London houses. If Barnabas asks, tell him I bought a lot of books today from Belltower, and I'm trying to follow something up.'

I made sure that Ernie had got all the details, urged him not to stay late in the shop but get down to studying because his exams were due – which was probably old news to him, come to think of it – and switched off. I checked my wristwatch and listened for noises from the next bedroom. Then I found Ernie's fax and rang the Frome number.

I was answered by what sounded like a child. I gave my name and asked for Mr Atyeo.

'Oh,' said the voice, 'my father will be home from work in an hour.'

My heat sank. 'Then I think I have the wrong number. I wanted a Harry Atyeo who's a retired policeman.'

'That's Grandpa,' the voice said promptly.

I controlled an impulse to let out a whoop. 'I think it must be,' I agreed politely. 'Does he live there? Or can you tell me his phone number?'

The voice said, 'He and Gram moved to Weston-super-Mare. Wait a minute.' I heard paper rustling. After a moment, the voice recited a number. I scribbled, thanked him and hung up. I thought about trying the number; then I thought about stopping to decide what to say. By the time that Ben was announcing his re-entry into the waking world, I had realised that it was good weather for a trip to the seaside. Party time, Ben was suggesting.

Sitting beside the low camp cot in the dim morning room, I launched into the story of Goldilocks for the third time, letting my voice sink into a soft monotone. Ben clutched his blanket with drooping eyelids, and when I let the story fade into silence, his breathing remained regular. In the reception room I could hear voices and the clink of glasses. Pre-dinner sherry. This was a formal occasion, even if there were only seven of us; but Helen and Rose had opened up the reception room and the big dining room, and lit fires against the evening chill. There was even a woman who had come in to wash up, though she remained invisible in the kitchen.

I stood and waited to see whether Ben would object to my going. Darkness was just falling. In the garden, a bird called sharply, and when I looked out I saw a man pausing at the edge of the drive and watching me through the window. He had been wheeling a bicycle, balancing a spade and a hoe along the bar. We stared at each other. Then he nodded and went on. I removed myself quietly and joined the others as they were crossing the hall to the dining room.

'There's a man outside,' I told them. 'With a bicycle. He was looking in.'

'With a bicycle?' Rose repeated. 'The gardener. He's late tonight. Teddy, take the head of the table, dear. Dido, will you sit between Teddy and Mickey? Of course we are a man short, but it scarcely matters among family. Lawrence, my dear, come with me.'

We grouped ourselves around the top end of the huge dining table, with the returned prodigal at the head in the place of honour, Lawrence silent at one side between his wife and his daughter, and the three of us non-residents facing them and the windows, where Helen had just pulled the heavy curtains to shut out the deepening twilight. On the table, the flames of the candles in two Victorian silver candelabra flickered in the draught. Helen and Lizzie began to serve cream soup from a tureen on the sideboard. The rest of us sat in silence. The uneasiness I'd anticipated was there, all right, and everybody was feeling it. I tried to think of some light-hearted *bon mot* to break the silence. The words, 'So, Teddy, this must be very different from your recent prison meals?' jumped uncontrollably into my mind, and I heard myself snigger. *Dido, will you pull yourself together?*

The Warings looked at me attentively, waiting to hear the joke. I opened my mouth.

'I may have forgotten something. Is your name Tracy?' It was the old man who had spoken. Startled, I looked across the table and found his eyes fixed on me. He smiled ruefully. 'I have trouble remembering, sometimes. Did I tell you I have been diagnosed with memory failure?'

I said carefully, 'My name is Dido. We've met before. I'm Lizzie's friend. Your daughter-in-law, Lizzie.'

'I know she is!' the old man said impatiently. 'You — what's your name?' He looked from me to Teddy and back again and his stare grew hostile. 'You weren't invited! Why have you brought her here, boy? I won't stand for it!' Suddenly, he was shouting.

Rose intervened sharply, 'Lawrence! Your soup!' Helen was sliding a soup plate quickly in front of her father. 'Aren't you hungry?'

She shrugged apologetically at me, but I was busy watching Teddy realise what had been happening to his father while he was away. He stared down at the table cloth, and when Lizzie put his soup plate down on that spot he remained motionless.

There was a banging somewhere.

Helen flinched. 'Back door,' she said, and fled to answer the knocker. We all, except perhaps for Lawrence, listened to her steps on the tiles, the sound of the back door opening, the murmur of voices. The conversation went on for a while; then she was back. 'I forgot it was Friday, with all the . . . It's Billy, he wants paying, and I forgot to get . . . Mickey, can you lend me thirty pounds?'

Mickey was getting up, flinging his napkin down. 'I'll pay him. You people go on.' He closed the door to the hallway as he went out.

But I was watching Teddy, who stirred in his chair. 'Billy?' he said. '*Billy?* He's working *here?*'

'We need somebody to keep the grounds under control,' Helen whispered. For some reason, she was angry. 'He does odd jobs for a lot of people.'

Then Teddy was on his feet too, facing her, straining forward like a runner. 'Are you mad?'

He strode towards the voices; but we all heard the sound of a door banging and Mickey coming back. He and Teddy met one another in the doorway, Helen fluttering at Teddy's elbow.

'Come back to the table.' Rose's voice was as hard as it was quiet. Everyone paused.

Lawrence said abruptly, 'I'm sorry to interrupt, but you've forgotten to give me my soup. You have given me an empty plate. Have you forgotten? I would really like a little soup now.'

'And you shall have it,' Rose said. 'Helen, give your father some soup, please. Teddy, sit down and finish yours. Mickey, will you pour the wine? We have visitors.'

That was a warning. The visitors, who seemed to be both Lizzie and me, threw one another a covert glance as the Warings rushed to do her bidding. I'm not sure about my own expression, but her face was a picture. We ate soup. As we did, Rose gave us an account of the history of Monksdanes and of the three houses that had borne the name: a ninth-century monastery, a Tudor manor, and the present Grade I Listed Georgian building. It was an interesting historical account, and a truly gutsy performance; and there was about as much chance that we could find the time to think about whatever it was that had just happened, as that Rose would suddenly climb stiffly onto the tablecloth and do a bump-and-grind striptease routine between the candelabra.

CHAPTER THIRTEEN

Sand

We were looking for one house out of the dozens of white bungalows with red roofs that sat along the tidy, sloping streets above the southern end of town. We found it by trial, error, and asking directions twice. There was a view.

Weston-super-Mare is an old seaside resort set on a shallow bay between two headlands: a traditional town with a pier, an aquarium, and amusement arcades mixed with small hotels, guest houses, fish and chip shops, and stalls selling buckets, sweets, sun hats, rock, hot dogs, candy floss, T-shirts and cans of soft drinks. The sea glinted a long way off beyond wide, muddy sands. The brightness made you squint.

I stopped in the empty road for the last time and consulted the dashboard clock. In fact we were two minutes early, but by the time we had unstrapped ourselves, got out, wiped Ben's face, and climbed the sloping path to the house it was two thirty on the dot. I pushed the bell. The chime was still vibrating when the door was opened by an upright, sixtyish, bald man straightening a navy cardigan on himself and looking expectant.

'Miss Hoare?'

I said that I was, and introduced my companions.

Lizzie's surname made his eyes narrow. He stood back for us. 'Please. Come inside. First door on your left. I'm on my own this afternoon; Franny, my wife, is shopping. I could put the kettle on . . .'

We said we were fine for the moment and let him usher us into a sunlit sitting room and settle us in a row on the sofa. He faced us from a battered armchair which was, obviously, his usual seat.

'You have a lovely view from here,' I said. Always direct and to the point. 'How long have you been living in Weston?'

My intended victim said briefly, 'Two years, thereabouts. Mrs Waring, I don't think we met in '94?'

Lizzie explained that in the spring of '94 she herself hadn't met any Warings. 'I met Mickey in Bristol that summer.'

'So.' I was watching a policeman shift into interrogation mode. 'So you don't know much about this business down here?'

Lizzie said bluntly, 'I only found out about the "business" a week ago. But then, Mickey and I only moved to Alford last autumn to be near his parents.'

Atyeo considered. 'The old man must be . . .'

'Seventy-nine.'

'I heard he has some mental problems.'

I sat up straighter: *he was keeping track of them* . . .

When the sound of Lizzie's voice stopped, I pulled myself together and asked, 'We wondered whether, since you're retired now, you'd mind talking about that case?'

He turned his attention to me. He was slightly cross-eyed, and I found myself not quite sure whether he was looking at my face or at a point above my right shoulder. After a moment, he asked, 'What do you want to know?'

'To begin at the end,' I said bluntly, 'I wanted to know about the sentence. Eight years?'

'You think that's not much for killing somebody?'

Now I was watching him very hard. 'It isn't enough for murdering somebody, but it seems a lot for accidentally shooting a burglar in your own home in a struggle in the dark.'

A smile hovered and vanished. 'I think I'd agree with that,

and there was no *evidence* of murder, or of any intention to murder.'

I took the bull by the horns. 'Then why wasn't he given a suspended sentence? Or a couple of years, if the judge really thought he'd been careless or reckless or needed to be taught a lesson?'

Atyeo was silent. I looked at him steadily: he had to understand that I would just go on waiting. After a moment, he looked away through the window at the bright sea. 'I'd say — mind you, I'm not a mind reader, His Honour had no reason to tell anybody what he really thought — I'd say there was some point that the trial didn't bring out. His Honour asked for reports before the sentence. Maybe something he read bothered His Honour. Do you know anything about court proceedings, miss?'

'A little. Not much.'

'Well, what happened here was that the accused didn't go into the witness box. His father did. He repeated what he said in his first statement to us and stuck to the facts. We didn't have much on our side. There were witnesses the prosecution could have called if any defence had been offered, but we had no *evidence* that would have affected the verdict, as His Honour pointed out to our side. Mr Edward Waring's plea of guilty to manslaughter was accepted, and that was the end of it.'

Something made me say, 'But you were uneasy.'

'Well, we were. The investigating officers.'

I had sat through more than one speech from policemen about their feeling that something in their findings had been incomplete, and how they were often proved correct.

He sighed and turned his wandering eye on me again. 'About two things. Three. First of all, the dead girl had told her family she was pregnant, and that it was the old man's doing. Now, the autopsy showed that she wasn't.'

'She'd had an abortion or a miscarriage?'

Atyeo shook his head.

'But there could have been a reason for her story – trying to get money from the Warings, or just trying to get attention.'

'That's right.'

'He didn't –'

'The postmortem report said the deceased was on the pill and hadn't been pregnant. Seemed like a dead-end. Funny business, but no way into it.'

I tucked the vanishing pregnancy away in my list of things to ask Mrs Molyneux and placed a small bet with myself that she would know all about it. 'There was something else?'

'May be,' he said deliberately. 'Times didn't fit. There was a delay, several hours, between the time of the shooting and the time the 999 call was logged.'

'You're sure?'

'Well . . .' A gesture commented on 'sure'. 'Something about that. You can never be entirely sure.'

'What my husband was told,' Lizzie said in a low voice, 'was that his father heard the shot and went downstairs and found Teddy there, very upset. It might have taken them a little while to calm down and decide what to do.'

'Exactly,' Atyeo agreed. 'You can never be sure what people will do in these circumstances, respectable people. Shocked. Blood everywhere. I said all that to myself. Maybe they spent a long time talking, maybe even wondering about Mr Waring slipping away. Maybe it took old Mr Waring some time to convince his son that the best thing to do was what they finally did.'

'But it bothered you?'

He said simply, 'It was never explained. I liked to have everything all clear.'

'What did they *say*?'

'Old Mr Waring said he wasn't sure how long they sat there. The defendant, in the preliminary interview, said they'd phoned right off, then later he wasn't sure, he was too upset to remember. That's possible. There was nothing to get hold of. And witnesses in sudden, emotional situations are unreliable.'

'You said *three* things.'

'Don't know about the last. There was mud. Mud on the carpet, under the broken window and near the body, tracked over to the body. Just a few smears, you wouldn't notice unless you were looking. Our scene-of-crime people got it, of course.'

'What did it mean?' Lizzie asked impatiently.

Atyeo answered slowly, 'Well, nothing, maybe. Just ordinary local mud with nothing to show when it got left there. But the dead woman's shoes were clean. I remember: pretty blue leather shoes. High heels. Nice and clean. The young man was wearing bedroom slippers, nothing on them. Or on old Mr Waring's. Only place we found fresh mud was on boots inside the back door. That was a wet summer, all the family wore wellingtons around the grounds. You might track mud in any time. They couldn't say that mud had anything to do with the incident. Seems funny?'

'But you couldn't prove anything, and nobody had the chance to ask about this in court. Wait a minute: high-heeled shoes? She broke in to burgle the house in the middle of the night wearing *high-heeled shoes?*'

'That niggles,' Atyeo said simply. 'One of the cases in my career that still niggle, you know. You just have to shrug your shoulders and walk away. Doesn't do to brood, Miss Hoare. Get on with the job, do your best, hope for luck and do better next time.'

'You can't win them all,' Lizzie added vaguely.

'Never a truer word.'

Out in the driveway, a car had appeared. Its driver, a middle-aged woman, turned off the engine, emerged stiffly and looked towards the house.

I said quickly, 'These worries — did the judge know about them? Are you saying that he took them into account when he was deciding the sentence?'

'They were mentioned,' Atyeo said simply. 'In my statement I mentioned what I could. I thought at the time it got lost;

afterwards, I thought His Honour noticed. Sharp man. And then, what was in those reports, eh? Now, I'd better go along and help Franny unload the groceries. Will you stay for a cup of tea?'

'We'd like to,' I said, 'but I think my little boy is getting restless.'

Atyeo considered Ben, who was showing signs of wanting to climb over the back of the settee and fall head first on to the carpet with tears. 'They get bored easy at that age,' he said. 'I remember it well, we had four. But it gets easier as time goes on, as Franny used to say, and she's often right.'

We gathered ourselves and Ben, and followed him towards the front door. I asked, 'Do you mind if I phone you, if I have any other questions?'

He said over his shoulder, 'Don't know that I'd have any answers, but you do that. We'll be here. We're always here, until we go to Frome, but that's not till school holidays. Family is important: we keep in touch. But you'll reach me here until July.'

I laughed and thanked him and said that I wouldn't be around that long myself.

'And anyway, Miss Hoare, Mrs Waring: if you should learn anything, I'd like to know – for my own satisfaction. So if you were willing to ring and tell me if you hear anything, I'd appreciate that.'

Well, well.

We gave Ben a little swing between us back to the van to compensate for his boring time. I'd been anything but bored. Well, well.

'Now what?' I asked my companions when we had shut ourselves into the van. 'It's still early. What shall we do? I don't think it would be wise just to turn around and drive home – not from Ben's point of view.'

'What you do at Weston,' Lizzie explained confidently, 'is go out along the pier and take one of the rides and then – we haven't finished the sandwiches we brought, we can buy some drinks, and it's warm enough to sit on the beach. We should have a picnic on the sands.'

'Have pink,' Ben agreed solemnly, settling it.

We re-entered Alford as the sun was setting, passed the cottage, and drove straight to the end of the lane, avoiding Barney as he sniffed at something in the weeds, and two boys pedalling their bikes in circles. We locked the van, and looked furtively at the face of the big house as we walked past. Teddy and Mickey were sitting with glasses in the illuminated morning room, their heads together. By unspoken agreement, we kept on going. Ben was dragging his feet even before we reached the gates; I picked him up and a shower of sand fell out of his clothing. The lights were on in all the houses on the lane, and the dog and the cyclists had gone. Something rustled in the undergrowth as we passed the stile at the end of a footpath. I yawned.

In the gloaming, we cut straight across the grass in front of the chapel. Lizzie was first through her gate, pulling out her keys as we went up the short path to the kitchen door. She stopped so suddenly that Ben and I ran into her.

'Dido . . .'

I woke up. 'What's wrong?'

'There's something here.'

I craned around her. 'What? Where?'

We edged up to the door and I examined her discovery. A heap of ragged fur was stretched across the step. Not a cat. A dead fox. I leaned over. My nose told me it had been dead for a while; my brain told me that it hadn't arrived on foot.

I said, 'Leave it. Get the door open. I have to get Ben inside.'

On cue, he started to grizzle with exhaustion. We stepped over the corpse, slammed the door behind us and switched on all the lights.

CHAPTER FOURTEEN

Low Profiles

Lizzie and I listened to water running and hand-washing in the kitchen. The noise stopped and Mickey Waring strode into the sitting room. I couldn't read his expression.

'I've wrapped it up and thrown it in the dustbin.'

When Lizzie remained silent, I said, 'I don't think you should have done that. The police might want to see it.'

'Police?' Mickey echoed. 'Why? Or, rather, why would we tell them?'

I'd been assuming all along that we would make a phone call to the Castle Hinton police in the morning. Well . . . 'What killed it? Did you look?'

'I didn't do an autopsy,' he snapped. 'It must have been dead for a few days. A dog might have got it. Or a car. God's sake, it might have died of old age for all I know!'

And why are you so cranky, Mr Waring?

'There's a joker around,' he said slowly, as though he had heard my silent question.

Lizzie said sharply, 'Well, we didn't think it had died on the spot, but it wasn't funny. Why would anybody leave it there?'

I said, 'You think it has something to do with Teddy coming back, don't you?'

He sat heavily in an armchair and stared at where the flames would have been if anybody had bothered to light the fire that evening. After a moment, he braced himself. 'There was a dead rat on the front doorstep at Monksdanes this evening. I nearly stepped on it when I was leaving. Teddy and I got it out of sight before Rose or Helen saw it.'

Lizzie was leaning forward. 'Mickey! You have to call the police!'

I said I'd second the motion.

'No! Someone's playing games. Teddy and I talked it over when we found the thing. Maybe even some kids – it's childish enough! What you do if somebody starts that kind of nonsense is ignore it. If I find out who it was, I'll take steps, speak to them or their fathers. What I *won't* do is fuss. That's just what they want. They're attention-seekers, these people.'

I said, '"These people"?'

'Whoever it is.'

'Mickey, it was *disgusting*.'

He looked over at Lizzie when she spoke and made a sound like a laugh. 'I know. I'm sorry, my love, but they'll lose interest if we ignore them. Make sure the house is locked up when the two of you go out, because a dead fox at the door is one thing, but you don't want to find one on the kitchen table. And don't worry. Look, I'll reassess the situation if anything else happens, but at the moment we want to keep a low profile. If we draw attention to the fact that Teddy's back, the next thing you know one of the newspapers will turn up; they'll print a little item on the dead animals, they'll talk about a vendetta in the village, and the manslaughter thing will get raked over again. If we can keep it quiet, that's really the best thing.'

'So that's what the family wants?' Lizzie suggested coldly. She had gone pink in the face.

'It's best,' he said defensively. Maybe too defensively, given that he could be right. 'Look, if you people don't mind, I'm going to have a bath and go to bed. It's been quite an evening. There's church in the morning, and I said I'd take Rose.'

'I'll go with you,' Lizzie said brightly. 'We'll see whether anybody will speak to us, shall we? Maybe the vicar will pull out his bell, book and candle when he notices us there.'

He looked at her, hesitated, turned away with a grim face and left us.

After a while, Lizzie sighed. 'I shouldn't have said that.'

I don't claim to be an expert on marriage, but I had to agree. Although in her place I would probably have made my feelings just as clear. More so. 'Maybe he's right,' I thought I had to say. 'If it is a prank, you should ignore it.'

'You make it sound like we're at school.' She pouted.

I probably did. But if somebody had a quarrel with Teddy Waring, that didn't mean Lizzie had to be involved. It didn't mean she should be quarrelling with her husband.

Lizzie said, 'I hate it down here.'

'Then why don't you both go back to Bristol? Now that Teddy's here, *he* can keep an eye on Helen and the old people. And if they decide that there's too much bad feeling locally, they can move. That's probably what your mother would say, if she knew about this business. I can't see why they haven't sold the house long ago, they can't afford to run it. They could take the money and buy a bungalow in . . . in Weston-super-Mare!'

We looked at each other. Lizzie snorted. A moment later, we were laughing harder than the joke deserved. 'I'll suggest that to Mickey,' she said. 'Dido, I'm going to make you some hot chocolate.'

I woke in the darkness, thinking that somebody had spoken, and lay there listening. After a moment I heard a voice next door. It was Ben talking to himself; he did that sometimes. I could hear that he was all right and if he needed me I'd hear that too. Maybe I was feeling lonely. He didn't speak again.

My wristwatch was on the bedside table under the silly lamp. I felt for it and read the illuminated face: just coming up to midnight. I felt as awake as though I'd already had a full night's sleep.

The thermostat clicked, switching the electric radiator on. I slid out from under the blanket, crept gingerly across the carpet in the dark, put out a hand to the little orange light and found the switch by touch. Off. Then I stepped across and slipped between the two halves of the thick velour curtains. The window was shut. I pushed the casement wide. Ivy rustled, and I leaned my elbows on the deep sill once again to breathe fresh air. In the distance a bell struck. I listened to it, counting to twelve. There must be a clock in the church tower; I hadn't noticed its chimes before; maybe it rang midnight to mark the beginning of Sunday.

There were no stars tonight. It had begun to cloud over as we drove back from the seaside, and even the moon was only a glow behind high clouds. I could just make out the line of the chapel roof and the hedgerows and trees against the sky. About twenty yards up the lane, facing my window, was the black shape of a car at the side of the road. I hadn't seen one parked in that spot before, so my eyes were hesitating on it when I saw the light inside. A little flame. I saw, and couldn't quite see, a face behind it. Somebody drew on a cigarette. After a couple of minutes, a spark arced through the air as the smoker tossed it out of his window on to the road.

At that point I remembered what Lizzie had said the first night. The Peeping Tom. Half of me wanted to pull on my trainers and a coat and creep downstairs, out the door, and around in the shadows of the chapel until I could read his number plate, after which a shouted threat or two might be pretty effective. The other half pointed out that I'd probably just encounter some sick flasher who would make me feel really stupid, and suggested crawling back into bed and pulling the blankets over my head. I compromised by doing nothing.

I was thinking of giving up when I heard the engine start. The side lights blinked on and the car rolled gently forwards. I leaned out as far as I could in the overhanging ivy and squinted at the dimly illuminated rear number plate. I only had time to read 'N981 . . .' in the fraction of a second before the angle became too sharp. It passed out of sight behind the house next door.

I pulled the window half shut and made sure the curtains were drawn tight. Then I switched on the lamp, dug a pen and my little notebook out of my shoulder bag, and wrote down the half of the registration number that I'd managed to get. I switched the light off again, listened for sounds from the next room, and finally crawled under the blankets to lie stiffly, listening for the car to come back, and fell asleep again, of course.

CHAPTER FIFTEEN

Roast Beef and Gravestones

The church party drove off at about ten twenty because Rose preferred to be in the Monksdanes pew in good time. I rinsed Ben's breakfast bowl under the hot tap and put it into the rack, then turned to watch him. He was reading a picture book upside down with every appearance of enjoyment, obviously feeling no great urge to do anything else.

I, on the other hand, couldn't settle. There wasn't even a Sunday paper, although Mickey had explained that by driving only three miles I could find a shop open: the twenty-four-hour, seven-day, London economy hadn't really taken hold in rural Somerset yet. I could spend the morning watching cartoons on TV. Or – it was still dry outside, despite a forecast of heavy rain – I could try again to wander about and bump into people. With Rose out of the way, I might even try to bump into Teddy. I ought to discuss dead animals with him, face to face. I might even find someone willing to fill me in on the old Peeping Tom story.

'Shall we go out and look for cows?' I asked Ben sneakily.

'Look dog,' he countered.

That was all right. Barney was probably holding down the middle of the road again on the way to Monksdanes. I told him it was a deal.

I locked up with the spare keys, and we set off towards the

centre of the village. Mrs Molyneux's garage was open and empty when we passed the chalet bungalow, and nobody was digging in the herbaceous borders. On the lawn of the tall brick house next door, a grey-haired, tweedy man was cutting grass with an old-fashioned hand mower. He stared at us as we passed and nodded gravely when I stared back. There was more activity at the council houses up behind the lilacs: people moving around in one of the tiny gardens, a couple of small children running and shrieking, and two fat women coming slowly down the path. It was probably my imagination, but I thought that they looked at us before they turned to talk to a man who had just appeared from a shed at the end.

I stopped beside the public phone box to consult Mrs Molyneux's map. It confirmed that the main part of the village stretched northwards, from the dead-end sign to where the church and a post office were shown. On the way, a short spur led off beside a stream. Mrs Molyneux's 'picturesque' Mill House was probably down there. We would find out. Beyond it, a minor track left the road, curving north and west towards the stream, where a ford and bridge sat side by side, then wandered off through farmlands to the next hamlet. I folded up the map and set off.

It was a morning full of interest for Ben, who spoke to a white Samoyed dog behind a gate, a Shetland pony being led down the lane, and enough cows to satisfy him, temporarily. I exchanged waves and smiles with a dozen people working in their gardens – Alford was not a very church-going community – and pursued conversations about the weather and the scenery with anyone who came closer than shouting distance.

At noon I gave up. The Five Bells had opened, so we strolled in, bought our drinks at the hatch in the passage, and made for the swings. The sum total of my discoveries was nil: this village was about as cosy and intimate as my own inner-city street. Maybe I should stick to London. I sipped a tonic water, pushed Ben, and watched the road for cars coming back from the church.

At about five to one, what was, for Alford, a stream of traffic arrived from that direction. In the best English tradition, at least half of it headed straight into the car park as their passengers sought secular refreshment. There was no sign of Mickey's black Honda, but I noticed a green Morris Minor pass in a stately manner and recognised the driver.

By the time we reached the bungalow, the garage door was shut. We went up the path and banged the knocker. The door opened abruptly: she had been standing in the entrance hall, taking off her coat and hat.

I said, diplomatically apologetic, 'I thought we'd say hello. I hope you aren't busy.' My instinct suddenly kicked in. 'I badly need your help, if you have a moment.'

The old lady straightened her glasses on her nose and looked at me closely. 'I'd be more than happy. Come in, the two of you. Can I offer you . . . squash for the young man, of course, and a sherry? I don't suppose you'd care to stay and eat with me? Unless you have other plans?'

An intense smell of roast beef hit my nose, and my stomach remarked that not only had I forgotten breakfast, I'd made no preparations for lunch despite having turned down an invitation to more Monksdanes soup and sandwiches. 'Are you sure?' I asked weakly.

Mrs Molyneux beckoned us into her living room with impatient gestures, her smile fading at my question. 'I have never,' she explained slowly, 'really adjusted to my husband's passing. I tend to find I have cooked for two by sheer force of habit. I've stopped worrying about it, I merely save half for the next day. So as it happens, there is a nice piece of roast rib, with roast potatoes and parsnips. And a cherry cobbler. Not fresh, of course, frozen. Still, quite pleasant, with cream.'

I told her truthfully that it sounded wonderful and settled in an armchair with Ben on my lap. We all looked at one another.

'Rose was at church this morning,' she observed abruptly, 'with your friend and her husband.'

'Was it all right?'

She knew just what I meant. 'There was a certain amount of looking the other way,' she conceded. 'Naturally, everyone was polite, but in point of fact the three of them were left to themselves, more or less. I spoke to them, of course, as did the vicar and one or two others.'

I asked a little mischievously, 'What would have happened if Teddy had gone with them?'

'Then,' she said drily, 'no doubt he would have been ignored, though a remark *might* have dropped, I suppose. There is a certain amount of curiosity in the village, and uneasiness, which I suppose is what you want to ask about.'

'Why uneasiness?' I asked carefully. 'Is it simply because Teddy killed somebody? Or is there more to it than that?'

She looked at me thoughtfully. 'There is more to it, of course. Miss Hoare, the meat will be ready in half an hour, and it won't take me a minute to lay two more places. May I show you something?'

I said she might.

'We'll drive,' she said. 'Perhaps you and the little one might be more comfortable in the back seat?'

The old Morris was a two-door model. She tipped up the passenger seat, and I struggled inside with Ben. The car must have been forty years old, and getting into the back was like clambering into a leather-lined bathtub. Mrs Molyneux settled into the driver's seat and rolled us gently into the lane; we headed for the crossroads and proceeded at our stately pace past the mill turning and on northwards, between the rows of old cottages, small fields and farm buildings; at a point just beyond our earlier wanderings was the entrance to a large factory farm with long, metal buildings.

'Pigs,' Mrs Molyneux observed briefly, 'as you will discover if the wind goes round to the north.'

At the far end of the village she swerved recklessly across the road and pulled up on hard standing in front of a lychgate at the bottom of a steep path. I clambered out and followed her up towards the church, carrying Ben. Alford's parish church sat in the middle of an old hilltop graveyard, surrounded by yews and leaning gravestones.

'As I mentioned,' she murmured, 'the exterior is relatively unspoiled. Perpendicular architecture, sixteenth century. Shall we go around this way?'

I put Ben down on his feet, grabbed his hand, and followed her. The path led us towards the church door, at which point a second one struck off around the walls. Our hostess plunged down it and turned off to wander up a line of old graves, pausing by the weathered headstones. 'You should notice the names on the stones. Do you see what I mean?'

At first I didn't. Then I noticed. The inscriptions went back more than two hundred years, and those were just the ones that were still unweathered enough to read. Those that were still in place, sinking crookedly into the ground, recorded the names of the village dead. A few surnames recurred over many decades: Bond, Winter, Holt. Around the walls of the church and along the side hedge leaned rows of other head-stones, removed when they had weathered into smooth silence. 'These are families who have lived in Alford for centuries,' Mrs Molyneux said: 'farm labourers, craftsmen. Hundreds of lives.'

I said slowly, 'But Monksdanes has stood here for centuries too.'

'Ah, yes,' my guide agreed. 'The Mortimers were granted their land at the time of the dissolution of the monasteries. They are buried in the family crypt; there is a fine Carrara marble monument inside you must look at, though perhaps not now — we should start back.'

'The Warings . . . ?'

'A northern family.' Mrs Molyneux turned down the path. 'Lawrence's grandfather bought the estate. I have a book, published in the twenties, which I must show you, with a section about Monksdanes which claims that he made a fortune horse-dealing for the British army during the Boer War, and bought the estate with the proceeds in 1905.'

I giggled at the information. 'Are you saying that the villagers regard the Warings as . . . as low-class incomers?'

Mrs Molyneux laughed, 'I wouldn't quite put it that way. Not in the way that your friend and I and three-quarters of modern Alford are incomers! They are outsiders, and they have money, or had. I would suppose that there might be some envy, some resentment . . .'

I burst out, 'What was Joannie Holt like?'

Mrs Molyneux considered my question. 'She was just a girl. Very young. Nobody in particular.'

'What made her try to burgle them?' I persisted.

We had got into the car again; Mrs Molyneux finished backing it into the road, then met my eyes in the driving mirror. 'Envy, wouldn't you think?'

I took the plunge. 'I've been talking to somebody who investigated her death. A policeman – Inspector Atyeo.'

Mrs Molyneux pursed her lips and pushed her glasses up her nose. 'Cross-eyed. I remember him.'

'He says that Joannie Holt had told people she was pregnant and that the baby was Lawrence's.'

My hostess expressed a ladylike, 'Tut!' followed by a confession: 'It isn't quite the first time I've heard that. There is no fool like an old fool!'

'But Atyeo says that she *wasn't* pregnant. Might she just have been trying to get money out of Lawrence Waring?'

Mrs Molyneux removed her foot from the accelerator, and the old car slowed to a crawl. 'How unfortunate if so!'

'Unfortunate?' I asked, though I knew what she meant.

'It might suggest that the whole business was less "accidental" than was put about, wouldn't you say?' She changed down, and we moved on again at modest speed.

'If,' I said very slowly, 'somebody who didn't believe the

shooting was an accident put it about that Teddy acted deliberately . . .'

I left it at that. The face reflected in the driver's mirror looked alarmed. 'Dear lord,' she said. She made the right turn into the dead-end and drove us silently into her garage. When we had disentangled ourselves and were heading towards the front door, she said, 'How exceedingly unpleasant. And yet . . .'

I prompted, 'Yet . . . ?'

'I was going to say that I could never see young Joannie as a burglar. Shop-lifting – perhaps: she was a very *feminine* child. I suppose that she might have become entangled with the old man; she was never all that bright, rest her soul, and her father died when the children were very young, so it is possible she was attracted in some way to older men. No, I mustn't, this is merely speculation. Dear me! Oh, dear!'

I was tempted to apologise for having upset her, but then I saw the glint in Mrs Molyneux's eye and realised that apologies were unnecessary.

'I was wondering,' I explained instead, 'whether there's someone in the village who might want to avenge her? Someone who might actually *do* something, now Teddy is back? Did she have a boyfriend?'

'I *must* take the roast out of the oven before it dries out,' Mrs Molyneux muttered. 'Will you . . . ? Come, come!'

I followed her into the kitchen, holding Ben, and stood well back while she donned oven gloves and began to pull roasting pans out of the largest oven of a cooker even more impressive than the one in the Barton. She forked a huge, sizzling piece of beef onto a platter and began to sprinkle flour into the pan and scrape together a gravy.

'Do what kind of thing?' She demanded.

I told her about the fox. The rat. The car in the lane. At the end of my account I was encouraged to see not merely a flush in her cheeks (which might have been caused by the heat of cooking) but a sparkle in her eye. She moved the pan off the plate and poured the contents gently into a gravy boat.

'That is . . . remarkable! I'm sorry, I should have said "unpleasant", but still . . .'

'The night I arrived, Lizzie told me to keep my curtains shut because there was a Peeping Tom about. Do you know anything about that? I was wondering whether it could somehow be connected.'

'I hope you both like parsnips. I seem to have outdone myself today. As a matter of fact, there was some such trouble once. I recall it had something to do with the Barton . . . somebody who lived there one winter. Major Hitchens, next door, mentioned it at the time with a great deal of indignation. He considered it an improper matter for a lady's ears. I hadn't heard anything more recently. What *are* we coming to?' She seemed more excited than alarmed. My suspicions were confirmed when she turned and beamed at me. 'Sit down. Wait, give me a hand with the vegetables, my dear. We'll eat before it gets cold. Then, if you will, we might consider our next step. You were quite right to come here for help! Wait again: do you fancy some mustard?'

We got ourselves and our feast to the dining table, and I busied myself for a while with the usual business of mashing up Ben's meat and potatoes, and supervising his table skills. Mrs Molyneux sat opposite, carving and serving deftly with what was obviously about a tenth of her full attention.

'Now, boyfriends,' she said eventually, showing that my interpretation of her silence was correct. 'Joannie went about with boys, naturally, but I don't remember that there was anyone in particular. Still, I shall call on her mother and have a little chat. Mrs Holt lives with her sister and brother-in-law in one of those council houses across the way. However, there is Joannie's brother. The two were very close, growing up, and I always think that blood is thicker than water, don't you?'

I told her that I definitely agreed and that I wanted to know about the brother. 'Does he still live around here?'

'Oh, indeed yes! You didn't know? He bought a tiny cottage some years ago: a rough little place, one of those you may have noticed on the unpaved track running from the eastern end of the green, so he is one of your friend's neighbours. You have probably seen him around the village on his bicycle: he works as a contractor for one of the farms and as a general handyman.'

I asked her what his name was, but I already knew what she was going to say, because it fitted. The situation was enough to give anybody indigestion.

'Billy,' she answered, right on cue. 'Billy Holt.'

CHAPTER SIXTEEN

Gentlemanly Conversation

I went looking for Lizzie and found her chopping onions in the kitchen.

'Is he all right?'

I told her that Ben had been sound asleep before I'd even had time to cover him, and that the heart-rending noises he had been making before that were just his way of communicating exhaustion and over-excitement. I added that she would find these things out for herself in time.

She worked on her new, soppy, inward-looking smile and changed the subject. 'Now, go on telling me what Mrs Molyneux said.'

I lied, 'I've told you most of it. We were going to call on Major Hitchens, but then Ben decided he'd had enough and I had to bring him back. I think she was going –'

'She's here.' Lizzie was looking over my shoulder at the kitchen window. I whirled around and saw Mrs Molyneux on the other side of the glass, gesturing imperiously. Her cheeks were pink and her glasses were sliding down her nose again. Lizzie waved onion-stained hands helplessly and we both shouted, 'Come in!' It might not have been necessary, because Mrs Molyneux was entering the kitchen before I had taken my next breath.

'Miss Hoare, will you come with me at once? They are about to go visiting, but the major has agreed to give us five minutes. I believe he has a tale to tell.'

I looked at Lizzie. 'If you don't mind keeping an ear open for noises upstairs . . . ?'

She looked frustrated and claimed that she didn't. I grabbed my jacket from the back of a chair and followed my leader down the lane to the tall house. When she rang the bell, the old man I had seen cutting his grass answered it briskly, nodded significantly at Mrs Molyneux, gave me a bow of recognition, and ushered us both to chairs in a pleasant sitting room overlooking a flower-filled garden. A white-haired woman sat there knitting. Mrs Molyneux introduced us all more formally. To my amazement, the major nodded at his silent little wife, who smiled, mumbled inaudibly, picked up her knitting and obediently left the room.

'Not,' said the major quietly, 'a proper topic of conversation for any lady's ears.' So much for me. 'Mrs Molyneux tells me that you've had an unpleasant experience. A spy, in the lane last night? A Peeping Tom?'

I folded my hands in my lap, crossed my ankles demurely, and attempted to look vulnerable. 'Lizzie told me there was one about. She warned me to keep my bedroom curtains closed at night. Mrs Molyneux says you know about something like this happening once before, a few years ago?'

The major sniffed into his moustache. 'That was altogether different.'

'Why?' Mrs Molyneux demanded.

'At the time, the Barton was let to a person, a woman, who purported to be a dealer in antiques. Name of Richards. Mrs. No husband, naturally. She drove a large estate car, did a great deal of coming and going with bits of furniture, pictures, etcetera. I believe she advertised in the local newspaper; you've seen the sort of thing: "Dealer buys old furniture, clocks, pictures, for export to the United States. Best prices." She bought some surplus furniture up at Monksdanes, I heard.' He suddenly looked shifty, and I realised that he was trying not to let us see that he knew about the Warings' financial problems.

'And somebody was spying on her?' Mrs Molyneux prompted him.

The old man cleared his throat. 'Mrs Richards was not what she seemed. A number of the local men discovered that she was, not to put too fine a name to it, a mere prostitute. Had a number of men acquaintances and brought them back to the house. The lane became rather busy at night. If you . . .' He was finding it hard to go on and threatened to stutter to a halt.

Mrs Molyneux made encouraging noises.

'If you walk up past the green after dark, you will find a point, or rather a space of fifteen or twenty feet, where it is possible to see straight into the Barton's upstairs windows when the lights are on. Some of the local lads, whose parents should have been keeping a closer eye on their whereabouts, took to gathering up there at closing time. She gave them an eyeful, I expect. A performance.' He seemed to shudder. 'I did hear she was involved with one or two of the local men, including someone who should have known better. But this was a few years back. Nothing in it to explain anything, er, you might have noticed more recently.'

'What happened to this woman?' I asked.

The old man shook his head. 'Went off. Lawrence Waring took a dim view and gave her notice. Heave-ho! Did a midnight flit, owing rent I don't doubt. The Warings eventually sent someone in to clean up – a pigsty, presumably, that kind of woman – and kept to short-term holiday lets thereafter. Families. Less problematic. I'm sorry, hate to push you ladies, but we are expected in Shepton in twenty minutes. Do call on my wife, ladies.'

We departed politely and paused for a moment just in front of Mrs Molyneux's gate.

'What a . . .' I reconsidered. 'What an old-fashioned man.'

'Rather past it,' Mrs Molyneux said brusquely, 'and not very perceptive, especially about women. His wife has twice his common sense. You noticed of course that I introduced him as "Major" Hitchens?'

'Isn't he?' I asked, incredulously.

Mrs Molyneux shrugged. 'He was an officer during the Second World War, but *not* in the regular army, and some people would think it pretentious to use the rank now. Still, I dare say he is right about one thing: it doesn't seem likely that last night's lurker could have any connection with events some years ago. You say that the tale came from Helen? Awkward, of course. And you don't want to alarm your friend, especially as she must be finding everything quite trying just now.'

She was right. But I would find a way to trace the story to its source, mostly in the interests of eliminating possibilities. Or else . . . 'What kind of car does Billy Holt drive?'

'He owns an old Mini. I'm not sure that it's taxed just at the moment, but it might be drivable. What kind of car did you see there?'

That was no good: I hadn't seen enough to identify the model, but it certainly hadn't been an old Mini. Even so, I needed to interview Billy Holt about his sister. As well as Teddy Waring, if I could just pin him down. I seemed to have left the awkward ones till last.

A gust of wind from the west brought the smell of rain. I left Mrs Molyneux with my thanks and her earnest offers of further assistance, and returned to the cottage, where Lizzie was still alone.

'Any problems?' I asked her.

'Not a sound. Oh, your father phoned. He wanted to know why you haven't been returning his calls. I told him that I thought you'd been out without your mobile – it's on the table in the other room – and probably hadn't noticed his messages, and you'd ring when you came in. He says he's at home and waiting to hear from you. Has it ever struck you how like my mother he is?'

'Very often,' I admitted. 'Do you think it's too early for a drink?'

'I don't,' she said. 'Now, tell me, what's going on?'

CHAPTER SEVENTEEN

Rain

Sunday evening: Alford closed for business by nine thirty, and by ten Lizzie and I were side by side at my bedroom window, lights off, curtains open. The others in the household were in bed, sound asleep in one case, but probably lying awake worrying in the other. Mickey had returned from Monksdanes just before seven, joined us at dinner with absent-minded politeness, and sunk into silence. When Lizzie challenged him, he claimed there was nothing wrong. He failed to convince us.

The lane was empty. One car had driven up it very slowly but without stopping. The lights in the houses were blinking out one by one.

I whispered, 'Lizzie, the night I came here, when you warned me about a Peeping Tom, you said Helen told you. How did she know?'

Lizzie hesitated. 'I'm not sure. Yes, I do remember: she was in the shop last week, and one of the customers was talking. A woman who lives up at the farm. She said there was a car hanging around the village at night, and that 'it's starting up again' and we should all be careful. Apparently there was some trouble once before.'

'She didn't say what kind of car?' I probed. I had the impression that Lizzie shrugged. A gust of wind rattled the ivy.

'What did you tell Uncle Barnabas?'

'Nothing,' I replied uneasily. 'He asked what we're up to, and I told him I was going for long walks. He made me promise to take my mobile with me from now on. In case he needs to contact me on business. He sends his congratulations, by the way.'

'So he's heard from my mother again?'

'She phoned to ask him whether he'd heard your news.'

We sat silently, contemplating the facts of family life. After a moment I asked, 'Have you told the Warings?'

'I suppose we'd better. I wouldn't want to cause bad feeling. Helen will be pleased for us.'

Helen? I let that pass.

'What's your next step?' Lizzie asked after a while.

I paused over the concept that taking action was my personal responsibility now, and decided to let that pass, too. 'I need to talk to Billy Holt. I'd say there's a ninety-nine per cent chance he's the one behind the dead animals. We ought to let him know that we know, and we aren't thrilled but haven't told Monksdanes yet. If we can do it the right way, we might manage to fix it. I mean, tactfully warn him to let up. Mrs Molyneux would bring pressure to bear, I think, if we asked her. She taught him at Sunday school.'

'She'd smack him,' Lizzie agreed, sounding relieved.

'We might not need to bring her in,' I said quickly. 'It would be better if I could speak to him privately, because I'd like to find out *his* take on his sister's death.'

Lizzie was silent for so long that I wondered whether she had fallen asleep in her chair and was startled when she said suddenly, 'Dido, maybe we should stop. Let's just tell Billy Holt to back off, and then drop it.'

'*Drop it?* But this was your idea in the first place!'

'I know.'

I said, 'It's too late. Don't you see that? How can you drop it now? What's changed?'

Eventually, she murmured, 'I don't want to risk . . . I mean, digging away at something that happened years ago can't really do any good, can it? It will cause bad feeling. This is a village. People need to live here.'

I wondered aloud, for the second time, what had changed her mind.

'Mickey and I are leaving, and it won't concern us. The six months' lease on our own house runs out at the end of June, and we won't take any more tenants. We should be able to go back to Bristol in July, because Teddy says he's going to stay here. He and Helen can look after Monksdanes between them.'

My own belief was that no human being could look after Monksdanes, at least nobody who wasn't very rich and very obsessive.

'You ought to encourage them to sell that place.'

'I know, but Rose won't even discuss it. She always says that they can't sell until Lawrence dies. What's that?'

It was a car rolling almost silently down the lane, probably the same one that had gone up a little while ago; they must have dropped off a passenger. Anyway, it passed without stopping.

Suddenly, it was raining hard. We listened to the water dashing against the tiled roof and rushing through the down pipes. Perhaps it was the weather, but nobody came near the spot where I'd seen last night's car. There would be no creeping out together as we had planned, reading number plates and asking the driver very loudly what the hell he thought he was doing. The wind was rising, rattling the ivy again. The last light down the lane went out and nothing happened.

CHAPTER EIGHTEEN

Down the Lane

Half an inch of water went swaggering down the flagstone path beneath the kitchen window and, alarmingly, vanished under the foundations of the cottage. There is a lot of weather in the country. Unless local stone could float, I could foresee a time when we might have to bale.

Lizzie and I had been lighting fires and turning up the settings on the stove in an attempt to make the Barton feel dry. She was in the sitting room now, improbably starting to knit something small and white while she kept an eye on Ben, whom I'd left on the sofa surrounded by his favourite junk and temporarily mesmerised by the Tom and Jerry morning on one of the satellite channels. I raised the mother's prayer of thanks for children's television, and wondered how long the rain could possibly go on pelting down this way. Maybe the weather was affecting me, but this was only the beginning of my second week of holiday, and suddenly I wanted to go home.

Out on the track that circled the green a figure appeared on a bicycle. It swooped past the chapel, head down and shoulders hunched under a hooded plastic cycling cape, and vanished in the direction of the muddy track across the fields. I was so dozy that for a moment I didn't react. Then I remembered.

'Lizzie? Lizzie, Billy Holt just came home! I'm going to try to catch him now, if you'll watch Ben?'

Her voice floated back to me from two rooms away: 'We're fine here . . .' Then, apparently, awareness dawned. 'Dido, are you going out in *that?*'

As a matter of fact, yes. I'd knocked on Billy Holt's door first thing that morning and got no reply. Now I knew he was at home, it would take more than Noah's flood to stop me talking to him. I grabbed an umbrella from the hooks in the entrance hall, plunged into the garden and splashed through the gate. Just past the pair of semi-detached cottages that were our immediate neighbours the paved lane swung back towards the chapel and a track plunged off between two ragged hedges. I stepped carelessly into a water-filled rut.

The last structure down this way was a tiny, drab-looking pair of semi-detached two-storey brick houses set back behind a hedge. The nearer of the two sat in a patch of weeds, with its windows and front door boarded up. The other was a different matter: with its woodwork freshly painted, it stood in a tidy cottage garden filled with rows of seedlings. A satellite dish looked up from the chimney. Dark brown curtains were pulled tight across the ground-floor window; they had been closed when I'd come earlier, but now I knew that Billy Holt was lurking behind them. I clattered the tinny door knocker and listened. There was a faint sound – voices – probably a radio or television set. I thumped the door with my knuckles, peered uselessly at the curtained windows, and finally had to accept that I wasn't getting a response. I stepped back and craned upwards. The upstairs curtains were open, but that wasn't much help.

A pebble path ran along the front of the house. I followed it around two corners and found myself standing between the back door and some rows of frail young carrot fronds. At the end of the rows were a couple of sheds, a compost heap, an outside toilet and, beside it, a kind of roofed shelter on poles. Inside it, a rusty green Mini had found its last resting place. At the far end was a hutch with a small run guarded by wire netting, and something inside that moved. The shed doors all bore shiny brass padlocks. The small back door of the house was also firmly shut, but there was an old-fashioned bicycle leaning beside it. I gave the door a thump with my knuckles and was almost tempted to find out whether that was locked up as tight as the sheds. Well . . . maybe not.

My feet were soaked. I squelched back towards the Barton, avoiding as many of the puddles as I could, asking myself crossly how long a man could hide out behind drawn curtains and refuse to answer his door.

Not long enough!

And why was he doing it?

He doesn't want anybody to see the mess, he doesn't talk to strangers, he doesn't like strange women, he doesn't like women, he's washing his hair . . . The question was how to persuade Holt that doing a Greta Garbo would get him nowhere.

Inspiration arrived just as I reached the Barton. Two black dustbins sat inside its garden wall, and I found a large, newspaper-wrapped parcel on top of the rubbish in the nearer one. Mickey had tied the fox's corpse up securely with string, I noticed, which was lucky. I dumped the lid back on and squelched into the kitchen, where nothing seemed to have been happening in my absence, and rootled among the stock of ballpoints, pencils and scissors in a mug on the Welsh dresser.

'Dido?' Lizzie called from the other room. 'What did he say?'

I shouted, 'He won't answer his door. I want to leave him a note; do you have some paper?' My fingers closed on the thick barrel of a waterproof black marker.

'There's some in the dresser drawer.' Her voice said she had lost interest. I found her pad of blue notepaper, tore off a sheet, and printed: 'I want to talk to you about your sister, so come to the Barton. *And I think this thing is yours*' I wrote my name at the bottom of the page, raised the umbrella again, stopped to pick up the corpse by its string, and splashed off around the green for the third time.

I didn't bother knocking, just positioned the wrapped bundle neatly on the doorstep beside the bicycle, tucked the note into the string, and made sure that the parcel was reasonably sheltered from the driving rain. Then for the last time I plodded back. I'd stopped even trying to avoid puddles.

Indoors again, I yanked my trainers off and left them upside down on the floor by the stove. My socks went over a warm rail beside the drying tea towel. When I stepped off the rush matting, my feet left wet marks on the flagstones all the way.

In the sitting room, Ben and Lizzie examined me thoughtfully.

Ben said succinctly, 'Wet.' His voice was fretful.

Lizzie announced, 'The television says there's a major depression over Ireland and this is going on for two more days. You wouldn't think it could, would you? It must be global warming.'

The cottage had begun to feel small, which when you compared it with my flat was ridiculous. Perhaps before I dried off I should go up the lane to Monksdanes and bring the van down. Maybe we should drive to the nearest cinema for the afternoon. Or if the waters rose, at least we'd be ready to flee.

The three of us turned as one to the nearest window and stared out glumly. We were in time to watch Billy Holt on his bicycle, head down and legs pumping hard, whizz past the cottage without even looking sideways and vanish down the lane. You'd think he was avoiding me. On the other hand, he hadn't stopped to complain about my leaving a corpse on his doorstep, however nicely wrapped, and that was significant. An admission of guilt, even. Yes.

CHAPTER NINETEEN

Visits

After lunch, bored with watching the rain-sodden landscape for signs of Billy's return, I left Lizzie in front of the television and climbed into a hot bath because there didn't seem to be anything else to do.

Therefore when the phone rang I was too far away to eavesdrop on the conversation. A moment later there were footsteps on the back stairs and a rap at the bathroom door.

'Dido?' She was whispering; Ben was having his after-lunch quiet time just down the passage.

I whispered back, 'Come in.'

She crept around the edge of the door with exaggerated caution and perched on the wicker hamper by the window.

'Rose just phoned. She said would we come to tea, and will you please give her a quotation for the books because she's decided they should sell. That's good, isn't it? It sounds as though Teddy's been talking to them about finances.'

I sank a little lower into the bubbles and thought about it. 'I can't make any promises. I mean, I can't even promise that I'll buy them, and I couldn't give her much money for most of them because they aren't my kind of thing.' Lizzie looked puzzled, and I decided to be brutally frank. 'I had a look at them the other day, remember, and a lot aren't worth taking away. To be blunt, I have an *antiquarian* bookshop, and most of those books up there are headed for a rummage sale or a charity shop. Or the bin.'

'They're not worth anything at all?'

I enlightened her about the realities of the trade.

She pondered. 'Look, I don't think you should discourage Rose, not if it means she's seriously considering their future. Won't you just come and look?'

No, no, no! my instincts chanted silently. Out loud, I said weakly, 'All right, but no promises.'

Lizzie nodded hard. 'Of course! You'll only offer what the books are really worth to *you*. Helen's making a cake; she makes very nice carrot cake – you and Ben will love it.'

'And,' I added quickly, '*you'll* have to keep Ben occupied if you really want me to do this. It will be good practice.'

'I said we'd be up there in half an hour,' she admitted, waltzing out of the room.

The rain had let up very slightly by the time we were ready to leave. Pushing Ben in his chair, with the hood fully extended, I manoeuvred out of the gateway and waited for Lizzie to lock up and join us. The sky was a uniform mid-grey with a layer of low cloud scudding from the west and a lot of rain still to come. A post office van splashed past the end of the chapel, but nothing else was moving. The birds seemed too wet to chirp, and Barney was absent: even a dog had enough sense to be sheltering somewhere. We splashed through the streams of water over-flowing the ditches and running down the edges of the road, Lizzie in her smart-looking green wellies and me in the old black ones I'd borrowed, with extra socks. They were more effective than my trainers. The gravel driveway at Monksdanes was comparatively well drained, and the garden washed green and empty. We circled the house and took refuge in the back hall to hang up our macs and change into the shoes we'd brought with us. A smell of baking filled the air. I grabbed Ben and led the way.

The Monksdanes kitchen was pure fifties: cream walls, glass-fronted cupboards, red Formica tops, and stains from rising damp in the plaster under the windows. Helen was there alone, elbow-deep in a great creamware mixing bowl.

'Making bread,' she announced when we burst in. 'I thought, why not? Such a miserable day!'

'Where is everybody?' Lizzie demanded.

Helen paused in her kneading. 'Father is upstairs resting. He's quite good today. He'll come down for tea. Mummy is sewing something, I think; anyway, she's in the sewing room if you want her. I think Teddy's with her, watching television. He's in a filthy mood. Have you come to look at the books?'

I said that I had, and that Lizzie was going to read to Ben while I worked, and she waved in a puff of flour and said that tea was at four and the library was open.

Somebody had been in there. The shutters were open, a two-bar electric fire glowed, and some of the more prominent surfaces had been dusted. The olive-green rug still sat in front of the hearth.

'Is that . . . ?'

I nodded and watched Lizzie slide over and lift one end gingerly. 'I don't see anything.'

I explained that there was really nothing to see, dug my big notebook and a couple of pens out of my bag, and decided to start at the door and keep going clockwise. I made good time because there wasn't a great deal that I needed to examine. Most of the novels had been published in the thirties, forties and early fifties. I pulled out a dozen obscure first editions, mostly without dust jackets. The children's books and annuals of the same period were collectibles; I knew a shop in north London that sold these for anywhere from eight pounds to three hundred. These particular examples were neither rare nor in very good condition, but I pulled out what I knew I could sell on. There were several Beatrix Potters on one shelf, all tattered late issues. The gardening books looked ordinary: either a specialist dealer or somebody with a big shop and lots of space might offer these things for a few pounds, but they were too problematic for me.

By the third wall, I was sure I was wasting my time. If there had once been better things here, then Belltower had got them years ago. The best thing Rose could do was phone and ask Kevin whether he'd like to come back and take the whole lot away for a few pounds.

On the fourth wall, up at the top and almost the last place I looked, was a stretch of dingy bindings not so very different from dozens I'd already scanned. I stood back and squinted. Shaw. Kipling. Hardy. If any of these were first editions, I'd jump at them.

'Have you found something?' Lizzie asked from one of the armchairs where she and Ben had settled, proving that she was not giving her full attention to *The Cat in the Hat.*

I said, 'Maybe,' and went to pull over the desk chair and climb up. A few minutes later, I was down again with a copy of Clive Bell's *Art*, a couple of minor Kiplings, Beerbohm's *Caricatures* and a book that bothered me: something called *Jocelyn*, by John Sinjohn, 1898, except that it wasn't. I had known something about that book, but I couldn't remember what. It seemed pretty certain that it was actually by *somebody*. I turned the first leaves and found a dedication to Joseph Conrad. Wasn't the author one of Conrad's literary circle? I added the lot to the pile of volumes I had stacked on the desk. Research time: I crossed to the armchair where I'd dropped my bag and dug into it for my phone. Which wasn't there. Damn! I could remember putting it . . . oh, on the dresser in Lizzie's kitchen.

'What's wrong?'

'I need to phone the shop. I'm going to pop back to get my mobile, because Barnabas or Ernie will have to ring me back about this. Take care of Ben — I'll just be five minutes.'

I made speed down the hallway, past the door of the kitchen where Helen was standing with her back to me, the telephone receiver to her ear. I heard her saying peevishly, 'I *said* they are, didn't I? I don't know why . . .' I crept past, pushed my feet into the wellies, shrugged on my mac, and let myself quietly out the back door. For a moment I considered driving, but the rain seemed lighter so I just kept on going. *John Sinjohn.* That had to be a pseudonym. *John . . . something?* It was the kind of thing that Barnabas was good at remembering and Ernie at digging out. On the driveway I broke into a trot. Maybe I'd been wrong about the rain letting up. I sped along the road, splashed past the chapel and cut straight across the ragged, wet grass to the Barton, where I unlocked the nearest door, dived inside, and pulled off my dripping coat.

Upstairs, something fell. Because the door had been locked when I arrived, I wasn't alarmed at first. But when I walked into the kitchen, I saw that the door of a little cupboard beside the chimney breast was open. We hadn't left it like that.

My mobile was still on the dresser. As I put my hand on it, I heard footsteps overhead. Someone was moving slowly and deliberately across the floor of the big bedroom, pausing at each step, as though walking on thin ice.

My own movements on the flagstones were noiseless. I slipped straight through the next room, took in the fact that the cushion from the window seat was on the floor, and went through the living room. I'd left each door wide open as I went so I could see the whole length of the cottage from the spot at the foot of the main stairs, where I halted and yelled, 'Mickey? You're home early! Anything wrong?' My theory was that if we really did have a burglar he would hear exactly where I was standing and run down the little back staircase to escape through the door at the far end of the cottage, while I took a good look at his face. Only it didn't happen that way.

'Lizzie?' A man in a waterproof blue jacket hesitated up at the top of the stairs. It was Teddy Waring, looking furtive. He peered round the banisters and recognised me. 'Sorry – Dido. I thought you people were out.'

'If you thought we were out,' I said coldly, 'what are you doing here? How did you get in?'

He was coming down slowly now, watching my face. He

seemed pleasantly unsure of himself. 'Mummy . . . we keep spare keys up at the house.'

I waited at the foot of the staircase wondering what to do. This wasn't my house. It was more his than mine, but even so . . . When he reached the bottom I tried holding out my hand, palm up. He hesitated but dropped a key-ring into it.

I put it deliberately into a pocket in my jeans and decided to take a chance. 'You were speaking to Helen on the phone a minute ago to make sure we were out of the way. I don't think Lizzie and Mickey will appreciate this.'

His eyes were blank. 'I was just looking for something.'

Snap. I asked, 'What, exactly?'

He looked at a point above my head and said, 'I'll walk you up to the house, if you're going back.'

'What were you looking for?' I persisted, not budging.

'Nothing!' he barked. 'Just a book I wanted. I thought it might have been left here. Shall we go?'

I said, 'Good idea. They'll all be waiting for us.' The phone call to my father could wait. 'We'll go out the other door so I can get my coat and lock up.'

I led him the length of the Barton, and he waited and watched me get my coat from the hook and put it on. Outside, he stood back and waited again while I made sure that the door was locked. Then we set off across the green in silence: this was not a man with a ready line in chit-chat. I remembered that I'd been planning to engineer a conversation so I could ask him all the questions I'd been collecting as time went on; but his silence made it hard to start. So did the fact that I'd just worked out what he was talking about. As we reached Monksdanes, I asked, 'What made you think that you'd find the *Peter Rabbit* in the Barton?'

The footsteps on the gravel beside me faltered, so I stopped too. After a moment, he said stiffly, 'It's not at home. We looked everywhere, years ago. I wondered, suddenly, whether it had got down there somehow.'

You what, you liar? I jeered at him silently.

Summary: Teddy had persuaded his mother to lure Lizzie and me out of the house. He had tried to search the cottage while they were distracting us with carrot cake and old books, so that we wouldn't know. His excuse – that as the book wasn't at the big house it must somehow have toddled down the lane and taken refuge in the family's other property – was so lame it was hopping. The question was why he thought I'd believe him, and why it should matter. Sooner or later, I'd have to work it out.

CHAPTER TWENTY

Visitors

———⟫•◆•⟪———

Lizzie had been right about one thing: Helen baked a good cake, the kind of cake that makes you forgive a lot. After tea, I slumped into one of the library's overstuffed chairs, listened to the rain blowing against the windowpanes and waited for Ernie to return my phone call while I thought about what I'd just witnessed.

Lawrence Waring had been 'quite good', as promised. For a while, he had told us stories about the war, which he had spent in the Royal Navy, mostly on convoy patrol between Liverpool and Nova Scotia. Somewhere between cucumber sandwiches and cake, a shutter had fallen abruptly, click! Teddy had been hanging on his father's stories, and I watched a shadow fall on him, too.

I did open my mouth once to broadcast Teddy's intrusion down the lane, but I couldn't bring myself to do it, and by now I felt like an idiot. An impatient idiot. It was a relief when my phone finally rang and I had something else to think about.

'Hey, Dido!' Ernie was saying, 'Listen, I got it! I looked up the title. There's a copy on one of the web sites: "Galsworthy, John, *Jocelyn* by John Sinjohn, Duckworth." '

'That's it! What does the entry say? Who has it and how much are they asking?'

' "Spine faded, some foxing, else v.g." Goldwater, they want nine hundred dollars for it. Is that OK?'

'It's good,' I reassured him. That copy sounded no better than this one, and at least my day wasn't going to be an entire loss. 'Have you got anything on the Beatrix Potter book yet?' He promptly listed some examples of current *Peter Rabbit* prices, but there was nothing like the Waring copy being offered. It had always been a long shot. 'I'll let you know if I need you to try again,' I promised.

The door opened, and Lizzie and Ben inserted themselves into the room to find me writing out a formal offer for my selected books on a sheet of Monksdanes' headed notepaper that I'd found in the top drawer of the desk.

'Good news?'

'One of these is worth a couple of hundred pounds to me. I've just added up, and I'll give this to Rose as we leave. She can sleep on it.' I threw a look and a kiss at Ben, who had decided to come and cling to my leg. He'd had enough of this place. So had I. 'I can only do more or less the same thing that Kevin did: I'll make them an offer for five dozen books. As far as I'm concerned, she can leave the rest of them where they are in case anybody wants a read. If she ever needs to clear the house, she'd better ring the nearest charity and ask them to take the rest away. Or maybe Kevin would take them for Belltower, if he has enough shelf space, but I don't suppose he'd give her more than fifty pounds.'

I went to hand my formal offer to Rose, who was still sitting alone in the morning room behind the cleared table. She barely glanced at it, though I understood from her manner that she had seen, pondered, and decided on my offer in the time that it took her to drop the paper carelessly onto the tablecloth. Without hesitating she said, 'Thank you, Dido. That's quite acceptable. When would you like to take the books?'

I understood that the real but vulgar question was, 'How soon can you pay me?' and told her I'd come back with my cheque book in the morning. I was going to pack up and take them away then, unless it was actually raining too hard for me to risk carrying cardboard boxes outside. There was plenty of room in the back of the van, even with the Belltower purchases. Rose nodded graciously, and I said our farewells and went to get our coats.

It was almost dark when we stepped outside the back door just after six o'clock. The rain clouds had lowered again, and it was pouring. I grabbed Ben's hand and ran him to the van. The three of us drove down the lane with our headlights on and the wipers waging a losing battle. I watched for Billy Holt's bicycle, though without much hope; he wouldn't be out in this down-pour. We passed four or five cars, each with a single passenger. Commuter traffic. A train must just have come in.

Probably reading my thoughts, Lizzie said, 'Mickey will be home in an hour. I suppose I'd better think about dinner.'

There was still the thing I hadn't told her. I took a breath. 'Lizzie, you'll find some things disturbed. When I went back for my phone I found Teddy there. He told me he was looking for *Peter Rabbit.*'

Liz gaped at me. I thought she'd forgotten. Well, say she lacked my professional focus. I reminded her about the Warings' missing book, and she still stared and said, 'Are you saying what I think you are? That Teddy got them to invite us up there so he could search the place without me knowing? Why?'

I said politely that her younger brother-in-law seemed to be as crazy as a jay-bird.

Her face grew thunderous. 'Cheek!'

I dug out the keys that I'd taken from Teddy, tossed them to her, and concentrated on circling the green and backing the van delicately on to the part of the verge beyond the garden wall that was just wide enough to hold it.

'What did he say when you caught him?'

I thought back. 'Not a lot. He didn't really apologise.' I thought back more carefully. 'In fact, he didn't apologise at all. He didn't seem to think there was anything wrong with what he was doing. So I locked up and made him give me the keys, which should put paid to more unofficial visits unless they have another set, and he walked back with me. All he'd say was that he thought the book might somehow have got down there when it went missing.'

'Why?' Lizzie asked, pertinently.

Yes, why? Presumably he did have some reason for what he was doing. If you assumed the man wasn't totally irrational. But maybe he was. 'Do you think,' I suggested slowly, 'that it might be worth *our* looking for it? Making a proper search tomorrow morning in daylight? However it could have got here, you've been living in the cottage for months now and at least you know all the places in the house where it *isn't*. If there's anything to this story, we have an advantage. Do you think there could be some hiding place in a cupboard, or the larder, say, that you haven't noticed? Or an attic?'

'There *is* an attic,' Liz admitted slowly. 'You have to climb through a trap door in the ceiling, and I've never been. Dido, we could start up there and work our way down. There are all *kinds* of funny places in an old house like this. I suppose we should look under the floorboards as well, and see whether any of the flagstones have ever been dug up. Maybe we should dig up the hearthstones! That's where they buried treasure hoards in stories: under the hearth! The only thing is – I still can't imagine why anybody would have.'

I suggested that we could ask that question with a lot more confidence after we'd finished our search. One obvious answer was that Teddy had left the book himself though somebody else had moved it. If he had, his motives needed examining. With *Peter Rabbit* wriggling, so to speak, in our hands, we could certainly bring pressure to bear.

If Lizzie still wanted to, that is, once she had worked out that getting an answer might not do her any good. Not in a family matter. She and Mickey were going to leave Alford anyway; this seemed like an excellent plan which couldn't be followed too soon.

We locked the van and hurried up the path, anxious to get into shelter. The Barton was still thoroughly and firmly locked up. We hung up our wet coats, turned all the lights on, filled the kettle as we passed through the kitchen, and made a circuit through the house, where Lizzie counted up signs of the intruder. Her face became grimmer and grimmer. The kettle was starting to whistle as we came down the little, twisting staircase by the larder.

'I've had enough tea,' she said as we returned to the kitchen. 'I'll make a pot if you want it, but I'm going to have a drink. Remind me to get some more tonic water in the morning. And another bottle of vodka.'

I said that was fine, because I was going to have to go to somewhere like an off-licence anyway to beg a few old cardboard boxes for my purchases. In the meantime, however . . . 'Lizzie, exactly how much are you going to tell Mickey?'

She answered immediately, showing that she had been thinking along the same lines: 'Nothing. Please, Dido, not yet. We'll talk about it tomorrow, after we've turned this place upside down.'

A car was pulling up outside. Mickey was home, and I was ready for the inevitable drink.

CHAPTER TWENTY-ONE

Billy

The kitchen was filling with smoke. Lizzie cried, 'I've burned the bloody chops!' Her tone was tragic.

Having finished my stint of potato peeling, I'd joined Mickey at the kitchen table where we were keeping the cook company and finishing the vodka. I had enough relevant cookery experience to make a practical suggestion: 'Cut the burned bits off. Slosh some ketchup over the rest. I'm not all that hungry, myself.'

Lizzie ignored me. 'There's some Cumberland pie in the freezer. I'll heat it up. It'll take about forty minutes in the oven. I'm sorry, I don't know what I was thinking of.'

I could guess, but didn't share the insight. And another forty minutes' drinking would leave me capable of nothing better than burning food too.

On the other side of the window it was as black as midnight. I wandered over to open the casement and let some of the smoke out. The light shining from the room behind me revealed that the rain had stopped again. I closed the curtains tight and said, 'He might be at home by now. I'm just going to have a look. I don't think Ben will wake up, and anyway I'll back . . .' I looked at my wristwatch. 'I'll be back by a quarter past at the latest.'

Mickey raised his eyebrows; but I ignored him and went to collect those borrowed wellies and my coat. Lizzie followed me into the hall and pushed a torch into my hand. 'Are you sure you'll be all right?'

I nodded firmly. 'If the lights aren't on inside, I'll be back in three minutes. If they are, I'm going to stand there and kick his door until he opens it. Don't worry.' And slipped out into the rain-washed evening while she headed to the freezer.

At first glance, Holt's cottage looked empty; but as I hesitated at his gate I saw a line of light under the curtain. I walked cautiously up the path to the door. It sounded as though a very quiet party was going on just inside, and this time I recognised the television programme he was watching. I flashed my light on the door, found the knocker, and banged it hard three times. The door swung unexpectedly inwards and revealed the object of my visit, silhouetted against the glow from the screen.

I said, 'Can I come in? I left you a note. I'm Dido Hoare.'

'I'm just going out. Meeting somebody.' The voice was a light tenor. It didn't sound bothered, one way or the other, but his face was in shadow and I couldn't read his expression.

I asked, 'Which way are you going? I'll walk with you. It will give you a chance to tell me how rude I am, leaving a dead fox on your doorstep.'

I hadn't expected his laugh. 'Well, it was wrapped up all nice, anyway.'

'Which way are you going?' I asked again. 'I'll walk with you if you're in a hurry.'

'All right,' he said almost without hesitation. 'I'm just going down the pub. I won't be a minute.'

He left me at the door but didn't quite shut it in my face. After a moment the television went dark and he was back. We set off down the track, with my torch illuminating the water-filled ruts. Trudging silently around the green, we passed the Barton, where Lizzie's frozen supper was presumably starting to melt by now, and turned towards the pub. My companion remained wordless, which was something I didn't have time for.

In front of the chalet bungalow, I said, 'You know Mrs Molyneux? She told me about you and your sister.'

'Nosy old bird,' he mumbled. After a second, he added more loudly, 'She's been good to my mum, though.' I let that sit for a moment, willing him to go on. 'What did she say, then?'

'That she liked you. And Joannie.'

That plunged him into silence again. We were opposite the lilacs when I judged it was time to attack. 'I know that you left that fox on our doorstep. Why?'

'Who are you?' he asked suddenly. 'Are you some relative?'

I told him about growing up next door to Lizzie in Oxford, as we paused beside the signpost. There was a little light shining from the public phone box on the corner and the lamp above the car park at the pub. I switched off my torch and found that I could still see his face. He heard me out. It was starting to drizzle.

'Look,' he said, 'I'll buy you a drink, if you like.'

I nodded, and we fell into step. I followed him through the break in the pub's garden wall, and through the car park, where he scanned the rows of parked cars. Apparently whoever he was meeting hadn't arrived; or if they had, he said nothing about it.

The place was full again this evening. Holt led the way into the saloon bar, beckoned me on, and pushed down the middle of the room to the last empty table, a little round one crammed into a convenient but insalubrious corner next to the women's toilets. 'What'll I get you?'

Suspecting that I'd already drunk more vodka than was wise, I asked for a plain tomato juice and watched him move towards the bar. He must have known half the people in the room for most of his life, but he ignored them. He greeted the barmaid, and they spoke for a moment. Then he leaned on an elbow until the drinks arrived and he could edge back to me and slide on to the wooden chair across the table, and all the time I was checking him out.

I'd originally put him down as my age, but he was a few years older. He wasn't tall, and he was wiry rather than muscular. His brown hair fell almost to his collar; it looked as though he cut it himself. He was wearing old jeans tucked into his rubber boots and a green waxed jacket with frayed cuffs. I made a mental note to be sure that I bought the next round and said, 'So: what's the dead animal thing about?'

'Call it a warning,' he said to his beer. 'Know what they did? I went up to the house Sat'day aft'noon, see if they wanted any help, all that rain, an' Helen gave me the push. Said they dun't need me any more. She was so twitchy, I asked why? Said they couldn't afford it. Maybe, but that was pretty sudden, I thought, so I said, "You tell me why!" 'S that bastard.' He looked directly at me. 'You were there Friday night, I saw you. Teddy. Come home, and he can't stand the sight of me, that's the plain truth. He poked his nose in and told her to. Din't he?'

I hesitated, but there was no other explanation and we both knew it. I said, 'I suppose he can't see you without thinking of what he did.'

He was staring into his beer again. 'Well, nor me him, but he dun't have to look. See, if I can take it, why can't he?'

'Because,' I said without even having to stop and think, 'he's in the wrong, and every time he looks at you, you remind him. So he's trying to make it easier for himself. It's . . .' I almost choked for a minute.

He stared at me. 'What? It's what?'

I said very carefully, 'It would be unbearable to be reminded every day that you'd actually killed somebody. You are her brother. Maybe he feels so guilty that he can't stand the sight of you?'

He said casually, 'Oh he din't kill Joannie. *That's* not Joannie, I don't care what they said, it isn't'.

I looked around, but as far as I could tell nobody was paying any attention to the madman. No time to think around it, just time to think, *This was what Atyeo meant.* I stared at him. 'Why do you say that? You . . . somebody must have identified the body.'

He shook his head stubbornly, wordlessly.

'There's something I'm wondering,' I said, trying to feel my way over this shifting ground. 'I don't know whether you remember a policeman called Atyeo?' I recalled what Mrs Molyneux had said. 'A cross-eyed policeman? I was speaking to him about the case a couple of days ago. He said that Joannie had been telling people she was pregnant, but the autopsy showed she wasn't.'

His lips moved silently. Then he said, 'Silly little cow, she let the old man screw her. Thought he was so posh he was doing her a favour. Dunno what she thought, stupid cow . . .'

'*But she wasn't!*'

He snorted. 'You din't hear her throwing up mornings in the sink. Our Mum was frantic, I was going crazy. I got her one of them test kits at the chemist's in Shepton; she was knocked up, all right.'

Maybe it was the vodka I'd been drinking earlier, but everything around us seemed to be growing quieter and further away. *Buy time, Dido. Think!* I shook myself. 'I'll buy you another drink. Best bitter?'

He said, 'Thanks,' and shoved his tankard towards me. 'I just need to have a word with someone. Back in a minute.'

For a moment I thought he was running, but he went past the outside door. I grabbed our glasses and followed, watching his back. As he reached the door of the public bar I saw that it was even more packed than the saloon, and the tobacco smoke was thick enough to cause fatalities. He shut the door behind him. I slanted my approach to the curved end of the bar, which gave me an angle to look straight down the serving space, past the hatch. I could even see a few feet of the other room. The landlord was down at that end, more or less blocking my view, but when he learned over I caught a flash of my escort standing beside a table, and somebody getting up and turning towards him. A face appeared in front of me saying, 'Yes?' and I had to focus on buying drinks. When I next looked, Holt was invisible, but he came back almost before I'd started my tomato juice, sitting down in front of his new pint.

'What're you going to do?' he asked. 'I'm sorry you and Mrs Waring come across the animal. Wasn't meant for you, anyway. Was she all right?'

'Surprised,' I said, 'but she's pretty tough. But I guess that if it happened again, or anything silly, she might have a word with somebody.'

'Police?' He looked sulky. 'You don't have to.'

I said airily, glad to change the mood, 'We didn't think of the police; we thought we'd tell Mrs Molyneux on you.'

He looked at me and his sullenness cracked. He had a rather nice grin. 'You're a hard case,' he said, 'I c'n see that now. Don't you do that, then, I'll be good. Look, walk you back – if you like.'

I looked at my wristwatch. A quarter to ten, half an hour later than I'd promised. They might be organising search parties. I said, 'Thanks.'

We struggled out just as more customers arrived and crowded in around the bar. The noise was growing. Outside, we struck off towards the gate.

I made another effort to wrestle this conversation to some kind of conclusion.

'The body wasn't your sister? Then why was it identified as Joan?'

'They asked our Mum to identify her. Shouldn't of done that, but she was next of kin, so. It was some girl – woman – in Joannie's dress and shoes. It wasn't Joannie, but I don't think Mum looked that hard. They shouldn't've asked her. They said it was Joannie, and Mum said there was no face, but she knew the clothes, and a locket Joannie was wearing, and she signed the paper. She still says it was Joannie, she won't admit it. That body – it's up there at the church under my sister's headstone; doesn't feel right. Not finished.'

My excitement at his story began to fade into doubt. My instincts said that Joan's mother would have known her daughter's body, and I doubted that this brother, with the bee still in his bonnet over four years later, could be trusted. I bit my tongue and wondered.

The car was parked out in the road just beyond the wall, with someone – two people – in the front seats, their faces turned towards the pub. We were halfway to the gate before I noticed the flare of a cigarette lighter. The face in its glow seemed familiar. A face I had seen somewhere once. It was only a glimpse.

I caught Billy Holt's sleeve and mumbled, 'Wait a minute: I need to look at something. Will you come with me?'

He started to speak, but I'd turned and moved back into the car park, edging around a van and keeping its high body between myself and the waiting car. Holt was behind me, crouching slightly, tiptoeing. It was a joke; I thought he was going to break into laughter. I turned down the row of cars, still keeping them between me and and the watchers. At the break in the wall I hesitated for half a beat, trying to read the number plate that was now only a few feet away. It was too dark. Lizzie's torch was in my hand again, so I put a finger on the button and just flashed it at the rear plate. The number began 'N981', and this time I got the rest of it.

'Do you know that car?'

Holt said, 'Why? No.'

I mumbled, 'I'll tell you later. I wish I could see a face.'

But the smoker was no longer providing any handy illumination. I moved closer to Billy to mutter, 'I'd better get back – I'm late. You don't need to come with me if you want to get back to your friends.'

'Might as well,' he said shortly. 'I'm done here.'

We walked silently up the lane towards the tin chapel and were pausing by the gate at the Barton when he said, 'Might as well be straight with you: I'm going to find Joannie. I'll do what I have to.'

I stopped. 'There must be a sensible – a better way.'

'You saying I should go walk up there, knock on the door, say Pretty Please to Ted Waring? Don't think so. And there's another thing. I've worked it out; whoever she was, somebody shot her on purpose. That wun't an accident.'

He took off and had disappeared while I was taking it in. I called, 'Wait a minute! What do you mean?' There was no answer, so I gave up and dashed through the door and into the kitchen, where Lizzie and Mickey were eating their pudding.

'Sorry. Has Ben been all right?' I evaded two pairs of questioning eyes and noticed that I was feeling sleepy. Possibly even drunk.

I heard Lizzie saying, 'I put yours in the warming oven.' I was vaguely aware of her moving, getting something, putting out a hand. 'Dido! Wake up! Eat! You're dead on your feet.'

I let myself be pushed into a chair, thinking, *Why would he bother to lie? Am I supposed to be impressed?* I was beginning to wonder whether I understood this business at all.

Almost certainly not.

The evening routine unrolled. We retired to the next room and watched *Poirot* on television for a while. When the Belgian detective finally called everybody together in the library and said, 'Well, *mes amis*,' a few times, then argued it all out and revealed a culprit whom nobody had identified until the last minute (not even Poirot himself it seemed to me), Lizzie and I said, 'Well, *mes amis*,' to each other, and called it a day.

In the small bedroom, Ben's eyes fluttered open for a moment, and closed. I heard Mickey turn on the water in the bathroom as I came out again. I went to shut my curtains so I could turn on the light, but before I reached the switch there was a flurry at the door and Lizzie burst in.

'Dido!' Her voice sank to a frantic whisper. '*What happened? Did you talk to him? What is he like, and what did he say to you?*'

I sat down on the edge of the bed with a thump, wanting to be asleep and not having to think any more for a few hours, but I made the effort, counting on my fingers: 'One, no more foxes. Apologised. He was upset because –' I got to the second finger – 'Helen fired him, and he lost it; he said Teddy made her, and thinking back to the dinner party, I guess he did. Three: wait . . .'

'What? *What?*'

'He said it's not really his sister's body, just somebody in her clothes. Wrong identification.'

Lizzie thought about it. She frowned. 'Well . . .'

'Wishful thinking. And last, he said the shooting wasn't an accident, and then he took off. No idea why, except he's a troublemaker.'

Lizzie stared at me. 'Why?'

'Ego. Personality.' I yawned at her. 'A bit sulky. I think he might be slightly crazy.'

'Oh, good,' Lizzie commented. Her voice took on its organising tone. 'Look, tomorrow morning we –'

I said, 'Talk about it, breakfast,' flopped down on top of the bed in an experimental way and was . . . out of it.

CHAPTER TWENTY-TWO

Old Books, Old Bones

The attic was a draughty space with a roughly boarded floor, where axe-hewn beams curved crookedly from outside wall to wall, and the remains of the old thatch had been carefully stuffed into every possible nook and crack. Liz looked around her and sneezed and explained that Mickey had said the builders used the old straw as insulation when they tiled the roof. Very economical. The problem was that everywhere had to be searched for a book which measured six inches by four. We took it in turns, since obviously Ben couldn't come up here however much he would enjoy it. It was nearly eleven o'clock before we had finished, and then we took it in turns again to throw all our clothes into the laundry bin and clean off the dirt. I was nearly dressed again when the phone rang downstairs. Lizzie banged at my door.

'That was Rose!' she called. 'She wants to know when you're coming up there and would you like to stay to lunch?'

I calculated. 'Tell her about half an hour, and thanks very much, no.' Reminded of business, I began to wonder where in Alford I could get half a dozen clean cardboard boxes.

The complications began when I picked up my mobile phone and looked at my messages.

The first two were family. I rang Barnabas at home, and he greeted me with a guilt-arousing, 'I presume you forgot?'

Obviously I had. I scrabbled through my memory and recalled the source of the second message. Pat. My elder sister. Married to a doctor, lives just outside London, two boys . . .

'Oh, shit.'

'It doesn't matter. I went there for the birthday tea, rapidly followed by birthday dinner at a hamburger chain. I took two gifts, nicely wrapped. At Pat's suggestion, you gave him a computer game. I gave him a book. Your gift was the better received. You owe me nearly forty pounds, hard as it may be to credit. What were you up to?'

I thanked him for covering for me, gave him a selective version of local events, said I was just about to go to pick up some books I'd bought, and started to discuss the weather.

A phone call to St Albans connected me to the family answering machine. I left a cowardly mixture of apologies and tardy birthday greetings. It wouldn't be the last I heard of this misdeed.

In a fit of guilt I went to tidy my bedroom and found myself remembering that Teddy Waring would have included it in his search. I sat down with a bounce on the edge of the spare bed and started to ask myself whether he might be just a pervert with a secret interest in my underwear. Because I still couldn't understand his story about looking for *Peter Rabbit*. Say it was true. What if he had found it before I turned up? Well, the book belonged to his father. But what if he meant to steal it? What if he meant to go away, leaving his parents to their own devices? What would I do in his place? Try a dealer in Bath or London? In any case, he would need to sell it quickly. I ought to cover that possibility.

I phoned Barnabas. This time, the number rang a dozen times without an answer. He had probably gone to the shop. I gave up and tried the business number again. Ernie answered promptly.

'When my father gets there —'

'He's been,' Ernie interrupted.

The statement confused me. 'Already?'

There was a little hesitation, and alarm bells rang faintly.

'The Perfessor came in first thing, an' then he went home. He said he had things to do. We got the second lot of orders off, and he told me if he didn't get in tomorrow, just pile up the cheques and the new orders and hang on to them.'

'Was he all right?'

Ernie assured me that my father had been bright and brisk when last seen and almost managed to persuade me that there was nothing funny going on.

I gave up and told him a half-truth about the Warings' *Peter Rabbit* which had been lost for a while and might just have been stolen. 'So I need you to phone the people who circulate reports of stolen books for the ABA and the PBFA – I can't remember the names, but they're in our business directory. Will you tell them that they may be offered a stolen first private edition of *Peter Rabbit*, with author's annotations and sketches, and get them to put out a warning about it?' We discussed exactly how much of a description he would need to give them; Ernie took notes and promised to get on with it.

I phoned my father again without success. Maybe he'd gone to the library.

Down in the kitchen, Lizzie provided a shopping list and directions to the village shop. 'Just ask,' Lizzie instructed. 'They have a back room that's always full of empty boxes. Don't forget the tonic water. Do you want to leave Ben here with me? He's no trouble. We could go up and start poking around the bedrooms until you get back. You're running late. Do you want me to phone Rose?'

I flung a look at the kitchen clock and said, 'Leave it. It shouldn't take more than a few minutes to get there, even with the shopping. If Ben gets whiny, give him a drink and read him a book. I'll get back as soon as I can.'

I flung a hug at Ben, who was deeply involved at the time in making coloured lines on old newspapers with a set of crayons. It did occur to me very fleetingly that I ought to warn Liz, but I was in a hurry.

The rain had stopped again, and the clouds were lighter and higher. Maybe it was finished. When I drove the van carefully down the lane, I was surrounded by minor floods spreading along both verges and out into every dip and pothole. I caught a glimpse of Mrs Molyneux standing in her garden, surveying a small pond that had appeared overnight in the middle of her lawn, and tooted; she was too absorbed to notice me. At the fingerpost, the lane descended into a puddle that had spread across the whole roadway and the van left a wake as I rolled through. The mud-coloured mill stream foamed just below the road, and ditches had overflowed. Having left my water-wings at home, I drove carefully and took a moment to find a parking space near the shop which didn't actually require me to wade from the driver's door to the footpath. On the up side, the shop was deserted except for the woman who was minding both the till and the post office counter. It wasn't much more than ten minutes later when I finally headed towards Monksdanes.

A stream of water was pouring out of that overgrown footpath with the stile, at the top of the lane. But Barney was out and about again, with some friends – two boys, eight or nine years old, who were wading through the floods, in over the tops of their wellies and screaming with glee. I suppressed an impulse to join them, drove soberly into the driveway, backed the van as close as I could get it to the front door, unloaded my boxes, rang the bell, and presented myself for business.

Twenty minutes later I put the Sinjohn-Galsworthy on top of the books in the last box, covered it with a couple of sheets of newspaper begged from Helen, and closed the flaps.

I was alone in the library. Helen had let me in, offered a cup of coffee, and left me to get down to it. Apart from that, Monksdanes could have been uninhabited. It suited me down to the ground, because I was in no mood to cope with Lawrence, much less Teddy. Teddy's appearance in the Barton was always at the back of my mind, but I wanted to sort out one thing at a time, and at the moment I had to pretend that I was merely a

book dealer. I made out a cheque to Rose Waring, placed it on
the desk blotter, and started the business of lugging the cartons
out to my van. Loading them involved leaving the front door
open, and it was probably the draught that brought first Rose,
then Helen, to see what was happening. We exchanged a few
thoughts about the weather. As though it had heard us, a wisp of
sunshine greeted my emergence with the final box. I slammed the
back door of the van, locked it, and glanced at my wristwatch. It
was just on twelve thirty: not bad at all.

I pulled out my phone and rang Lizzie to tell her I was
finishing. 'Any problems? Is Ben all right?'

'He's fine,' she replied. I thought she sounded odd, and
enquired sharply. 'No, no, Ben's fine. It's just . . .'

'*What?*' I shrieked.

'I only left him alone for a minute, Dido, I swear. I'd been
through the bedrooms, and brought him down with me, and we
both had some apple juice, and then I suddenly remembered the
top of the water tank in the bathroom, so I just put him down on
the floor with his things and dashed up to check, but when I got
back he'd been drawing on things. There's no problem, really.
You don't know how to get crayon out of rush matting, do you?'

Burn it? I thought cynically. I said aloud, 'I'll be back in five
minutes.' That's the kind of promise that offers hostages to
fortune.

Helen appeared. 'Mummy says thank you for the cheque. Are
you sure you wouldn't like anything?'

The noise was just beyond the gates. A dog was barking
wildly, almost drowning out two shrill voices. Something in the
sound made me run. I was in time to see the two little boys
scrambling over the stile towards me, while Barney bounced and
barked and wagged and got underfoot. The children stumbled
and struggled, landing with a splash on the path and rushing on
to the road.

I got in their way. 'What's happened?' Two faces turned to
me, muddy and panicky. '*What's wrong?*'

For a moment I couldn't make out what they were babbling. Then the bigger one burst into a wail, and the other said, 'We found a *skeleton!*' He pointed towards the stile.

I grabbed a handful of the nearest jacket and said as calmly as I could, 'Show me. Come on, you aren't scared of old bones, are you? Just show me where it is.' My voice sounded insultingly calm in my own ears; but bones in a farming landscape meant a dead sheep or something – didn't they? I looked hard at the boys, watched the panic subside, and reminded myself that I was a responsible adult whose duty was to exude calm and control, and protect small children.

'How far is it?' I asked quietly. 'Just over the stile?'

'It's in the ditch,' the bigger one hiccupped. A grin started to struggle to life. 'Up the corner of the field.'

I said, 'Good. Then come and show me: let's find out what it is.'

The little one said, 'It's a *man.*' His tone indicated that grown-ups are badly dim-witted.

I said, 'Gosh! Come on, let's see.' That meant wading through the flood in my trainers, but they'd recovered from their first experience and might again. I climbed over the stile and was relieved to see them follow me. Barney wriggled through the gap and bounded ahead, all bounce and tail – one of us was enjoying this. The branches of the overgrown hedge brushed my sleeve as we followed the line of the flooded ditch up along the Monksdanes wall. Ahead I saw open sky, with the first patch of real blue in days. The boys were just behind me when the hedge took a turn to the right and the weed-tangled drainage ditch slanted off beside it before it climbed a slope through open pasture. The water must have been rushing down the ditch for the past two days, because it was clogged with muddy debris. At the corner by the hedge, the dead branch of a tree had jammed and partly blocked the flow, and there had been a fall of earth from the bank.

'It's there,' one of the boys said shrilly. Suddenly they were overawed again, hesitating, crowding together and looking down at the ditch. I joined them slowly.

It was covered in slime. Not a sheep. The delicate bones of a human foot had been washed clean. I made out the rotting remains of plaid fabric, a blanket maybe, and a rounded shape, the head with a matted hank of short, colourless hair still attached, and an eye socket choked with mud.

'Let's get it out!' one of the kids suggested.

I stopped marvelling at childish resilience and snapped, 'Not on your nelly!' in tones sharp enough to stop them jumping down. I grabbed Barney's collar and a boy's at the same time. 'What we do now is call the police.' When they were under control, I pulled my mobile out of my pocket. 'Then we're going to take Barney back to the lane and wait, and you are not to let anybody come near, all right? You're guards. And when the police come, you can show them where it is, if you like.'

They nodded. The bigger one relieved me of Barney's collar, and they both watched with interest while I switched on and dialled 999.

'Will they use their sirens?' the smaller boy asked.

I said I thought they were bound to, which pleased him. The operator's voice asked, 'Which service do you want?' I started to herd the boys and the dog back towards the road and told her. And we did hear a siren coming all the way from Hinton, and it only took them ten minutes to arrive, but they weren't the first on the scene.

CHAPTER TWENTY-THREE

New Questions, New Answers

We heard Helen calling even before we had reached the stile. She fell silent when she saw us and hovered by the path until we had scrambled over and joined her.

'Dido? What is it?'

The boys jostled one another and competed to tell how they had found a body in the ditch, their voices rising.

She looked at me, startled. 'Not a person, Dido!'

I said that it had been once.

She said breathlessly, 'I'd better go and call an ambulance.'

'*She* did,' one of the boys said. 'She has a mobile phone! She called them right there.'

'Not an ambulance,' I said. 'It's been dead for a long time.'

'What has?'

I hadn't heard the sound of the bicycle, but when I turned around, Billy Holt was behind me, one foot on the ground and one on the pedal, as though waiting to take flight. He nodded stiffly at Helen, who flushed and nodded coolly back. 'What's dead, then? You 'n' your brother find something, Jackie?'

The boys rushed to him, clung to his bicycle, and started to pour out their story. I watched Billy focus suddenly. He swung his leg over the bar and dropped the bike on to the road, and suddenly he was running for the stile. I shrieked, 'Don't touch anything!' He was out of sight before I'd got beyond the second word.

Then, across the fields, I heard the siren and started to wonder how long it would take them to find this obscure dead-end lane off a little side road; but I'd underestimated them. We listened to the sound approaching. It changed tone as they turned into the bottom of the lane. The black and white car appeared around the bend, braked in the middle of the roadway; two uniformed men climbed out unhurriedly. I saw them look at the fallen bicycle and jump to conclusions about traffic accidents.

'It's along the path, in the ditch.' I pointed.

'Can you show us?' the driver asked. He nodded to his companion. 'Stay down here, keep them clear.' He cast an inclusive eye over the scene: Helen and the two restless boys, the six or seven people who had heard the siren and were already heading towards us. He jumped to the wrong conclusion again and said to Helen, 'Keep your boys here.' And to me: 'Lead the way, please.'

I scrambled as neatly as possible over the stile and led him, slipping in the mud, down the wet path. Billy was standing motionless on the eroded bank, looking down into the ditch, and the bones were just as I'd left them, though I'd half expected to find him digging them up frantically or covering them over again: Billy had an interest in dead things. He looked up and stepped back as we arrived; the policeman looked down and stepped back too. 'Keep away,' he said.

'That's been there a long time,' Billy said tightly.

'Never mind that.' The driver was scanning the empty fields as though he thought he would see a killer, running. 'I'll stay here. Will the two of you go back to the car and tell the constable to radio for back-up? And then wait, please. They'll want your names before you leave. Live in Alford, both of you?'

I said, 'Yes,' which was accurate enough for his purpose,

looked at Billy, and found him staring at empty air in front of his nose. After a moment he turned away. I followed.

The situation had developed in our brief absence. The boys had been retrieved by someone who was certainly their mother, since she was gripping each of them by an arm and informing the constable that they were recovering from chickenpox, which was why they weren't at school, were now soaked to the skin, and were going home with her right this minute to be dried out, whatever the Avon and Somerset Constabulary thought about it. Helen and Teddy were just inside the gateposts, while fifteen or twenty other people and three dogs were buzzing around, including Barney who was being restrained on a length of rope by one of the newcomers. Another car arrived and pulled into the driveway of one of the bungalows opposite, and its driver got out and leaned on his roof, talking to a neighbour. Carnival.

Holt gave the message to the constable, who looked harassed. 'You do it,' Billy said. 'I'll stand here. Nobody will go past.' He leaned on the stile, blocking it; I decided to lean beside him for a minute or two.

'Who do you think it is?' I asked him softly.

He didn't reply, and after a few moments my mobile rang. I switched on.

'Dido?' Lizzie's voice. 'Dido, what's happened up there? Are Rose and Lawrence all right? I heard a siren; and everybody in the world seems to be running that way. What is it?'

I realised I'd been careless and explained the situation. 'You and Ben might as well walk up too, if you want,' I said. 'Everybody else is. I can't leave until they take my name, since I'm the first person to have seen it apart from a couple of little boys.'

'Maybe I will just have a look. Are the family all right?'

I told her that Helen and Teddy were keeping an eye on things and there was no sign of the others. And that if she turned up, I'd walk back with the two of them. It was obvious that I wouldn't be able to get my van down the road for the time being.

Lizzie and Ben arrived with the push-chair almost at the same time as two more police cars and a van. Suddenly the road was full of police, moving everyone to the far side of the roadway, unrolling tape to close off the footpath, carrying what looked like poles and tarpaulin up towards the corpse. A dog yelped, and a fight started and was stopped by men shouting. I made sure that Lizzie and Ben had got themselves safely through the mêlée and taken refuge in the driveway, and turned back.

The last car to arrive obviously belonged to the CID, and was driven by a man whose face I somehow knew. He spoke to the driver of the first car, and then turned and looked in my direction and I made the connection: this was the detective sergeant I'd spoken to at the police station when I'd gone looking for Atyeo. I dug around in my memory and came up with the name: Cole – DS Cole. But what was particularly interesting to me was the car he had just parked on the far side of the lane: N981 had just turned up again – in daylight at last. I was so busy adjusting my ideas that he must have spoken two or three times before I realised that he was asking for my name and address. Just for a second, I may have given the impression that I had no idea who I was. Then the name clicked with him. He looked at me hard. 'You were asking for Harry Atyeo.'

I agreed.

He considered the notebook in which he'd written my details. 'I'll drop by in a little while to have a word. Where is the Barton?'

I told him, and then he turned to Holt while I slid past him and escaped through the gates.

'What is it?' Lizzie asked soberly. 'What's happened?'

I met four pairs of eyes. 'Bones,' I said briefly. 'The boys found a body. A skeleton, like the little one said; it's been there for a while. I think that the flood must have washed it out of the side of the ditch.'

For a few minutes we watched them unrolling tape. The waiting crowd chattered in undertones. Billy Holt lounged against the fence of one of the houses opposite, talking to the man who held Barney. His eyes, as he talked, kept returning to the path, although there was nothing to be seen there.

Helen grew restless. 'I haven't started lunch. I should get on with it.' She tried to smile at us and turned towards the house. Teddy hesitated for a moment, then started to follow.

I couldn't read his expression, but I was standing in his way, and something made me remember that I'd been keeping an urgent question for him. I muttered, 'You know, I just keep on wondering about you. Why did you say that *Peter Rabbit* was hidden at the cottage? Did you put it there yourself?'

'Keep your stupid, pointy little nose out of my business!' I barely caught the quiet words, but the tone was condescending. I discovered that I was raising my hand to feel my nose and turned it into a rub.

Lizzie was staring. '*What* did he say?'

I told her I hadn't heard; but I was happy, because I'd found a raw nerve, and that alone was enough to tell me that there was something to all my suspicions. But a person was beginning to demand attention at knee level. I pulled myself back to the moment. 'Ben's hungry and bored. I'd better take him back. Are you staying?'

'You can tell me about the body,' she said. 'There isn't much to see here.'

I made sure that our route took us past N981, where I checked the full registration number again, unnecessarily. I could hardly wait for Cole to turn up; I had questions to trade for his. Probably this was another man who would wind up telling me to keep my pointy nose out of other people's business, but I meant not to hear him, either.

Lizzie shook off her abstraction as we started across the green. 'I meant to tell you, I went around the whole of the first floor, Dido – all the bedrooms, the landing, the cupboards. But then I remembered that the cottage was redecorated the year before we came down, and I just don't believe there's much chance anything's still hidden, unless it's plastered into a wall, or hidden under a floorboard.'

I told her solemnly that could well be, and we might even have to tear up the floorboards. Oddly enough, she seemed to welcome the idea, and to me it looked easier than the alternative of searching Teddy Waring's bedroom.

CHAPTER TWENTY-FOUR

Traffic

From the chair at the head of the cot I could see through Ben's window to watch the comings and goings outside. It was quiet in the small bedroom, and I didn't feel like going back downstairs, where Lizzie was clattering dirty dishes and waiting to speculate with me about corpses. I needed to get my ideas in order. My day seemed to have turned up a mountain of unfinished business.

I knew as clearly as though he had got around to answering my question that Billy Holt believed this body was his sister's. I'd been assuming that his story about a mistaken identification was simply deluded, but now I wondered. That dead foot had been shoeless: it probably hadn't walked to its grave. The corpse had been killed somewhere else? I hadn't seen enough, through the muddy silt, to know whether the body was entirely naked. But if it was, and if Billy Holt was right that the body up in the churchyard was not really his sister's although it had been dressed in her clothes, then maybe this new corpse was naked as well as barefoot?

Say that *two* women, not one, had been killed that night in 1994. One of them was Joannie Holt and the other one was . . . Well, that was the point, wasn't it? Whose body had been dressed in Joan Holt's clothes, and why?

When I looked again, DS Cole was stepping out of his car in front of the cottage. I watched him read the name above the door and move in. I got stealthily to my feet and leaned over the cot. Ben looked at me. One thumb and a good lump of the blue blanket were in his mouth and his eyelids were heavy. I blew him a kiss and crept downstairs.

'Look,' I said to Cole, when the simple and cooperative part of our business was finished, 'I have a question.'

An air of officiousness snapped down like a security shutter. 'I'm afraid I can't discuss the case,' he said.

'It has nothing to do with the case,' I told him pleasantly. Maybe not so pleasantly. 'I want to ask you why you've been lurking around Alford at night. Why you've been looking in at our windows. The whole village is talking about a Peeping Tom. What I happen to know, and they don't, is that he's you. I've seen your car parked just up the lane where you can look into my bedroom. I've seen it outside the pub, too. I've taken your registration number twice.' I caught his eye. 'I think it's time for me to make a formal complaint to your superiors, don't you?'

The security shutter vanished and was replaced by something else. At first I assumed it was fear or embarrassment. Upon consideration, it looked more like anger. 'Miss Hoare, you've jumped to conclusions. *If* you have noticed my car—'

I stared him in the eye and interrupted. 'It's not "if", and don't think that I'm the only one who's seen you. Perhaps you need help. You should speak to your doctor.'

His face became an interesting rose colour. 'As I was saying, if you've noticed my car here, then I was on duty at the time. We're responsible for keeping order in the area, and we do occasional patrols, naturally.'

I laughed at him. 'The CID does routine patrols in outlying villages? That's original.' I stared again. 'Now I know who I've been seeing, I am going to spread the news. I only have to tell —'

'Can I ask you not to do any such thing?'

His voice had risen, and Lizzie appeared in the doorway, looking startled. I glanced at her; she read my mind and vanished. I turned back and waited.

After a moment, he said, 'There's a surveillance being conducted. I'm one of a group of officers involved.'

Oddly enough, I believed him instantly. I said, 'I wish I could believe you.'

'Will you wait until tomorrow before you say anything to anybody? I'm going to ask a superior officer to confirm what I've just said.'

I let him see me thinking about it. I said, 'If I leave it, just to show goodwill, would you return the favour?' He looked evasive again. *Really!* 'Remember, I saw that body down there. It's just something that I can't stop thinking about. I know I saw a bare foot. Am I right that the body was naked?'

Cole blinked, and I could see I'd confirmed his idea that I was an unpleasantly morbid busybody. He snapped, 'Maybe she was', and got to his feet. 'I'll ask the Inspector to ring you here in the morning.'

Lizzie was waiting to show him out and rush back for a briefing. I let her do that while I digested things, especially the news that the corpse was 'she'.

'Dido?'

I made up my mind. 'I have to go and find Billy right away. I'll come straight back.'

She was objecting loudly as I rushed out the nearest door and hurtled down the footpath. I'd left without noticing that it had started to drizzle again, but I kept on going because I had seen Billy Holt cycling towards his house twenty minutes before, and I wanted to get there before he could do another of his disappearing acts. I was damp by the time I knocked at his front door, wet when I realised he wasn't going to answer it, and wetter still when I'd circled the house and found that there was no sign of his bicycle at the back. He had got past me somehow. Mr Invisible. Since I was going to have to change my clothes anyway, I trailed down the narrow path to the sheds, peered through a couple of crude windows at the shapes of gardening tools and sacks, checked the padlocks, determined that the chemical toilet was unoccupied, and paused by the hutch. A young brown rabbit started up from a feast of cabbage leaves and gnarled bits of carrot, thought about hiding, and slowly decided not to bother. I left quietly so as not to frighten him again. By the time I had reached The Barton, even Lizzie could see that I had to change my clothes before I answered any questions, so she followed me upstairs and into the bedroom to quiz me about DS Cole.

Sitting sideways on the window sill, she crossed her legs, fixed me with a stern gaze, and asked, 'Why were you winding him up?'

I didn't see that my promise of confidentiality extended to Lizzie, so I told her what I had been finding out.

She blinked. 'So Billy Holt may have been right all along?' She thought about that and opened her mouth, but whatever she intended to say was lost when she glanced quickly at the window and turned it into: 'Mrs Molyneux. I'm sure she's coming here. She'll want to hear all about the . . . what you saw.'

I said, 'Good!'

Following the strategy I had just used with Cole, I let Mrs Molyneux have the first turn, and gave her a complete account of the day's discovery. She sat with us at the kitchen table; the three of us finished a pot of tea and a plate of chocolate digestives while we debated the situation.

'Mother naked!' Mrs Molyneux sighed. 'Of course you understand what that means.'

I tried to look puzzled.

'Well, let me see. Let me speculate. If – and I say *if* – this body is indeed young Joannie, then she was certainly killed at the same time as the shooting in the library, because that body wore her clothing. Now: why? To hide *her* true identity from the police, of course. Now, if *her* clothes were to be found buried there with this new corpse, with Joannie, mightn't that be revealing!'

'If that's so,' I said, 'it would certainly prove that the two killings were part of the same event. But they may not be there, of course. I didn't see anything like that.' I was thinking about Billy's story. 'Isn't it strange that Mrs Holt made the wrong identification? Is there something suspicious about that?'

'You mean –? Oh, no, I shouldn't have thought so. You're a city girl, I imagine. You will never have seen the effects of a shotgun blast at close quarters. They are terribly destructive! Oh, I assure you, the face would have been *destroyed*. This is not entirely speculation, by the way: I remembered that Mrs Holt spoke to me, back then, about what a terrible sight it had been, what an ordeal for her. As soon as I heard about this new discovery, I went across and called on her at once and mentioned that I had been wondering whether some kind of mistake might have been made. She denied it, which is why I asked her to remind me precisely what occurred. She described the corpse. Terrible. But she will not accept that she might have been wrong.'

Lizzie said, 'You'd think they would have been more careful about it. There'd be dental records, fingerprints . . .'

Mrs Molyneux said gently, 'Why, I don't doubt there were dental records, but in the circumstances would they have been very reliable? And why bother, when the mother had already identified the victim so certainly? Then I don't suppose that her fingerprints would have been on record. Mine are not.' She looked from Lizzie to me, and we agreed that we too had never had our fingerprints recorded. 'On the other hand, there are DNA tests. I have phoned Chief Inspector Wills, in Shepton, whom I knew quite well when he attended our church, and suggested that in the circumstances they should arrange the testing of both bodies. He has nothing to do with this investigation, but he assured me that in the light of today's discovery the pathologist would certainly arrange testing. I gather that it could take some time. Months, possibly.'

Lizzie said harshly, 'Teddy must know who she was.'

'Not necessarily.'

They turned to me. I explained, 'If the story Mickey heard is true, it was very dark, Teddy was probably nervous, somebody he didn't see jumped him and tried to take a loaded gun away, and he fired. By the time he turned the light on, the corpse was – well, as you've described. If Joan Holt's own mother couldn't tell the difference, how could Teddy? He might not have had any idea who he'd killed.'

Mrs Molyneux pushed her spectacles onto the bridge of her nose, examined me closely, and said, 'But why on earth would this mystery woman have exchanged clothing with Joannie?'

I had no answer to that; you couldn't even rule out some wild possibility that the two women were friends and had done so for their own obscure reasons. Every answer raised more questions.

When sounds of life began to come from upstairs, Mrs Molyneux gathered up her bag and got to her feet. 'You will be busy with the baby, and I must get back. I look forward to seeing you both – and the young man. Please call at any time if there is any way I can help.'

We accompanied her to the door, watched her retrieve the umbrella she had left drying in the larder doorway, and saw her out. As she turned for a last farewell, Billy Holt rode along the far edge of the Green and swerved into the track. Lizzie and I exchanged looks. This time I decided I would waste a moment putting on my raincoat before I chased him to ground. Then I ran. By the time I had reached his gate, he was wheeling his bike around the corner of the house. I was only vaguely aware of the taxi that had appeared across the Green behind me as I ran into his garden and shouted. He waited for me to catch up.

'You are bloody hard to get hold of,' I panted. If I sounded cranky, I was past caring. If he was looking stressed, I didn't care about that, either. 'I need to ask you about something you said the other night.' Watching for a reaction, I saw him relax. Hmm. I plunged ahead. 'While we were coming back from the pub, you told me that the shooting in the library wasn't an accident. Why not?'

He leaned his bike against the wall of the house and looked at me guardedly. 'Common sense.'

I persisted. 'Why?'

He hesitated. 'I c'n show you.'

I said, 'All right, then, do.'

He hesitated again, looked at me hard, and then stepped between two rows of seedlings. He had used stakes to mark the line of some beans, and he pulled the nearest out of the ground, came back, and tapped it to shake off the mud. Then he pointed at a spot on the wall of the house. 'The light switch's there. I'm going to turn the light on and then shoot you, so you better grab this shotgun, you better stop me. All right?'

He turned away, and before he had taken more than a step, I jumped and grabbed his arm. I held on with both hands, and we stumbled and struggled for the stick. After a moment, he gave me a shove. I wasn't expecting it; he broke my grip and I staggered backwards. That gave him enough room to raise the stick to my face; he said, 'Bang. You're dead . . . Are you all right?'

Panting, I answered, 'I'm fine. Let's try again.' We went through the motions for the second time. This time I held on tighter, pressing close to him and not giving him enough space to raise the stick. We staggered around for what seemed like a long time, until he finally said, 'All right, stop, you're messing up my beans.' We broke apart and faced one another, and this time we were both panting. Deliberately he raised the stick and pointed it at my eyes and said, 'And bang, you're dead. See, I mean it.'

I saw that. I made myself ignore a little trickle of fear. The third time, I got in front of him so I could watch his eyes, pushing the 'shotgun' sideways. That might have worked if he hadn't stepped backwards and made the same annoying little speech. It was proving to be strangely difficult to get myself shot accidentally, simply because of the length of the stake that represented the barrel of the shotgun. I couldn't find any natural way to get in front of the muzzle while we were still struggling. The final attempt saw us with our hands on the stake, wrestling for control. My blood was up, and I really meant to be the one to say, 'Bang, you're dead' this time, because it was time to stop. Instead I had to say, 'All right; I believe . . .'

I was interrupted by a crash and a roar. When I saw Holt's eyes widen, I let go and whirled about. Barnabas had burst through the gate and was charging straight across the rows of seedlings, shouting like a madman and holding his rolled umbrella in front of him like a spear. I flung myself at him, grabbed for the umbrella, and started to laugh so hard that I couldn't speak, especially when Lizzie came panting up to the gate shouting ridiculously, 'Dido? Dido! Uncle Barnabas is here . . .'

CHAPTER TWENTY-FIVE

Bad Manners

Lizzie said coolly, 'That policeman, Billy Holt — men don't *like* women beating them up — they think it's bad-mannered.'

'I don't see what you thought you were doing,' my father chimed in fretfully, 'mud-wrestling with that chap.'

Following the old principle that when two friends are criticising you simultaneously you can't hear what either of them is saying, I commented, 'We'd better move the cot into my room, and then Barnabas can sleep in the nursery.'

'I can find myself a bed-and-breakfast somewhere,' Barnabas said apologetically to Lizzie, and they began the social sparring which allowed me to ignore them for a while.

The 'wrestling match' had left me with a kind of instinctive, physical conviction that Billy might be right. I had to keep reminding myself that he could never *prove* that the body in the library was not the victim of an accident — negatives are unprovable, and something might have happened that today's amateur dramatics simply hadn't brought out. Or more likely, in the darkness, Teddy had heard a movement, thought he was being attacked, turned and fired at the sound, and then invented a struggle to justify himself? Perhaps it hadn't occurred to him that a shotgun would be such an unwieldy weapon at close quarters. Or Lawrence could have proposed the story. It was hard to imagine the old man up at Monksdanes being in control of any situation, ever, but back then he might very well have decided it would be best for Teddy if there had been an actual struggle. It might even explain the delay in phoning the police: Lawrence had been persuading his son and making sure he had his story straight.

All right. That still left a problem. Unless it was two problems. The change of clothes. The unexplained traces of mud at the scene. If I tried adding all this together . . .

'Dido?'

I woke up and found them both staring at me.

'What is it?' my father demanded.

'Then it's decided?' I asked sweetly. 'We'll move the cot out of the little room before I put Ben to bed this evening.'

A car stopped outside the house while I was speaking. We all turned to the window and discovered that Mickey had arrived. He wasted no time joining us, and barely hesitated at the sight of Barnabas sitting on a chair in his kitchen, drinking tea.

'I . . . hello? Helen phoned me at work. She sounded worried. I thought I'd better come home. What happened? Who is it?'

I said quickly, 'The body hasn't been identified yet,' and inserted an introduction. My father stood up and the two men shook hands, but Mickey's attention wandered.

'I'd better get up to the house and see what's happening.'

Lizzie rose deliberately. 'I'll come with you. Maybe I can help. Dido and Barnabas can bring each other up to date about the bookshop, and things.' She looked at me.

I nodded appreciatively. A spot of assertiveness from her might be quite useful. Not to mention a line of communication with these family councils that kept happening. 'We'll be fine,' I said. 'You get stuck in and see what you can do.' We exchanged a thoughtful look, and they left. Then I turned to my father.

'Now then,' we chorused.

I dived in. 'Why didn't you tell me you were coming? What if there hadn't been a taxi at the station? I could have met your train.'

He looked at me ironically. 'If you hadn't been too busy elsewhere. Why did I come? Pause a minute. Consider. For the past four or five days you have been nearly unreachable, except for mysterious conversations during which you claimed to be spending all your waking hours going for long walks without your phone. Bunkum! Then Ernie and I have received a constant stream of requests for information about men who need to be traced, stolen books of considerable value, and for him to notify the associations that such a book may be offered about. I spoke to Lizzie on the telephone and got the clear impression that she too was keeping something from me, presumably covering up your misdemeanours – as she used to do in the old days, now I remember. Her mother then phoned to say that she has become increasingly uneasy that something is being kept from her, and begged me to investigate. I tactfully omitted to tell her what you had said about the arrival of a hitherto-unknown brother-in-law, a man of dicey reputation and a prison record, but I feel that Lizzie might phone her, if she can work out a good story to tell. Shall I continue? I have come down to find out what the blazes is going on and whether you are likely to be arrested for it, and to take charge of my grandchild in the event that you are. And I find that you have a corpse and all my suspicions were entirely justified! Now –'

I bit back the observation that I had been more than ten years old for quite a long time, and turned it into, 'I *must* do something about Ben. He's been awake for the past five minutes.' The noises coming from the floor above were starting to resemble a jail-break. 'I'm going to go up and wash and change him, and then while I give him something to eat –'

'I'll come and look on,' my father said firmly. 'You can start telling me about it. Begin at the beginning. This may take some time, so we should make a start. They'll be back soon, I presume, and we don't want to be interrupted.'

Personally, I thought that this might be one Waring family conference that would run and run, but I had my own urgent reasons for wanting to develop the Hoare version. I felt as though I were sitting on a rubbish tip full of gobbets of information and speculation, and I found out long ago that relating a mishmash like this to my father – a good teacher because he always forces you to work out the meaning of things for yourself – is the best way to make sense of a big mess.

I got to my feet, waited for him to retrieve his old leather overnight case from a spare chair, took a deep breath, and started the whole story. Barnabas remained remarkably patient and fairly silent until I brought events up to the experimental re-enactment with Billy Holt of the killing in the library. In the course of this, we moved from the kitchen to the little bedroom (Barnabas tested the narrow bed gingerly), to the bathroom, back to the bedroom, and down to the kitchen again, with Ben making cheerful contributions about cows and the seaside. The three of us finally settled around the kitchen table with a pot of tea, a mug of milk, and a slap-dash bowl of assorted mashed vegetables and chopped chicken leftovers for Ben.

'. . . and I realise that it proves nothing,' I admitted, arriving at my ending, 'but I'm pretty sure that there's something seriously wrong with the official version of that murder.'

'Oh yes,' my father said, watching his grandson with a satisfied air which suggested that he had been missing his company. 'It must be a fiction from start to finish, and I imagine, from what you say, that your retired policeman guessed that at the time. Lengthy professional experience is a very reliable instinctual guide. Take that problem of the anonymous manuscript poem which Tullet insisted on attributing – never mind! A pity the pathologist wasn't a little more patient and a little less inclined to accept the obvious; but then they were presumably pushing him for results. And having a penitent culprit who readily confesses to the crime and begs you to convict him – why would you reject a solution that insists on dropping so economically into your lap?'

Ben applied apple sauce to his mouth and nose, and I wiped

his face and hands when necessary and listened to the sounds around me: the Rayburn rumbling, an intermittent scratching which suggested that Lizzie had a mouse, one or two cars outside . . .

Barnabas roused himself. 'How extraordinarily quiet it is here! The lack of traffic noise is disturbing. I find it hard to concentrate.'

'There's a fire in the living room,' I said. 'We could go in there and turn the television on and I'll read aloud to Ben, if that will help.'

'Disturbing,' my father repeated to himself, promptly getting to his feet and leading the way. By the time we had joined him, he was in the armchair by the hearth, fiercely examining the flames. Ben and I settled ourselves and tried not to interrupt his train of thought.

After five minutes, he said, 'Mrs Molyneux: I should like to meet her. And the present vicar, perhaps? And the Warings, of course. You must take me up there tomorrow, you and Lizzie. I should very much like to see the old library. It might be interesting, and descriptions of course are never quite sufficient.'

'I could say that I'd like to take one last look to make sure I haven't missed any books, and that I'll need to consult you.'

'Good.'

Silence fell again. Ben abandoned the little plastic blocks which he had been building into a three-storey construction and joined me on the settee, demanding, 'Me read.' We selected a pop-up book and began. The Waring family conference, as I'd anticipated, went on and on and on. Barnabas thought, asked the occasional question I couldn't answer, or dozed.

It was nearly eight thirty when the front gate clattered and we heard voices raised outside. Judging by the tone, it wasn't so much a quarrel as a debate. The far door slammed, and then the voices were in the kitchen. I picked up a sleepy Ben and went to join them.

Lizzie turned quickly. 'Dido, I'm so sorry. Is Uncle Barnabas all right? Aren't you hungry? I'm sorry about dinner. I'll have something ready in half an hour; there's some stew in the freezer.'

She was interrupted by Barnabas, who appeared in the doorway and avoided hitting his head on the low lintel at the last minute. 'Don't concern yourself. I often eat this late. I trust everything is well?'

Mickey said, 'Yes,' just as Lizzie replied, 'No.' They exchanged looks.

'The police were up there for a long time this afternoon. They had a chat with Teddy –'

'A long talk,' Lizzie interrupted. 'There were two of them; one was the man who came here.'

'Apparently they had a lot of questions. It's bad luck that body was found so close to Monksdanes. It was bound to make them think back to the . . . the last time.'

Barnabas threw Lizzie a glance. 'I don't suppose that anyone let anything useful drop about this present corpse? I mean to say, whether the police believe it to date from the same period as the old shooting? Did they confirm that the body is indeed a female? How did she die?'

Lizzie shook her head. 'I don't think they said anything. Teddy said they just banged on and on about whether he had any idea who it might be, whether he knew of anyone who disappeared a few years ago. "A few years ago" – I think that's what they said. Helen said that they didn't seem to believe anything she told them. Rose just said that the men "displayed poor manners", as though they thought they were speaking to criminals.'

'And it all upset Helen so much that she phoned you?' I asked Mickey.

'Not just that. Mummy suddenly said to her that they'll never have any peace here again and their only option is to sell up and leave Alford for good. "Why not?" she kept saying to us. "The time has come." It made Helen panic. I don't think she can see what they'll do if they leave here.'

'Neither do I,' Lizzie muttered. 'Where will they go?'

Mickey said abruptly, 'I'm going to give Tris a bell and let him know what's happened. He'd better come down, if he can get away. Excuse me.' He sidled past Barnabas and vanished into the next room, closing the door, and we heard him on the phone.

'I should very much like to know whether they have made any useful discoveries about the skeleton,' Barnabas announced once more. 'Dido, you haven't by any chance established lines of communication with the local CID?'

'Not really,' I admitted, 'but I know who has. Well, not the local CID, but a local Chief Inspector. That might be even better. She's known him for a very long time. Why?'

'Because,' Barnabas said, 'if nothing else, they must know whether or not that corpse was pregnant.'

I said, 'She won't have gone to bed yet. I'd better phone.'

The directories were on a shelf under the kitchen phone, and Mrs Molyneux's number was listed. I sat at the table, cradling Ben's sleepy head against my shoulder, picked at the buttons on my mobile, and made the call. Mrs Molyneux's ringing voice answered, and I tried to explain. I gave her the number of my mobile.

Lizzie said, 'That sounded as though she thought she could find out, all right.'

It had. I looked at Barnabas. 'She'll phone me in the morning, after she's spoken to him. She seemed happy to help.'

'I could hear that,' Barnabas remarked. 'Piercing. Very piercing.'

Efficient, too. Mrs Molyneux returned my call while we were still at breakfast. Her message was brief. What the rains had washed up was the decomposed body of an unidentified, young, naked and pregnant female who had been dead for several years; the cause of death had not yet been determined. Mrs Molyneux had sounded uneasy. She probably wouldn't be the only one when this news got out around Alford.

CHAPTER TWENTY-SIX

Pieces

Barnabas sat at the kitchen table, making it difficult to clear the breakfast dishes. I watched him place two of Lizzie's blue and white striped mugs side by side and position the honey to one side of them and the marmalade jar close by. After a moment, he set the pepper pot a few inches away and laid two teaspoons – slightly used – to right and left of the formation. Lizzie raised her eyebrows at me. The corners of her mouth twitched, and she crossed from the sink and pretended to be reaching for the dirty mugs. Barnabas caught her hand and patted it tolerantly.

'All right, Uncle B, I'll ask you, if Dido won't.'

'What? Oh, of course. Is there any tea left?' My father was a morning tea drinker, unlike Lizzie and me.

'I'll put the kettle on,' my friend said. 'It was stewed black when I emptied the pot five minutes ago. What are you doing?'

'Putting the pieces together,' Barnabas said. 'There were a great many pieces in Dido's story, all with a disconcerting tendency to slip and slide. Remind me – did you say that your sister-in-law was *not* at Monksdanes at the time of the shooting?'

I'd already realised what he was doing and intervened. 'No, she came just afterwards, when they called her. She may know something she hasn't told Lizzie. She was the first person Rose contacted, so she's closer to what happened than Mickey and

Tris, unless somebody confided in Tris because he's a clergy-man.'

'I don't catch much of a whiff of the religious in this,' Barnabas said drily. He moved one of the spoons further from the mugs and added, 'It's a nasty, arrogant, cruel business, isn't it!' He put a fingertip lightly on one of the mugs and fell silent.

I returned to my seat and waited. Lizzie joined us; I noticed that she was keeping a slightly nervous eye on Ben, who was on the floor with sheets of old newspaper and his crayons again. As I understood this, he had recently entered an Abstract Expressio-nist period and seemed to be finding straight red lines so satisfying that they ran off the edge of the paper in moments of enthusiasm.

'Two bodies. Two women,' Barnabas said after a moment. 'One was Joan Holt, and the other one was substituted for her. Why did that happen? That is the centre of this conundrum. If we had the answer we might, I believe, understand everything. The story that the corpse was burglarising the house is, as Dido suggests, wildly unlikely.' He looked at me hard. 'Now, I can see *her* doing something of that kind.' He utterly ignored my ironic bow. 'But as she admits, she would not herself undertake the project wearing her best frock and high heels.'

'Only in a terrible emergency,' I interrupted, trying to be objective.

'What kind of terrible emergency would require an entry *into* the house in the middle of the night?' Barnabas asked cogently. 'No, one thing that puzzles me is why all this had to happen in – at what time, exactly, did it happen? – when the household was a-bed, at any rate. You will say . . .' He threw a glance in my direction, but I refused to rise. 'You will point out that this is the conventional time for burglaries, although I read somewhere that many if not most occur during the late afternoon while the residents are out at work. And then, what was the girl proposing to steal? There is no suggestion that she had parked even a wheelbarrow outside the window, much less a pantechnicon. Am

I expected to believe that she was proposing to roll up a large Aubusson carpet, or dismantle a fifteen-foot antique mahogany dining table, and carry it down the lane on her head? While wearing high heels? Obviously not. So unless she was looking for the family jewels –'

'There aren't any,' Lizzie interrupted, 'but she might have been looking for *Peter Rabbit.*'

'But that went missing some time before,' I reminded them.

'That story,' Barnabas repeated in measured tones, 'is not necessarily to be believed. Perhaps we should ask again. The Belltower man actually saw it when he bought the other books, so they had it then. I'd quite like to know exactly how long that preceded the killing.'

I said, 'Six months? I can check that.'

'Do.' My father nodded. 'However, barring some astounding new evidence, I shall maintain my current assumption: this business had nothing to do with burglary. Nonsense!'

I was looking at the mugs. 'So, two women were killed, presumably at the same time? Because of the clothes, I mean. One was Joan Holt, who had nothing to do with burglary, and the other was somebody else whose own clothing hasn't been found, who might have been a burglar, I suppose, though nobody has any idea who she was?'

'Not local,' Lizzie pointed out, 'or she would have been missed.'

'*Probably* not local,' Barnabas corrected her. 'Might there have been a missing persons report at the time, for some local whose link with this story has not been noticed? Enquiries should be made, no doubt. Now: I have used the two jars to represent the men involved. Whatever did happen, Teddy Waring must know about it, and probably his father also knew. The pepper pot . . .'

'Rose,' I guessed. 'Very appropriate. Wait until you meet her.'

'I look forward to it,' my father commented. 'I have placed her a little further away from the victims, but I'm not sure . . . I suppose it isn't outside the limits of imagination that she was central to the business and protected by her son and husband. Dido assures me that the Warings are a very close family.'

Lizzie said, 'She's an old lady.'

Barnabas sniffed. 'And therefore helpless? Like your mother, no doubt. Or myself?'

Lizzie held up her hands and laughed sourly.

'No, she is not beyond suspicion,' Barnabas announced darkly.

'The teaspoons?'

'Probably peripheral; but Helen may know more about this than she has ever said, and the same is true of Joan's brother. The man is obsessed, if we can believe Dido's story. A clearer understanding of his motives and emotions could be illuminating. His behaviour is very odd: the fact that he has been working at Monksdanes, the games-playing and evasiveness. It does not, I should say, add up. Is there any chance that he is either a little simple or a little insane?'

I was about to say, 'Neither,' when the telephone rang. Lizzie rushed to answer, greeted Helen Waring, and then listened. Eventually she said, 'No, no, of course, I'll be there in ten minutes,' and hung up. Then she sighed at Barnabas and me and said, 'I forgot it was Wednesday. Helen was wondering whether I'm too busy to take her shopping.' She explained the weekly excursions to Barnabas. 'So unless you'd like to come with us and grill her, I suppose . . . Dido, could you make the tea? The water's just starting to boil.'

Barnabas broke up his model and said that he thought he would refuse the opportunity, and that he had stopped wanting tea, too.

After Lizzie had gone up to get her bag from the bedroom, I said, 'What?'

'You were about to say?'

I shook my head. 'You're on the wrong track. Billy Holt isn't either mad or stupid.'

There was something else, but Barnabas frowned and changed the subject before I could put my finger on it. 'We spoke of visiting the house, looking at the scene of the crime, and perhaps conversing with the killer. Would this morning not be the time?'

I said, 'It'll take me a couple of minutes to get ready, if you'll just keep an eye on Ben. Don't let him crayon the matting again.'

'Too late,' my father commented.

As usual, I was over-optimistic. I was halfway up the stairs when my mobile phone trilled. I pulled it out of my pocket and switched on. A man's voice said, 'Miss Dido Hoare?'

I agreed cautiously that I was.

'This is Detective Inspector Bruce Clark, Castle Hinton CID. DS Cole asked me to ring you.' He paused, but I saw no need to comment. 'I understand that you've noticed one of our cars in Alford village on various occasions? I wanted to tell you there is no cause for anxiety. DS Cole has official business there. I'd appreciate if you'd keep this confidential, it could compromise an investigation. I wonder whether you happen to have mentioned it to anyone?'

I told him quite honestly that I'd mentioned a peeping Tom to a few people, but the story had been around the village long before I had got here. 'But I won't say anything about it being police,' I promised. I had a thought. 'I presume that if I called in to the station I'd be able to see you in person and check the accuracy of the explanation?'

'I'll be happy to see you.' He sounded more resigned than happy, but it seemed straightforward. Cole had mentioned a 'surveillance', and this confirmed it. Who were they watching, and why? Teddy?

I was brushing my teeth when the phone rang for the second time. I spat vigorously, switched on, greeted the caller – Ernie – and spent a few minutes discussing business matters.

'Er . . . Dido, you haven't forgotten?' he asked solemnly. ''S my first exam on Monday morning.'

I felt a pang of embarrassment. Looking after a business

probably wasn't the ideal situation for a student. 'Will you be all right?' I asked quickly. 'No: look, close the shop. Put up a sign saying we're shut for a few days.'

''S not the shop,' Ernie said anxiously. 'I di'n't want to close for Saturday, but what I'm really worried about is the book fair.'

Book fair. He was talking about the monthly two-day event in Bloomsbury, at which I always have a stand. I'd originally planned to get back in time for it, but I'd been distracted. I started to wonder just how far downhill my business had slipped while I was enjoying myself in Somerset.

I thought fast. 'Don't worry, I was coming back for it. I'll be there by Saturday, and I'll pack the books and do the fair. You do what I said: put a sign on the door saying we'll be open again on Saturday morning, and go upstairs and revise.'

He hooted, 'You sound like Mum.'

Unpleasantly reminded that Ernie's mum might have some words to say when she caught up with me, I rang off, gave my teeth a promissory rinse and headed downstairs.

CHAPTER TWENTY-SEVEN

Bloodstains

It wasn't until the three of us left the Barton that we realised just what was going on. Even from the front door, we could see the two police cars drawn up on to the grass outside the chapel. Its big doors stood open for the first time since my arrival, and uniformed officers were emerging just as we reached our gate. We watched them consult a clipboard and then head off on foot. When we reached the end of the grassy oval, we noticed a third car parked down in the lay-by under the lilacs. Four people, two in uniform, were slowly descending the steps at the bottom of the path from the council houses. We stopped to watch while they climbed into the car.

'Wait,' Barnabas said softly.

We waited. The car rolled towards us. Reaching the green, it turned past the Barton and its immediate neighbours. A woman officer was at the wheel. They hesitated at the beginning of the track, and the motor died. We watched the driver emerge, open a rear door and help a fat woman in a red cardigan to climb out. On the far side of the car, an even fatter woman appeared, her head down. The second policeman offered her his arm, and they all set off slowly into the rough track leading to Billy Holt's house.

'Joannie Holt's mother,' I guessed. 'And the aunt. Mrs Molyneux said they live up there. The police have told them about the body, that it's probably Joan, and they're all going together to tell Billy. I wonder what he'll do?'

Up the lane, we paused at Ben's suggestion to say hello to Barney, who was investigating the police tape across the stile. As we turned away, the officers we had followed were ringing a doorbell at one of the small bungalows opposite the footpath.

'They're interviewing the whole village,' Barnabas observed with interest. 'Obviously. I wonder whether anyone will help them with their enquiries?'

Perhaps it was the rain, but the air inside the library was as dank as on my first visit. I abandoned my pretence of looking at slightly damp books after a few minutes and retreated to sit on the floor with Ben and watch Barnabas prowl.

The house was silent. Helen had let us in on her way out with Lizzie, too preoccupied with her grocery list to ask questions. I divided my attention between Ben and Barnabas and keeping an ear open for other Warings. My excuse, if I had to give one, would be that I was making one last search for buyable books, but that might not convince anyone who happened to walk in and find Barnabas on his hands and knees with the hearth-rug rolled back, poring over the ragged hole in front of the fire. After what seemed like a long time he unfolded himself, got to his feet, and began to wander in a widening semicircle, stopping occasionally to lean down and place a fingertip gently on the carpet. I couldn't imagine what he was doing.

'It was years ago,' I decided to point out.

'What?' He looked at me and frowned. 'Ah, well, true, but the remarkable thing is that—' He broke off and rolled the hearth rug back.

I said, 'What?'

'My hearing,' he remarked mysteriously, 'has recently been tested, and I'm pleased to be able to say . . .'

Then I also heard the creak of floorboards, and by the time the door swung open I was examining the title page of a yellowed copy of *Cottage Economy* while my father leaned against the mantelpiece with a patient smile. 'It's not really good enough,' I said to him. 'It's too badly foxed.'

We looked up at the same moment to find Teddy Waring in the doorway, looking flushed and heavy-eyed as though he had only just woken up and hadn't yet washed. I scratched the tip of my nose, introduced him to Barnabas, and watched the two men make a polite inspection of one another. 'Do come in,' I urged him. 'You're not disturbing us.'

'I thought I heard Helen's voice.' He made an effort and almost smiled politely.

'They've gone. Barnabas and I are having a quick look around before I move my van in case there's anything else here that I can handle. Is it true that your mother is talking of selling the house?'

'Yes. Probably. There's nothing else to do.' He seemed less edgy today.

'It would be a relief for her to have a smaller place to look after,' I speculated. 'Where will they go?'

'That depends on what Tris and Mickey come up with.'

When I'd worked out what he meant, I said, 'But Monksdanes will fetch a fair amount, surely, even if the buyer does have to spend on repairs?'

He shrugged. 'I think they've been living for the past ten years by remortgaging. Look, if you don't mind . . .'

I lied, 'I'm sorry, I didn't mean to pry.'

He shrugged as though he knew my apology was meaningless. 'I'm going to make coffee. Want a cup?'

'That would be welcome,' Barnabas intervened smoothly. 'If we were to follow you in a few minutes when we have finished here?'

'It's just instant,' Teddy said shortly and went away.

This Waring lacked the genteel impulses of the rest of his family; we traced him to the kitchen by the sound of the fridge door slamming, discovered him shovelling coffee powder into three mugs, and found our own seats around the table.

'Of course, if you could locate the Beatrix Potter,' Barnabas said, as though continuing an uninterrupted conversation, 'that should solve your parents' problems for a few years more. I imagine that you know its value?'

Teddy returned the kettle to the cooker, took his seat, pushed a half-empty milk bottle and a bowl of lumpy sugar in our direction, and dealt with his own coffee. After a moment he said, 'Somebody once told me it was worth five or six thousand.'

'Who said that?' When he didn't answer, I added, 'It must have been a while ago. If it's the edition I think, it would fetch five times that.'

That startled him into looking at me directly. 'You're having me on!'

I could have sworn that he really hadn't known. I asked tentatively, 'Do you remember the book? The pictures?'

He frowned. 'The pictures? As I recall, they were mostly black and white drawings. What do you mean?'

My father pursed his lips.

'What?' Teddy asked hoarsely.

I told him, watching his face as I explained. Maybe prison had trained him in the art of giving nothing away. When I'd finished, he even managed a twitch of his lips, as though something I'd said was mildly amusing. I would have gone on watching him until he said something if Ben hadn't intervened.

'Drink,' he announced vigorously, and the chance was lost while we set about finding some orange juice in the old fridge. When we settled back in our chairs, Teddy's expression had glazed over again.

Barnabas said suddenly, 'Dido and Lizzie have searched the cottage, I believe, and Dido tells me the book isn't there.'

I was watching for some sign of guilty triumph, so I caught the look of barely camouflaged disbelief. So did Barnabas, I thought. Teddy said, 'There are a lot of nooks and crannies in an old place like that.' His unspoken message was that he wouldn't trust anyone but himself to do that job the way it should be done.

I pushed my half-empty mug of warmish stuff away and made my point by wondering aloud, 'Have you ever been up in the attic? It's full of the old thatch.'

He looked at me for a moment. Pointy nose. 'I'd better have a word with Mickey about coming over and going through the whole place with him properly. It would be . . . a life-saver for Mummy, if you're right about its value.'

'I can imagine,' I said, and we stared at each other coldly again.

He got to his feet abruptly, scraping his chair-legs on the floor. 'Well . . . I'd better get on. I'm doing some clearing in the grounds. I don't know what Holt's been doing around here all spring.'

He nodded at us, hesitated, and crossed the kitchen to the door that led into the little lobby. We could hear noises: something dropped, a couple of cupboard doors slammed. Then the back door. When he reappeared outside the kitchen window, he was wearing an old waxed jacket and rubber boots and carrying a gardening fork and hoe and an old pruning saw. He walked away without looking back.

'We almost spooked him into telling us something,' I said aloud.

'I believe we did,' my father mused. 'We've learned that he took advice on the book at some time without showing it to the dealer, or at least without showing it to a competent dealer, since the point about the private printing apparently escaped somebody.'

'Somebody was probably trying to cheat him. He didn't sell it, though. But whoever saw the thing might have stolen it?'

'Unlikely,' my father suggested. 'There is only one credible answer: if the man really believes it is in the Barton, then he must either have hidden it there himself and then, incredibly, forgotten where, or have cause to believe that another member of the family did.'

'Lawrence? Before his memory went! Only why would he have done that?'

'I have no idea. But do you think we might leave this rather depressing kitchen, or better still the house?'

'It's a lovely house, really,' I said vaguely, and remembered something. 'Barnabas, what did you mean, back there, when you said something about "the remarkable thing"? What thing?'

Barnabas hesitated. 'Somebody had cleaned up the big carpet, but I could still just make out where it had been marked, stained – splattered, if you will. I saw where several brownish spots had been washed out, not entirely successfully, presumably because the blood had dried. You have to look at it in the light.'

I shrugged my shoulders and couldn't help pointing out that there had been a shooting.

'So I believe,' my father agreed. 'So everybody claims, at any rate. A nasty shooting. A young woman's face destroyed in an explosion of shot and gunpowder, a body left in a welter of gore, life blood soaking into the beautiful and valuable rug – you are quite right, it does look like an Aubusson – tragic! So we had a puddle of blood, cut out and removed, either beyond cleaning or more likely, from the appearance, because somebody found that blood so terrifying and repulsive they were frantic to get rid of it, and . . . a few odd drops?'

I said, 'Ye-e-es,' but didn't get as far as 'So?' because the answer was intruding on my imagination. 'You're saying there should have been a lot of . . . splash? Well, they took the trouble to wash it.'

'Yes,' Barnabas said, 'of course they cleaned it up! It was just that I am sure I could *see* where some of it fell; but it seemed too little. Surely somebody must have noticed! And now I suppose I might be wrong about this, being no expert, but I can't help picturing a body being carried into that room, bleeding and dead, and placed neatly in front of the hearth.'

'Mud!'

My father raised his eyebrows at me until I told him what

Atyeo had said about traces of fresh mud. Barnabas said, 'Ah! Well, Teddy Waring entered the library through the garden window, we know about that.'

But that was wrong, and now I knew why. I told him, 'The soles of his shoes were clean because there's a gravel path along the back of the house. And Joan's shoes were clean, too.'

'Then how it happened is entirely beyond me, for the moment, but it is not a picture that I can easily forget. It makes no sense yet. Although a sequence of events may be becoming marginally clearer . . .'

Yes. Or a mid-sequence, anyway. Apparently everything had been wrong: wrong corpse, wrong clothes, wrong scene of the crime. Wrong killer?

I got to my feet. 'Barnabas, I think I'd just like to take the van and drive somewhere.'

My father looked at his wristwatch. 'It could be time for an early lunch.'

CHAPTER TWENTY-EIGHT

Wading Through Treacle

We stayed at the Woolpack until Ben began to complain and I remembered that Lizzie would probably have returned from Yeovil by now. The long lane into Alford was deserted, and nothing moved all the way up Dead End. As I edged on to the verge in front of the cottage, I noticed that the police cars had gone and the tin chapel was shut up again. The cottage was also empty and silent, with no sign of either Lizzie or her groceries. I filled the kettle and placed it on the boiling plate, retrieved Ben from my father's grasp, and removed us both to the bedroom for some quality time, which involved falling asleep.

When I woke after a few minutes, I heard the kettle whistling. I swung my legs over the side of the bed, checked on Ben in the cot, and went looking for Barnabas. The whistle faded before I reached the ground floor, and I found my father scooping Lizzie's Earl Grey into the teapot and covering it with water which had gone off the boil.

'What's happened to Lizzie?'

'Oldish blue estate?' Barnabas asked. 'She drove around the green and honked a minute ago. Went on up the lane without stopping. I presume she will return in due course.'

The news made up my mind for me. I grabbed a mug of tea, splashed it with milk, and headed towards the door. 'I need to have a word with somebody. Listen out for Ben, will you?' I managed to get away without being questioned and stood a moment later in front of Billy Holt's front door. When it popped open, I was so surprised that I just blinked.

Billy looked down at me, at my mug of tea, and at a spot behind my back. 'The old boy not with you today?'

I shook my head. 'You're safe; my father is baby-sitting.'

'So you say,' he commented. 'Brought your own tea, did you? Want to come in?'

Repressing a gasp, I nodded casually and stepped past him into a dusky room. He shut the door behind me.

I'd been expecting some kind of dark den, crammed with a jumble of nineteenth century wooden chairs, an old range, a few pitchforks and a couple of black cats. Instead, I was in a tiny, carpeted sitting room crowded with chintz-covered furniture and dominated by a huge, black, new-looking television set. The place was almost obsessively tidy, if you discounted the large glass ashtray parked on a chair arm and full of ash and smelly ends from a dozen roll-ups. Billy removed it quickly, offered me the other armchair, vanished through the far door with the offending item, and returned without it. He hesitated, sat down, and indicated that he was waiting for me to say something.

'We saw the police here this morning. Was that . . . was one of those people your mother?' He hesitated and nodded curtly. 'Is she all right?'

'What d'you mean?'

I took a mouthful of Earl Grey to gain time. 'The body,' I said finally. 'Yesterday. They think it was your sister. I thought they brought your mother and aunt here to tell you.'

'Worked that out, did you?' There was something in his tone that made me suspect my pointy nose was to blame again.

'So who was the other one? The body in the library wearing your sister's clothes?'

'Better ask that . . . Ted Waring, ha'nt you? He shot her.'

I decided to gamble a bit and said, 'Maybe, but do *you* really believe all that story?'

Billy looked at me without any expression. 'Said he did. You think he was joking? Funny old joke.'

'I think he could be lying.'

'Well?'

I waited, but that seemed to be that. This was like wading through treacle, but I thought I'd try one more question. I drained my tea, got to my feet, said, 'I'd better get back in case Ben wakes up,' turned to the door, and turned back quickly. 'Oh, something else entirely. I was wondering whether you knew the woman who was living in the Barton a couple of years ago? Mrs . . . Richards, was it? Major Hitchens told me a pretty colourful story about her. He said she was a prostitute, and half the men in Alford spent the evenings either in her bed or spying on her from across the green. Were you living in this house, then?'

I stared because he gave a kind of strangled snort. My question had obviously been very funny.

'You want to take that old bug— chap's stories with a pinch of salt. The Major's a'most always wrong about a'most everything.' His mouth was twitching.

I widened my eyes at him. 'Really? Why, what *was* she doing?'

'Dealing — mostly speed.' I didn't have to pretend astonishment now. 'Surprised, then?'

'Gobsmacked,' I agreed unsteadily. 'Are you serious?'

He was laughing at me openly now. 'You ask your friend's in-laws. The old man found out and gave her an hour to get on her bike. He stood over her and watched everything she packed, said he'd make sure she din't take anything of his. I helped her load her car. She was mad as hell, but scared he'd call the police,too. I told her calm down, he wun't want trouble, wun't want police around making him look like a fool, if she just got out and kept quiet. She had a brother, went to him for a bit before she moved on. Tell you what, though: Ted Waring might know. He was seeing her, and he didn't stop just because his dad blew his top.'

I said,'Oh.'

That covered it. It even covered my idea that I'd just heard the reason why Teddy Waring had been looking for *Peter Rabbit* in the Barton. To me, of course, it was perfectly clear that if the evicted lady dealer actually had the book in her possession, she would have managed to get it away from there. Did she know what it was worth? She was supposed to be an antiques dealer, so she probably had an idea, and in her shoes I certainly wouldn't have left it behind even if Lawrence Waring *had* been standing over me, fuming. It would have been an immensely satisfying revenge to remove the family treasure from right under his nose. Personally, I'd have shoved it down my bra.

There were some hows: how she had seen it in the first place, how she had got it out of Monksdanes . . . Wait: Teddy Waring had been 'seeing' her?

I came to and saw Billy Holt watching me.

'That's very interesting,' I said. 'I'd really like to talk to her. Is her first name Tracy, by any chance? Lawrence Waring spoke of a Tracy, once. Do you know where her brother lives?'

'He's gone,' he said. 'Went off last winter. Could be anywhere now.' His tone said, London, Timbuctoo, all the same thing, and he wasn't going to say any more. He saw me to the door in silence.

I wandered helplessly down the path. Nobody was going to get to the bottom of all this without calling on some serious resources. A medium-sized police force might just manage.

Which reminded me: it was three o'clock and still nothing was happening anywhere. Apparently the constabulary had chatted to people and gone away. It all seemed a little casual, even for a long-dead corpse. Possibly they weren't trying very hard?

Lizzie's blue car was outside the gate. I emptied the last drops of tea out of my mug on to the track, and headed back, frustrated.

A medium-sized police force? Maybe not.

I went in through the first door, listened to the sound of Barnabas and Lizzie talking in the kitchen at the other end of the house, and crept silently upstairs. I'd left my shoulder bag in the bedroom, where Ben was just beginning to stir, but managed to grab it and exit before he noticed me and retreated to the bathroom. Atyeo's telephone number was scrawled on one of the pages in my diary. I sat down on the edge of the tub and punched the number into my mobile. He answered; we exchanged civilities.

'Have you heard the news?'

He didn't pretend not to know what I meant, or why I was phoning. 'There's an item in the *Gazette*, just a paragraph. "Children find body in Alford village. Victim had been buried in a field for some time. Foul play suspected." And so on. I made a phone call to a friend at Hinton. Do you —'

I said, 'Billy Holt and his mother were told that it's probably Joannie's body. Whoever it was, she was pregnant.'

There was a little silence before he said, 'Then there's not much more I can say. Forensic tests take a while. Then they'll act according. You don't need to worry about it any more, you and Mrs Waring. It's in good hands.'

Maybe. I said, 'Something has come up. It's a question about the shooting at Monksdanes. Can you remember whether there was anything wrong about the scene of the crime? You mentioned unexplained smears of mud. Was there anything else?'

I listened for a long moment to the sound of the open line.

'What kind of thing?' His voice was cool.

'About the bloodstains,' I said.

'What about them?'

'Was there anything unusual about the . . .' I scrabbled for the way to put this. 'I mean, about the pattern of the blood around the body?'

'Pattern?' There was definitely something evasive in his voice.

I said, 'I don't know what you call it. There doesn't seem to have been much blood, except maybe in the one place where the body lay. There's been a great hole cut out of the carpet, so I presume there must have been a pool of blood around and under it. But not enough . . . *mess*, considering the damage that was done to the body. The shotgun. Am I right?'

The something in his voice was still there, but now he had made up his mind. 'Miss Hoare, it wouldn't be right for me to say anything more to you. The case is a live one again, you see, or it might be. I could say in general terms that, yes, you would expect a fair mess from a shotgun blast hitting a . . . large body at close range. They call it "splatter pattern", I've heard. But that could be affected by various factors, I guess. Couldn't comment specifically. Not my field. Do you understand?'

I did understand. A simple 'no', or 'I don't know' would have worked, if he had really wanted it to. He hadn't said I was wrong. It was all that I'd get. I thanked him warmly enough, switched off, and sat thinking.

The immersion heater in the hot-water tank above the bath had switched itself on, and I could hear its faint murmur. In the kitchen below, the voices went on. Something rustled in the ivy outside the bathroom window, and out in the lane somebody was laughing.

CHAPTER TWENTY-NINE

Grave Matters

By Friday morning, the police investigation had apparently ground to a silent halt. Frozen. Vanished. Lizzie was monosyllabic and withdrawn at breakfast, and I could feel myself getting edgy: it was time for a push. Anything. So we had gone to church, so to speak.

Walking around a corner of the building, I discovered Ben and Barnabas sitting in the shade on a bench outside the west door, sharing a newspaper. Barnabas was focusing on an item in a lower inside corner. It was hard to say what, on his page, had caught Ben's attention, but he was copying his grandfather's serious face. They both looked up and saw me,

Barnabas said, 'Well?'

'He's got somebody with him, but his wife said he'll come over in a few minutes. What have you found?'

'Nothing.' He folded the paper into quarters and passed it over to me. It was a tiny item, a paragraph at the bottom of the inside column under the attention-grabbing heading, 'Body Found'. The single paragraph contained the basic information − Somerset village, children playing, woman's body − but made no connections and offered no speculation. It had taken two days to get even this much into the national newspapers: Alford's ferment of shock, horror and gossip seemed unimportant in the national scheme of things.

Ben dropped his section on the ground and seemed bored.

'Shall we go and have a look at the grave while we're waiting?' I suggested. 'It's over at the north side. I can remember where it is.'

In fact, as we discovered when we had followed the path up into the newer part of the graveyard, Joannie's grave was now well marked by a conspicuous mound of earth and a big yellow tarpaulin.

Barnabas halted in his tracks. 'Ah. That was quick work. I see that they are not being quite as neglectful as you thought. Mind you, I should think that things will be quiet for a while. There must be complex tests and investigations, what with two old cadavers to deal with. At least this time they should get answers.'

I was looking at my wristwatch, but I needn't have bothered since the bell in the church tower immediately started to clank midday. Time was passing, and I'd wanted to get into London before rush hour traffic built up along the Marylebone Road. Footsteps crunched on stones behind us, and the parish priest sidled through a gate in the hedge which separated the graveyard from the vicarage garden. He was a middle-aged, florid man in a black suit with a dog collar, his red hair softened by grey.

Barnabas took charge and introduced the three of us. 'We're grateful that you can take a moment,' he said, man to man; 'I would imagine your Fridays are busy.'

The Reverend P Wilkes, BA, as the church's sign had named him, smiled, shrugged, and exuded an air of half-controlled anxiety. 'Two weddings tomorrow. I have to have a last word with them all today.' His eyes strayed to the mound of earth. 'How can I help you?'

'We're here on behalf of my niece, Elizabeth Waring. And also of her mother, whose health does not allow her to travel to Somerset.' Barnabas had obviously decided not to offer the unnecessary information that ours was a historical, rather than a blood, relationship. 'I'm sure you can understand how disturbed Lizzie was to discover, only in the past fortnight, something' –

he threw the vicar a significant look – 'of the recent events in her husband's family. We are here to give her support.' He was getting into his stride and, under the influence of present company, his voice was beginning to take on something of the rolling tones of a sermon: the vicar could only nod understandingly. 'But to be frank, I don't think she can be easy in her own mind until things are brought to a conclusion. In her present state of health . . .' More significant looks, which Wilkes seemed to adjust to: if there was something here that he was supposed to know, he wasn't about to admit ignorance.

Barnabas' oration rolled on. 'You were here, I understand, when it all happened. Joan Holt.' The two men turned to glance at the empty grave. I kept quiet: Barnabas seemed to be doing brilliantly. 'I can assure you that I understand your duty of confidentiality to the dead.' He was staring earnestly into Wilkes' eyes by now. 'Clearly, that must be respected. But is there not a duty to the living, as well as the dead?'

'What are you suggesting?'

'The whole village knows by now that the body found two days ago is really that of the girl believed to be buried in this grave. That poor woman, her mother, must be grieving all over again. Now there is the matter of the other young woman, whose unidentified body has been lying in this churchyard for over four years. I believe it is vital to my niece and the whole family that this matter should be cleared up, finally and correctly. Justice . . .' He stopped himself, possibly realising that he was about to go over the top.

Wilkes cleared his throat uneasily and said that he agreed that, for the spiritual health not only of the Warings but of others too, it was time the matter was resolved. Something in his voice told me that he was tempted to add, 'The police are on it.'

I intervened. 'Did you know Joannie? You see, they say she was pregnant, and that the baby was Lawrence Waring's.' I hesitated, and plunged into the way it seemed to me. 'Her brother says that she was fine with that: that she seemed to think it was an honour, or something, but I don't believe him.'

'And you're asking me whether I can give you any insight into Joan Holt's thinking?' The vicar fixed me with a weary eye. 'Miss Hoare, do you think this is a question I haven't asked myself? But I have no idea. Our parishioners usually vanish from our ken just after First Communion, if they get that far, barring perhaps an annual appearance at the Carol Service. Joan Holt was no different from anybody else in that respect. They often reappear, asking me to marry them, but that, of course, didn't apply in this case. And they will surface again at about the time when they qualify for their pensions, looking sheepish and saying something like, "Well, Vicar, I know I haven't been to church for a while but." In other words, they expect me to bury them.' He shook himself and abandoned what was obviously a favourite topic. 'Oh, this place is like any other C of E parish in the land, and no, I have no special insight into Joan's mental state. I really didn't know her.'

That seemed clear enough, and perhaps an apology was in order; I said, 'I'm sorry we've taken up your time, it was just that Mrs Molyneux gave me an idea that you might be able to help.'

'Ah. Did she?'

We looked closely at one another, and I could swear that his eyes twinkled, or something.

'I'm surprised that Mrs Molyneux would feel I know more about the situation than she.' It *was* a twinkle. 'I can say that Mrs Holt did not encourage gossip. She's an old-fashioned woman who would feel shame and anger at her daughter's situation. She was, and is, quite conservative. There would have been no question of a termination. I did get the impression . . .' He hesitated. We waited. 'I should say that this is a confidential matter, except that I was not the only person to whom she spoke, later, at the time of the funeral. Mrs Holt's idea was that Joan should ask Mr Waring for enough money to allow her to go and stay with a cousin in Poole until the birth, give up the baby for adoption, and return with a little nest-egg to tide her over until she found other work or training.'

I was bewildered. 'Didn't anybody ever connect Joan's death with her pregnancy?' I meant that it offered a motive for killing her, but Wilkes seemed to miss the point. Maybe he meant to.

'I thought,' he said simply, 'that it seemed an old-fashioned approach, Victorian, even, but reasonable from everyone's point of view.'

Victorian? No – feudal. I tried not to let him see how I felt about it. But in any case, it hadn't happened. Perhaps the Warings saw Joan's demands not as reasonable, but as blackmail. I said neutrally, 'The Warings don't seem to have any money.'

The twinkle turned into a cynical smile. 'They certainly have more than any member of the Holt family has ever seen. Furthermore, the sons could have been called upon. Admittedly Ted has always been disinclined to earn his keep, but both Michael and – what's his name? – Tristram could have helped, in the circumstances.'

For a moment, we all watched Ben, who had found a squirrel that had ventured out onto the rough grass and was stalking it enthusiastically as it retreated towards a nearby yew.

'So if Joan Holt got all dressed up in her best clothes and went up to Monksdanes one night, you think she might have been putting that plan to Lawrence?'

We all contemplated the question.

'I couldn't say. Nobody can, now, not even Lawrence Waring.' He consulted his wristwatch. 'I have an appointment in ten minutes. The second happy couple. I think I need a cup of tea before they arrive. I'd offer . . .'

'We should get back,' my father said, 'but I thank you for everything.' His voice was subdued. The priest strode back towards the vicarage. The Hoares watched the squirrel vanish overhead and then strolled down towards the road.

I said, 'Poor Joannie,' as I unlocked the van.

My eyes fell on the solitary figure of Mrs Molyneux as soon

as we reached the green. She was standing stock still in the middle when I noticed her. Then she caught sight of us and hurried forward. Her expression was so odd that I for one couldn't take my eyes off her face. I backed half on to the verge, fell out of the driver's door and opened my mouth, but she was already pointing silently at the Barton.

At first I thought that the mellow fieldstone of the cottage had been splashed with blood; but it was only crimson paint. Somebody had flung a bucketful of gloss paint against the wall, where it had run down in rivulets and formed little, gaudy puddles on the earth among the wallflowers. Like a bloody face.

Mrs Molyneux said, 'Lizzie asked me to wait here in case you came back. She called me when she came down from the house and found it like this. She's gone back up to make sure they're all right.'

Before she had finished speaking, I heard a shout behind me. Teddy Waring was galloping across the grass, clumsy in his rubber boots. He came to a halt in the middle, staring at the cottage. His face was rigid and entirely unreadable. He stared at the paint for a long beat, then looked directly at us and whirled and stomped off towards the track. He was going to Billy's place.

I said, 'Take care of Ben,' and ran. By the time I got there, Teddy was pounding the door knocker. I stopped inside the gate. He stooped and picked up a big stone and pounded it on the door. I could see scars multiplying on the green paint. After a moment, he froze and waited, head down, listening. I decided to bang the gate, but stayed back beside it. He glanced at me.

A voice behind me said quietly, 'Miss Hoare?' Mrs Molyneux had joined us. I stopped holding my breath. Teddy looked at us, came down the path and went through the gate. He seemed perfectly calm as he passed us without a word or a look and headed off towards Monksdanes.

'Dear me,' Mrs Molyneux commented, 'for a moment . . .' She sounded breathless.

I said, 'Lucky Billy isn't home. Come on, we'll – put the kettle on and wait for Lizzie.' We set off rather briskly towards the cottage. 'Mrs Molyneux, will you keep an eye on Lizzie over the weekend? We have to go back to London for a few days on business. She may need somebody.'

Mrs Molyneux was emphasising that of course she would when we reached the van and found Barnabas still clumsily disentangling Ben from the child seat. They both looked fed up. My father slammed the door, and the two of them turned and fixed me with glares. Mrs Molyneux's presence may have saved us from some plain speech; all my father said was, 'Too much leaping before you look.'

I sighed. 'I only looked. That was all I ever meant to do.'

'Fine words butter no parsnips,' my father observed obscurely.

I said, 'I'd better not go.'

'Rubbish!'

'Barnabas, I don't like what's going on!'

'You don't *know* what's going on,' Barnabas observed, sounding grumpy.

'That doesn't make it any better!' I shouted.

Mrs Molyneux looked from one of us to the other and observed, 'There might be something I can do?'

I thought there was. 'You have to talk to Billy. Make him stop! I don't know what he thinks he's up to, but he has to stop doing these things before Teddy Waring kills him.'

I'd said that casually, the way you might say, 'I was so angry I could have killed him'; but I was talking about a man who had really killed someone already, and who had just demonstrated what a scarily short fuse he had. We all looked at the damage again; then we turned to one another cautiously.

'Are you sure Billy did that?' Mrs Molyneux asked, sounding disturbed. 'Are you sure?'

I had reason to be. Probably . . .

'I am not going back with you,' Barnabas announced abruptly. 'You and Ernie will have to manage without me somehow. Try not to do anything too rash. I shall stay here and comfort Lizzie and I will make sure that nothing happens.'

I made up my mind. 'I won't go.'

Mrs Molyneux shook her head decisively and then had to push her glasses up onto the bridge of her nose again and say, 'Nonsense! Do you think that Professor Hoare and I can't cope with things here?'

Well, I had my doubts. But I didn't quite believe my own worst-case scenario, either. I tried telling myself not to be melodramatic. My inconvenient internal critic sprang into life suddenly, sneering, *What makes you think that any of this story you're imagining is going to come true, or that you could stop it if it did? Do you think you're the Household Cavalry, or something? Grow up!*

I just repeated pathetically, 'Try not to do anything too rash,' and went to put the kettle on, finish packing and then worry about everything while I did something about lunch.

CHAPTER THIRTY

Mondays Can Be Difficult

———◆———

A voice speaking somewhere above my head said, 'It can't be that bad. I'll buy a book. Show me something. Or better still, I'll buy you a drink.'

Realising that I'd slumped into the folding chair in a more than usually glum posture, I straightened up and identified the speaker as my old friend Jeff Dylan, a bookseller from Swansea.

'Or both?' I suggested hopefully, and explained to him that my pose of despair was caused, not by anguish at the slowness of trade on the second day of the book fair (which is only normal), but by other and more serious worries which refused to lie down even though I had phoned the Barton repeatedly over the weekend. I had talked to Barnabas and Lizzie already this Monday morning, and been assured that everything was so peaceful down there in Alford that they were seriously considering going to visit Wells Cathedral that afternoon. Whether I believed them was another matter.

When I'd left Somerset on Friday afternoon, I was just glad to escape. By Saturday, I was too busy running the shop on the busiest day of the week and arranging two days of serious babysitting with the college friend of Ernie's who had covered for me once or twice before to brood. Equally on Sunday, when Ernie and I had set up the stand at the book fair before I sent him home to do some last-minute cramming, I'd had no chance to worry about Alford. But today, with time on my hands . . .

Uncontrollable curiosity. Pointy nose. *Grow up, Dido!*

Forty-five minutes, two spritzers and a chicken sandwich later, I left Jeff in the hotel's comfortable bar talking to some of our hung-over fellow booksellers, wandered restlessly back into the ballroom, and waved my thanks to the woman two stalls along who had been keeping an eye on my stand. In my absence she had sold one of the Monksdanes volumes for me, and there was a cheque sitting on top of the paper bags under the table. I looked at my watch. Just after three. Another four hours here and I could . . .

'Hey, Dido!'

I jumped. 'Ernie! How did it go?'

But I could already tell from his grin. He just said, 'Piece o'cake, that one. You want me to take over?'

I hadn't planned it that way, but yes, as a matter of fact I did. I fumbled in my shoulder bag and pulled out my wallet. It was unusually fat with banknotes, mostly yesterday's cash takings. I split the pile in two halves and shoved one of them into his hand. 'I'm going back to Somerset. You pack up and take everything home by taxi, will you? Just dump it all in the office and leave it. I'll have left by then, but I'll put a sign up on the door that we're on holiday, and a new message on the answering machine. Lock up when you've unloaded, and get on with it.'

'You don't haveta go,' Ernie protested. 'No problem! Is it?'

Actually, the last two nights with Ernie on the couch in the living room, Ben and me in my small bedroom, and the three of us falling over one another everywhere else, had been a small problem; but that wasn't the point. I told him grimly that unfinished business was waiting in Somerset. He looked wistful: I'd told him what was going on, and Ernie enjoys excitement.

I growled: 'Study. Serious concentration. Exams, exams. Apart from that, I just need you to make sure that the shop is secure, and that's all. This is important for you. Right? Yes?'

He grinned sheepishly, because we both knew exactly what I was saying. I fled, sooner than I'd hoped to get away and a lot happier.

As usual, it took me longer to leave than I'd expected, and longer still to get through the roadworks on the western outskirts of London. I'd had to stop at the motorway service area to feed and change Ben, and the sun was low by the time I reached the turn-off. I considered phoning the Barton, but there wasn't a convenient place to pull over; and anyway I hadn't bothered to tell them we were arriving today, so they wouldn't be worrying about our non-appearance. Ben was silent, probably sleeping. No point waking him, I reminded myself, and kept on going.

When we emerged on the open hillside above the railway station, the sun had just set. The western sky still glowed with red light. Shepherd's delight. I switched my headlights on, glanced at the clock on the dashboard, and swept into the bend over the railway line. At the Woolpack, where the car park was again almost empty, I turned left and switched on my high beams. There was no traffic in the lane. In the deeper darkness between the hedgerows, my headlights were suddenly reflected in a pair of red eyes by the ditch. Cat? Fox? Wandering dog?

The blockade had been set up at the T-junction: a couple of torches were bobbing around a police car parked at an angle across the road, its blue lights flashing. I braked, then crept forward and pulled up just short of them. Someone ran a torch beam briefly over the van, and then came to my door. I already had my window down.

'Is it an accident?'

'Nothing to worry about.' (I repressed my instinct to repeat the question in an attention-getting shriek.) 'I'm afraid that you can't go on for a little while. Can I ask where you're heading?'

The second policeman was at the other side, flashing his light into the back of the van. The beam crossed Benjamin's face, and he woke up with a squeal. The policeman beside me pulled back and said something sharply across my bonnet, and the other torch retreated. Ben decided to begin to cry experimentally.

'Sorry about that,' the near voice said hastily. 'Do you live in Alford?'

'We're holidaying here with my friend,' I said rapidly. I undid my seat belt, leaned into the back, and gave Ben a pat. To my astonishment, he seemed to decide that this meant everything was all right.

'Address?' the voice persisted.

'It's a house called the Barton. It's just ahead. On the green. Can't I get there?'

'Not just now. I am sorry, I know you'll want to be getting the baby to bed, but I can't let you through. There's an operation being carried out just ahead, and it might not be safe. If you'd like to turn back a few yards and pull into one of the field entrances, you won't be bothered there, and we'll be opening up the road as soon as we're finished.' He sketched a kind of salute and stood back.

I made a slow 180-degree turn, conscious of the ditches lurking in the twilight on either side of the road, and drove off. I'd better phone Lizzie now; but I'd passed the first two field entrances before I saw them. I did see the wider break in the hedge to my right in time to approach it at a crawl. It was the rutted track I'd noticed once before. There was no gate to open, so I swung the van straight across and got it well off the road before I switched off the ignition, cut the lights, and climbed out. I could still see the blue flashes up the lane, but nothing suggested what was happening beyond them. I switched my mobile on, hesitated, switched it off again and put it away. Because I knew how to get Ben to bed now, despite them all.

My emergency torch was in the glove compartment. I flashed it at the ground and moved a few yards. As far as I could tell, the track was bending slightly northwards, the direction I needed. Big clumps of weed and grass were a problem, but the ground at the bottom of the ruts seemed level and clear. I wouldn't risk driving this rough, deeply rutted track in darkness, but it was walkable.

I went back and slid the side door open, unstrapping Ben by feel. His plastic bag was on the floor between the seats. I pulled it out and slung that and my own bag over one shoulder, and hoisted him up on the opposite hip. He grabbed a hunk of my hair in one fist and said something unintelligible. His head nodded against my neck.

'Come on,' I whispered. 'This must go straight into Alford. It's probably the other end of that track that runs to the green, and we can't be more than ten minutes from your bed. You coming?'

He yawned into my collar. I locked up, pocketed the car keys, and shone the torch on the ground ahead. Our dark shadow loomed on the hedge behind me. I set one foot lightly ahead of the other, watching for treacherous dips, but the ground remained flat and the track was almost straight now.

A half moon hung over Alford. Only my torchlight kept me from seeing through gaps in the hedges and across the rolling fields. There were noises everywhere. Some large beasts were breathing heavily in the field to our right, and a faint shriek in the opposite hedge said that life-and-death struggles were going on all around. I was starting to hear a different kind of noise up ahead, like the rumble of a distant crowd.

I had reached Billy Holt's low hedge before I even noticed the outline of his roof against the sky. Then I felt the paved surface of the lane under my feet and switched off my light. The tin chapel was just a dark hulk, but all the other buildings around the green seemed to have lights in every window, and there was a murmur in the air, as though the crowd was closer now. Ben was getting heavy, and my curiosity faltered. I arrived outside the Barton, hurried up the path, and rang the bell.

Barnabas opened the door abruptly, said, 'Good lord!' and pulled us inside. The telephone was ringing in the next room.

I blinked in the light. 'Barnabas, what's going on? There's a police block on the lane: I had to walk the last few hundred yards!'

My father unloaded the bags I was carrying and decided not to try unloading Ben, who was asleep. 'Two or three people have rung Lizzie to ask just that. The village is full of police. Mickey phoned an hour ago to say that he couldn't get through from the station. He's waiting at that pub on the main road where we had lunch, I believe.'

Then Lizzie exploded out of the sitting room, saying rapidly, 'Mrs Molyneux – oh hello, Dido – says the Major rang to tell her the police are at the pub! He went down to have a look, but they're keeping everybody back. The lane is full of police vans, and they seem to be arresting people.'

'Oh hello, Lizzie,' I countered. 'You mean, it's a raid?'

The telephone rang again. Lizzie nodded wildly and went to answer it. We followed her in, listened to her telling somebody, 'I haven't the foggiest. no . . . no.' That call was brief.

'Would you like some food?' she demanded. 'Or something to drink? We've eaten, but I've kept lots for Mickey, and he's probably eating at the pub, did Uncle Barnabas say? Or . . .'

I told her that I would put Ben to bed and then be ready and grateful for food.

I heard the telephone ring twice while I undressed Ben's limp body. He didn't wake up enough to need much attention, so I left the bedroom door ajar and crept downstairs.

They were in the kitchen; my father seemed bemused. 'It appears,' he announced, 'to be a drugs raid, for heaven's sake! Or so Mrs Molyneux has now decided. You don't seem surprised?'

No. I wasn't. Various things suddenly made a lot of sense, like police cars lurking outside at night and the unlikely crowds at the Five Bells the two previous Monday evenings. Mondays, for crying out loud! Shopping sessions! I might even admit that I'd been a little naive when I'd accompanied Billy Holt on his visit there last week. I couldn't help laughing.

'What?' Lizzie asked.

'Nothing,' I told her. 'Just . . . this quiet little village beats London for criminal mayhem, doesn't it?'

'You don't want to go down and have a look?' Barnabas asked suspiciously. 'Maybe take part? Perform a citizen's arrest? See —'

I ignored him. 'Food and drink, you said?' I asked Lizzie. It turned out to be a good move.

I'd had a busy, hard-working weekend and an active and exhausting day, and was asleep by nine thirty. When I woke abruptly, I listened first to Ben's regular breathing, he hadn't disturbed me, but I was pretty sure there had been a noise outside. I consulted the luminous dial on my watch. It was a quarter past twelve and I'd had just enough sleep to be wide awake. I turned and shut my eyes, letting my ears take over. I could hear a heavy engine, a big vehicle moving somewhere. Blue lights flashed suddenly on the curtains. For a confused moment I was back in the lane and the pub raid was still going on. I slid on to the floor and crept to the open window. There, I caught the faint smell.

Fire.

I pushed my feet into my trainers and stuck my head into the corridor, sniffing. Nothing there. Whatever was burning wasn't indoors. My jacket lay on the spare bed, where I'd thrown it earlier. I grabbed it and slid out the door, down the stairs, and into the kitchen.

Nothing.

Blue lights were flashing again. I decided that my oversized T-shirt was just about long enough, on a dark night, in a possibly serious emergency, to wear outside the house. The second vehicle had already disappeared up the lane, but the smell of burning was getting stronger. A light sprang on in an upstairs room next door: I wasn't the only one who had been wakened by the . . . the fire engines, of course. There had been two of them and they had been going up . . . I ran to the end of the green and looked towards Monksdanes. The blue lights had vanished by now, but I might be seeing a glow up there.

'Who's . . . Dido?' A torch shone on my face, blinding me, but I recognised Mickey's voice. He switched it off and said quickly, 'Sorry. Teddy just rang. There's a fire up at the house. I'm going now. Will you wake Lizzie and warn her that I might have to bring them all down here? She might want to put a kettle on.'

Before he could move, something rushed towards us in the darkness: a bicycle with a front lamp so feeble that it barely glowed. It was too dark, now that the moon had set, to recognise the rider, but he turned past the chapel and vanished into the shadows at the far end of the green. Billy.

I shifted uneasily. 'I'd better get back.' But Mickey had already gone.

CHAPTER THIRTY-ONE

Morning After

The birds woke me before five. The first dirty, pre-dawn light was slipping in through the crack in my bedroom curtains, and a cock was commenting loudly from nearby. I closed my eyes firmly.

When I crawled into consciousness for the second time there were voices just outside the house. Hushed. Furtive, even. But after a minute I recognised disagreement, and it was getting louder. I rolled out of bed and slipped over to the window to see Lizzie and Mickey Waring standing in the lane beside Mickey's car. My wristwatch said that it was nearly seven thirty and my eyes admitted that the sun was shining. I hadn't had enough sleep, but when a bang at the window to my left announced that they had also wakened Barnabas, I opened my casement and leaned out.

Mickey threw me a quick wave and escaped. Lizzie grimaced.

'Is there coffee?' I asked. Another grimace, but it looked hopeful.

'I'm sorry I fell asleep last night,' I told her when Ben and I descended into the kitchen ten minutes later. 'I couldn't help it. Did somebody have to put me to bed?'

'You walked,' Liz assured me. 'Well, anyway you staggered. Don't you remember?'

I told her that I didn't think so, settled Ben and myself into our chairs, and yawned until Lizzie provided milk and coffee. We fell on our cups.

Then suddenly I woke up. 'What happened? I take it that Mickey didn't bring the whole family back here last night?'

'It was just a shed behind the house,' Liz said flatly. 'Gardening tools and things.'

I swallowed quickly. 'What? How?'

'Well, Teddy and Mickey smelled petrol. The firemen agreed. The police will be around this morning again, with some people from the fire department – investigators. Look, Dido, Mickey says you and he saw Billy Holt coming from the direction of Monksdanes last night.'

Barnabas appeared in the doorway. 'You did?' he asked me sharply.

I delved into my confused memories from the previous midnight and nodded.

'Well, Mickey told Teddy, and Teddy is going to tell the authorities, and . . . I suppose they'll want to talk to you again. Mickey wondered about staying home today, but I told him that you were quite grown up and perfectly capable of dealing with them. If they want him too, they can come back later. He'll probably be early this evening anyway. He's worried.'

I said slowly, 'So his idea . . . their idea is that Billy tried to burn Monksdanes down – out of revenge?'

'I don't think he can have thought the shed would take the house with it,' Lizzie said frankly. 'I think he was just trying to make a point. Like with the fox and the paint.'

'What point would that be?' my father asked sharply. I noticed that during my weekend off he had trained Lizzie to provide a pot of fresh tea when he appeared in the morning. 'I should have thought he would be content, now everyone knows that he was right about his sister all along.'

'He might want to push them for an outcome,' I suggested. 'He's been waiting a long time to know the truth.'

'He might just want to be a bloody nuisance,' Lizzie added.

'He's a funny man. Sulky. Who knows how he thinks? Don't you think? Oh, I wish I hadn't stopped smoking!'

I made wordless noises meant to be encouraging and also noncommittal, and accepted a couple of slices of toast. In my experience, Billy Holt could be seen as a funny man, and sulky. Not stupid. I kept my mouth shut, basically because I was facing the window and had just caught sight of two cars passing the end of the chapel: one of them was red, with some kind of logo on the door; the other was a marked police car. Time was short, and Ben and I had things to do before any outsiders appeared. Especially me.

Luckily, officialdom moves deliberately, so we both had time to eat, bathe and dress before the bell announced its arrival. DS Cole, Teddy Waring and a police constable were gathered on the doorstep when I opened the door. Cole's expression was something I'm familiar with, having met it on other occasions on other policemen. Roughly translated, it means that I'm around too often to suit them and am therefore probably up to no good.

'If I could have a word?' Cole asked without preface. 'Privately?'

I looked at his companions, and then realised that both Lizzie and Barnabas were hanging over my shoulder.

'We could take a walk around the green?' I suggested innocently, stepping outside and weaving among them towards the gate. Cole followed me silently as I strolled off along the roadway. When we reached the end, he said, 'Mr Waring suggests that you might have seen something here last night that would interest us.'

I stopped. 'So it *was* arson?'

'Probably. I'm interested in knowing whether someone was up at Monksdanes last night who didn't belong. Mr Waring was told by his brother that the two of you saw a cyclist at about the time of the fire?'

I nodded, not very happily. 'We were standing just about here, wondering what was going on. The fire engines woke me when they went past and I came out of the house to look. While we were standing here, a cyclist rode down from the direction of Monksdanes. He turned beside the chapel and rode on around the green, but I didn't see where he went; he didn't have a rear light.'

'Did you recognise him?'

Now that I'd had the time to think, I was sure of my reply. 'It was too dark. I couldn't even be sure that it was a man, though at the time I assumed so.'

'Did you come to any conclusions about who it might have been?'

Careful! I said thoughtfully that as Billy Holt was in the habit of riding around the green, my first idea had been that he was the cyclist. 'But I don't know,' I said very clearly. 'I could easily have jumped to conclusions. By the way, where do you think Teddy Waring is going?'

Cole turned around and took in what I had just noticed: Teddy striding off towards the far end of the green and Billy Holt's cottage, followed a little slowly by the constable, who was looking our way for instructions. Lizzie and my father seemed to be restraining each other. Colt left me abruptly, sprinting across the grass. I trotted after him, counting on his being too preoccupied to argue. I saw Teddy glance at Cole and continue on his way. We arrived at the gate immediately behind the constable and a moment behind Teddy, who had found Billy in his garden among the vegetable rows and seemed to be shaping up for a fight. I saw that it wouldn't actually get started, mostly because Billy was holding a spade horizontally in front of himself with both hands. I suspected that spades must do a lot of damage at close range. I could see that Teddy had drawn the same conclusion.

Cole clattered through the gate shouting, 'Mr Waring?'

Teddy stepped back.

Cole said, 'Thank you,' in a glacial voice, and then turned to Billy and looked at him until the spade assumed a less defensive angle. 'Mr Holt.'

Billy nodded slowly.

'I was just coming around to have a word with you. Shall we go inside?'

Billy looked at him. 'Out here will do me.'

'All right.' Cole gave the impression of a man too busy to argue. 'I'm DS Cole, Castle Hinton police. Did you hear about the fire up at Monksdanes last night?'

There was something about Billy's look. He nodded.

'We're trying to clear up the matter. Can you –'

'Somebody set that, did they?' Billy interrupted. 'Deliberate?'

'Possibly,' Cole said icily. 'Can you tell me where you were last night between, say, ten o'clock and twelve thirty?'

Billy seemed to be having some trouble with the question. 'Ten o'clock and late?' he asked at last. 'Town. Hinton. Got held up there. I was there most of the night.'

Teddy let out a growl which Cole quelled with a look. He turned back. 'Anyone who could confirm that?'

'Oh, pro'bly,' Billy said easily.

Cole said, 'Names?' and waited.

'Don't know their names,' Billy said.

'Then it might be hard for me to check your story. Where were you, exactly?'

'Exactly?' Billy wondered. Then I saw he was playing games. 'We-e-ell, most of the time, some waiting room, Hinton police station. When they walked into the pub last night, your lot were real pissed that I had an eighth o'grass in my pocket. Seemed to think it's a crime.'

Cole froze. 'You were arrested at the Five Bells?'

Billy shook his head regretfully. 'Caught red-handed. You think I'll be charged? I'm hoping for just a caution.'

'We'll have to see,' Cole said politely. 'Thank you.' He was looking at Teddy Waring's face. So was I. It was worth seeing.

I said, 'I'd better get back to the baby.'

Billy winked.

CHAPTER THIRTY-TWO

Very Funny

Barnabas seemed more amused than alarmed. 'That chap has a surprisingly short fuse, you know: we were standing at the door, looking at what's left of the red paint, when he suddenly glanced over in your direction and then took off. Curious – he has been around here a good deal this weekend, and I'd put him down as a little stolid, if anything.'

'Around?' I handed Ben a mug of juice and told him that he was behaving angelically.

Lizzie nodded. 'He and Mickey spent the whole weekend searching the cottage. They even tore most of the thatch out of the attic, and then they had to put it back. Of course they couldn't find *Peter Rabbit* any more than we could. I told Mickey I was feeling fragile and went to bed in your bedroom and read a couple of books. You wouldn't believe the mess; Teddy and Mickey had to Hoover and dust our bedroom afterwards. Then on Sunday they had a go at that paint, but they decided it needs sandblasting to get it all off. Uncle Barnabas went out while they were at it. I believe he spent most of the weekend entertaining Mrs Molyneux.'

I stared accusingly at my father, who seemed slightly alarmed, slightly amused.

'I was being given a tour of the area,' he said. 'Did you realise that the whole village is situated on an ancient network of overgrown footpaths and hedges? The farmers have grubbed up a lot of the hedges, I know, but I believe you could get from any point to any other in this place without being seen, if you needed to. Were you aware that ancient ditches are still used to mark the borders of properties, and there seems an unnecessary uncertainty as to which part of a ditch is the legal boundary? It appears to depend on your point of view.'

'Did you see the Mill House?' I asked nastily. 'And the ford?'

Barnabas said, 'Naturally. And spoke with Mrs Holt, who was incoherent and no help to anybody, least of all herself. She has taken this new discovery very hard. And the church is indeed very fine Perpendicular, though the interior is rather heavily restored for my taste.'

Lizzie was looking from him to me a little oddly; I took pity on her and started to explain Mrs Molyneux's list of tourist attractions, but Ben created a diversion with the mug and its remaining contents.

'I'd better go and get the van,' I realised some time afterwards. 'I'm blocking a farm track. It didn't look as though it's being used, but I don't fancy the idea of someone with a tractor deciding to push me out of the way.'

'And then we'll go for a walk and a look,' Barnabas said smoothly. 'Go on, then, I'll read an improving book to him. Don't be long.'

'Ten minutes,' I said. 'Thanks.'

Negotiating the track beyond Billy's cottage was a good deal easier in daylight. The sunshine lay on rolling fields. Rustlings in the leaves were caused, visibly, by small birds; and the breathy animals were a herd of cows, now grazing in the middle of a dandelion-blazing meadow. Docks, more dandelions and coarse grass grew undisturbed on the high central ridge between the ruts, and there was nothing to suggest that anybody had driven along here in months. I plodded along with the sun warm on my shoulders, thinking vaguely about the enigmatic Billy Holt and the equally enigmatic Teddy Waring.

It was a broken branch in the overgrown hedge that grabbed my attention. It leaned across my path at waist height, and I knew I hadn't run into that last night in the darkness. I put a hand on it and pulled, and although it didn't snap, the movement disturbed the branches around it. I gave it a shake.

There was a wheel. I pushed into the branches and found an old-fashioned black bicycle jammed upright into the hedge. The hedge had been pushed in to hide it. Automatically I reached to haul it into the open – and stopped myself just before my fingers touched the mudguard. The machine looked like Billy's. But if it was his, what was it doing down here? Why would he have wheeled his bike here just to abandon it? It seemed equally improbable that anyone would have stolen his bike for a hundred-yard ride to nowhere. But a mysterious cyclist had ridden away from the fire at Monksdanes, so DS Cole would be interested. I reached into my pocket for my mobile and didn't find it. *Damn!* I could picture it, now I stopped to think, on the chest of drawers in my bedroom. Barnabas was right: this carelessness must stop.

There was a patch of deep purple just beyond the next bend: my van, sixty feet away. I pushed the branches back in around the bicycle and made for it.

It took me a few minutes to back cautiously on to the lane and complete the circuit to the Barton. To save time, I avoided questions by climbing the little back staircase, found my mobile in the bedroom where I'd left it, got the number of the Hinton police station from the operator, and was telling Cole in person about my find a minute later.

'Wait there,' he said. 'I'll come as fast as I can. Don't go near the spot again until I arrive.'

I said, 'I thought maybe I should just go back and keep an eye –'

'Wait there.' It wasn't a request; despite that, I made a bed or two and then descended to bring the others up to date. It took Cole half an hour to arrive and park his car prominently outside the cottage. It took him another five minutes to make sure of his facts, and five more to make his way along the track behind me and find the hedge broken down at the place where the bike had been. Somebody I hadn't noticed might have observed my interest and taken his chance to retrieve his property.

'Can you describe it?' Cole asked me as we hovered there uselessly.

'It was a man's bike,' I said brightly. 'Old-fashioned. Upright. Black.' And went home to complain, with only the briefest detour to Billy Holt's front door where I got no reply to my knocking, and his back door where there was no bicycle in sight.

'Astonishing,' Barnabas remarked sourly in response to my story. He looked as impatient as I felt.

'What do you suppose that detective is doing?' Lizzie commented. 'He's gone past. He's left his car here.' She pushed the casement window wide and leaned out. 'Oh. He's going next door. He won't find anybody there, not at this time of day. He's trying the next one.' Under the force of her running commentary, Barnabas and I took the other window and watched Cole making his way around the houses on the green. He got an answer at his fourth attempt. I could see somebody shaking a head, and the door snapped shut. Cole went on and vanished into the lane, turning down towards the signpost.

'Asking whether anybody saw anything this morning?' I speculated.

'Looking for Billy?' Lizzie speculated too. 'I haven't seen him since he left at about eight. He must be working somewhere.'

'Was he on his bike when you saw him?' Barnabas asked her casually.

'Oh, yes. He went off . . .' Lizzie stopped and turned pink. My father said, 'Very funny.'

'That looks almost like an alibi,' I said after a moment. 'You could run after Cole, or you could tell him when he comes back for his car.'

'Or we could leave a note under his windscreen wiper,' Lizzie added brightly. 'I was thinking that I might go to Monksdanes and just check that everything's all right up there this morning. Mickey thought they might need company. Do you two want to come?'

Barnabas was looking vague. 'I don't suppose that either of you could suggest a source of cartridge paper?'

'Cartridge paper?'

'Or similar. I find myself in need of some large sheets of sturdy paper of some kind – say about twenty-four inches by eighteen? Cartridge paper.'

Intrigued, Lizzie and I demanded enlightenment.

Barnabas sighed. 'It seems to me that our problem, here, is – for want of a better term – woods and trees. We have a historical puzzle. Seemingly unconnected dribs and drabs of information come from various sources and stretch back to 1994 or beyond. What is required is a major intelligence-gathering operation. I feel the need to find a very large writing surface on which to list all known facts and dates pertaining, because it does seem to me that if everything were somehow placed in order, links might become more obvious and understanding might ensue. I shall need large pieces of sturdy paper, therefore, with pencils, erasers and a flat surface on which to lay them.'

'Ben would like some of that paper, too,' Lizzie said a little wistfully. 'There's a stationery shop in Hinton and it has art gear. I'm sure we could get some there. We could drive in after lunch?'

'Mrs Molyneux possesses a remarkable motor car,' Barnabas said slowly, 'as well as much gossip, some of which is relevant. I wonder?'

Lizzie looked at me. 'I'm sure she'd drive you in to town,' she said. Her voice wobbled.

'Very funny,' I said to her. 'All right, and in the extremely unlikely event that she's too busy to help you, we'll all go to Hinton when we get back from Monksdanes. Barnabas, you'd better look out there! And we'd better leave a note under Cole's wiper.'

From somewhere not too far away came the sound of a shot. A second followed it.

After a moment, Lizzie said, 'Somebody's shooting pigeons. They're a pest. You hear guns quite often. It's a country thing, after all.'

I'd noticed.

CHAPTER THIRTY-THREE

Silence

In the darkness, the fire engines had driven straight across the lawn, scoring deep tracks from the gates to the far end of the house. Lizzie and I exchanged a look and veered off along the scar. The grass had reached ankle height in the aftermath of Billy Holt's departure, and the push-chair came to a sticky halt before we had got far. At the same time, Lizzie gave up. The ground was wet, and her heels were sinking in.

'There's a collection of wellies outside the kitchen,' she said. 'I need to borrow some.'

Lizzie turned the handle of the back door confidently and seemed surprised when she found it locked. Not me. We completed our circle of the building, finding the shutters of the music room and the front reception rooms also closed tight. The house looked blind or asleep. Or besieged. I lifted Ben out of the push chair, wanting to keep him close, and watched Lizzie bang the lion's head door knocker.

It was Rose who answered.

Lizzie asked, 'Has something happened? The back door is locked.'

'Come into the morning room, Elizabeth. Dido, you're back? I hope that your weekend was successful. You were at a book sale, I understand?'

Chatting, we followed her into the entrance hall and on to

the morning room, where the shutters at least were open and the sunshine shimmering through the window glass. A pot of coffee was waiting on the hot plate, as though she had known we were coming. I sat with Ben on my lap and let Lizzie hand me a cup.

'I'm so sorry about last night,' I said experimentally. 'It must have been terrifying.'

I accepted two digestives for myself and Ben while Rose fixed her cold eyes on me and shrugged. 'In fact, I knew nothing about it until the fire engines arrived. I sleep at the front of the house, and I'd taken my pill, as usual. I've had trouble falling asleep for years, now, so I take my sedative every night.'

'And . . . is everybody all right?' Lizzie asked tentatively. 'Father? Helen?'

'Lawrence was alarmed by something last night and wandered downstairs; Helen found him at the back of the house when she went to call the fire service. We've decided it might be best to keep the outside doors locked. He is becoming—' She broke off and made herself busy with her coffee cup. 'He and Helen are both resting now. But it was nothing, really – vandalism. I was not particularly alarmed.'

I looked at her incredulously. She sat upright in the carver with her back to the window, almost expressionless. In her cardigan and pearls and nicely curled white hair, I found her incomprehensible. It was impossible to imagine her panicking about anything, and even if she had wakened to find Monksdanes itself on fire, I could see her sitting calmly among the ruins looking queenly, tough and unperturbed, passing a plate of biscuits.

I'd heard nothing, but suddenly Teddy Waring was watching us from the doorway. His silent approach was explained by the socks on his feet. There was mud on his hands and the knees of his jeans; he had been working outside and had taken his boots off at the door.

He said, 'Coffee?'

His mother gestured, and he came in to help himself. He

hesitated at the biscuits, but took one in his dirty fingers. I saw the look on Rose's face; he did, too.

Lizzie said quickly, 'We've just come up to have a look. Can we do anything to help?'

Teddy shrugged and swallowed. 'Nothing to do. I'm to leave the place alone until they've looked at it. Or do you mean, with the "situation"? I'm not going to be scared away, so we just have to get on with it, don't we.'

That was interesting. 'You think it was done by somebody who wanted to get at *you?*' I asked.

'I thought it was done by Billy Holt. If it wasn't, then I think he got one of his mates to do it. I told the detective, I know the law. If they threaten me or the family or our property, I'm allowed to use "reasonable force" in self-defence. I told Cole, arson is a threat to life and limb, and if I have to scare anybody off with a shotgun, I'll do it.' He looked sideways at Rose. 'I'll try not to shoot anybody; but they'd better believe that I will if I have to.'

Helen's arrival, unlike Teddy's, was heralded by running footsteps overhead, the sound of clattering heels on the main staircase, and a kind of breathless gasping, so that we were on our feet by the time she appeared in the doorway.

'Father,' she whimpered, 'in his room . . .'

With Ben to carry, I arrived last and found them all in the bedroom at the head of the stairs. It was a strange tableau. Lawrence Waring was sitting frozen in a wing chair by the window; staring at the air. Helen and Rose knelt on either side of him. Helen had taken her father's hand, and Rose was peering into his face.

'It's all right,' she said harshly. 'It's just another . . . episode.' She glanced at Lizzie, frozen at the foot of the bed. 'A very, very minor thing like a tiny stroke. He'll be all right in due course.'

'I've called Dr Perry,' Helen said in a little voice. 'He'll come as fast as he can.'

I was just inside the doorway, with Ben in my arms and

Teddy beside me, his back to the wall, his eyes fixed on his
father's frozen face. The attention of the Waring women was
focused on the old man, and I was pretty sure that I was the only
one who knew that Teddy had just whispered to himself, or to
his ghosts, as quietly as breathing, 'I wish to God he'd die.'

CHAPTER THIRTY-FOUR

The Grand Plan

By the exertion of my sharpest detecting skills, I traced Barnabas to Mrs Molyneux's bungalow and found him leaning over the dining-room table, which now held his grand plan in the form of two sheets of cream-coloured cartridge paper taped together, and a handful of coloured pencils and felt-tipped pens.

He looked up quickly. 'Where is Lizzie? I need her.'

Behind me, Mrs Molyneux was saying, 'I saw Dr Perry driving up the lane – he wasn't by any chance called to Monksdanes, was he?'

I manoeuvred around the table until my father's scrawl was the right way up. He had drawn a chart of vertical and horizontal lines and written the years down the left-hand column, beginning with 1993. Broad columns were labelled, 'Joan Holt', 'X', 'Peter Rabbit', and 'Misc'. Across the bottom of the plan, he had a numbered list of people's names. They were labelled 'Witnesses'. I saw that I was number seven, whereas Mrs Molyneux occupied the number one spot.

'Is Lizzie still up there?' my father persisted. Witness number six, that was.

I explained that she and my son had returned to the Barton to start Ben's lunch. 'Good,' Barnabas commented vaguely. He selected a black marker and poised it above the paper. 'At the moment, Mrs Molyneux and I are attempting to fill in all that she knows. We'll need Lizzie soon. And you, of course.'

He stood back and surveyed his work. I took my chance to tell Mrs Molyneux about Lawrence Waring's 'episode'.

She heard me out, pushed her glasses up, and explained that these little events occurred regularly and were either the cause of Lawrence Waring's mental deterioration or an effect. 'Dr Perry says there is nothing to be done,' she added, leading me to wonder whether she had taken the trouble to discuss her neighbour's health improperly with their mutual physician. Barnabas was entirely right to be starting with her.

'Wait!' my father said suddenly. 'I may be wrong. Dido: do you know exactly when it was that your friend – you know who I mean – purchased those books from the Warings' library?'

I started to say 'No', caught myself, and cast my mind back to my first visit to Monksdanes. The catalogue that had been lying on the desk, with the offer for a thousand books: that had been dated . . . I found myself crunching up my eyes as though it would help me to visualise the cover. 'Some time in the winter of '93 to '94. I could probably find his offer, if it's important.'

Barnabas mumbled, 'Probably good enough,' and got to work at the top of the plan. 'All right. The *Peter Rabbit* was still in the collection? He saw it there himself?'

'That's what he said.'

'Good. Then we have a starting point.'

'What are you doing?' I demanded. I pointed to the columns.

'We have three crimes,' my father announced. He had shifted into his lecturer's mode. 'The murder of Joan Holt, the murder of another girl whom I have called X, though I imagine that you are as well aware as I of her identity; and the theft of a rare and valuable Beatrix Potter, still missing despite the fact that Teddy Waring seems sure it shouldn't be. I will rule out for the moment any chance that the theft was committed by some casual passer-by who turned up collecting for charity. The rest – fires, vandalism and intimidation – are all connected with those three crimes.'

I opened my mouth to say I was not *as well aware* at all. But I was. Joan Holt was NOT the only one who was no longer around. My eyes went to the bottom of Barnabas' great plan. Billy Holt was witness number two. That seemed right. And I wanted to talk to him myself – wanted it really badly.

'Mrs Molyneux, do you have any idea where Billy is working today?'

'Tuesdays,' she said, 'he usually helps out in the garden at the Mill House. However, they do not give him lunch, and in normal circumstances he might be at the pub now.'

I mouthed, 'I'll just go and look for him.'

'But the pub,' she swept on, 'is closed. The word is that the brewery will be removing Mr Bond from his post, as he could scarcely have been unaware of what was going on, and will reopen with a new manager as soon as possible. I shouldn't have thought . . . not before next week at the earliest.'

I thought fast and said, 'I'd better get back and see how Ben is doing.'

'Send Lizzie,' Barnabas muttered at my back. 'Mrs Molyneux, I would be most grateful if you could confirm the date . . .'

I let myself out. I was still rearranging things in my mind, and I needed solitude, so I turned left at the footpath and strolled down towards the pub. Mrs Molyneux had been right, as usual: its door was shut, a chain immobilised our favourite swing and blocked the slide, and the car park, as I arrived, was empty except for one car which had just driven in, braked, and was now reversing to leave. The driver, when I glimpsed his face, looked bereft.

I'd have to get back. Not that I didn't trust Lizzie with Ben. Absolutely. But I'd send her down to Mrs Molyneux's, and then Ben and I would try to catch Billy Holt, who had probably been forced to go home for food, and ask him the right questions.

I might just have started to shape my own grand plan. I couldn't stop now.

CHAPTER THIRTY-FIVE

The Other Dead

Having knocked on Billy Holt's front door with the usual success, and listened, and heard the sound of his television, Ben and I wandered unhurriedly round the back. My quarry was down at the pen, delivering a metal plate full of chopped carrot and cabbage, and talking to the little brown rabbit as it ate. The rabbit noticed our arrival and froze. Billy got gently to his feet and walked up the path.

'No point you going on at me,' he said quietly. 'That policeman of yours found me. We had our talk. He went away.'

'I'm sorry about that,' I told him. 'He isn't my policeman, but I did call him when I found a bike hidden down along the track. It had to be the one that I saw somebody riding last night at the time of the fire. By the time Cole got there, though, it had gone, so he rushed off to talk to you. But Lizzie saw you with your own bike, before I even found the other one, so I think you're in the clear. We've told them.'

Billy considered. 'Well, he wasn't pushing it, anyways. Don't seem he can work out what's going on, any more'n I can.'

'Can't you?'

He looked at me sharply. 'Now what?'

I said, 'You know lots. I think you've known what's been going on all along.' We stared at each other. Ben said something.

I put him down, and he wandered over to the pen. He and the rabbit considered one another, and Ben sat down abruptly on the path.

'Not good pets for kiddies,' Billy warned. 'They scare them.' He turned back to me.

I said, 'This will just take us a minute. Listen, why did you start working up at Monksdanes last winter? It can't have been pleasant for you, even while Teddy was still away.'

'Di'n't have to be nice,' he countered. 'They offered, last Christmas; I accepted. Season o' goodwill. Why not?'

'Why?' I countered.

He looked at me coldly. 'Some of us have to work for our living.'

I looked coldly back. 'You have other work, and you probably get income support? Housing benefit?'

'Up on the benefits system, are we?' he sneered. 'You know I was looking for Joannie.'

'But you didn't find her.'

'You know I di'n't.'

I decided to believe him, for now.

'What was in the shed that was burned out last night?'

'Nothing! You asking if I looked there? Course I did; looked through all the outbuildings first off. Had the floors up and put them down again. Nothing. Nowhere.'

'Then why would somebody set fire to it?'

'Making a point, maybe? Ted Waring's not liked 'round Alford, I'll tell you that for free, Miss Dido Hoare. I'd say he should move on.'

'People are wondering whether you got a friend of yours to do it.'

He looked at me silently.

'Did you? I'm not even asking who.'

'Might've done if I'd thought. Good alibi. Just di'n't know I was going to be arrested, did I! You got any other questions? I better get back.'

'One. Who was the girl who was shot and dressed up in your sister's clothes?'

He shifted his feet and turned again to look at Ben. I just went on waiting.

In the end, he turned back and said quietly, 'How sh'd I know?'

'Want me to say?'

He kept his mouth shut.

'Obviously, the woman that Lawrence evicted from the Barton. Tracy? You said she went to stay with her brother. Have you ever seen her since she went? What's the brother's name, and where does he live now? I want to know where she went afterwards and whether he's heard from her. Because I think she's probably been dead for four years.'

For some reason I didn't understand, I'd flummoxed him. I watched him hesitating, shifty and speechless.

I pushed it. 'You told me she moved on. Did she come back? Why? Had she left the Warings' copy of *Peter Rabbit* hidden in the Barton? Did she come back for it?'

I suddenly realised that he wouldn't know what I was talking about and I'd need to tell him about the family's missing heirloom, but Billy beat me to it.

'Well, maybe she did,' he conceded. 'How would I know that?'

Hadn't he just admitted that he *did* know? I said slowly, 'You and she were friends? Or more?'

'Me and her brother are friends,' he muttered.

All right. For the moment. 'Who *is* her brother?'

He smirked suddenly. 'Mac? He was the licensee up at the Woolpack then, so she moved in there for a bit, said she had to sort something out before she moved on.'

'Sort what?' It was like digging coal out of rock with a soup spoon; but I believed I knew already. I lowered my voice a little and repeated, 'Sort out what?'

'Ted Waring. Asked her to marry him.'

In the end I made my voice work well enough to squeak, 'He can't have!' But he might have, he could have; Lawrence Waring, at that awful dinner, Lawrence Waring had . . . 'Why did he let his father throw her out, then? Was it true, the story you told me about drug-dealing?'

'Oh, that was true. Everybody here knew that. People calling around, evenings, to buy gear off her, cars driving round the green, the kids hanging around in the lane, Too many people knew. By the end, she thought they were on to her. Couple of strange cars turned up, hanging round in the lane; somebody taking notes. The old man was the last to find out. Blew his top. Having his son tied up with her made it worse.'

'Teddy dumped her?'

'Not exactly.'

I wanted to scream, *What then?*

'Thing is,' Billy said, obviously interpreting my expression correctly, 'that lot dun't have any guts. You better warn your friend Lizzie what the old ones say goes. Lawrence, Rose – they say "Hop", then Ted and Helen and Mickey hop. Always have, always will.'

I caught myself shivering in the May sunshine. *I wish to God he'd die.* I said, 'Look, can you just *tell* me the brother's name and where he is now? I know he's not at the Woolpack any more.'

'Mac? His name's Jerry McGregor, and right now he's in custody, far as I know. He's been living in Hinton, past few months, working for a mate in a shop there. Aerial installations, satellite dishes, that kind o'thing. Always visits the pub on Monday evenings, regular, more fool him. Understood?'

I'd squeaked, '*McGregor?*' before I could stop myself.

Billy looked at me out of the corner of his eye. 'Know him?'

I said, 'I've heard the name.' My voice sounded odd, even in my own ears, so I added, 'I think I've seen his van at the pub.'

'Well, you better ask Mac. Maybe he can tell you about Tracy.'

Maybe he could tell me about *Peter Rabbit.* Maybe Barnabas

should find out whether it was possible to visit Mr McGregor even if he was still in custody. My father was the man for that job: Barnabas Hoare, Emeritus Professor of English from Oxford University. Very, very respectable.

Ben let out a wild shriek, and we turned to the pen. My son was scrambling to his feet, red-faced, holding out his hand in front of him. I ran and grabbed him and inspected a little red mark on his finger.

'Bit him,' Billy said succinctly. 'Rabbits – look all cuddle-some, but not good pets for babbies. Good to eat, though.'

I couldn't tell whether he was joking and I didn't care: kissed the bruised finger, picked its owner up and comforted him all the way home.

The Barton was empty when we got there. Lizzie was still being interviewed by Barnabas and Mrs Molyneux, which suited me – gave me a chance to think. I wiped various parts of Ben, checking again that no skin had been broken, and put him and his blue blanket to bed in the cot. It had been a busy, over-exciting day for us both, and he would drop off to sleep in a minute. I was just looking at my own bed when the doorbell rang.

I could think of quite a few people I hoped I wouldn't find there, but naturally one of them was standing at the door when I opened it. Teddy Waring was in his scruffy gardening clothes, and it struck me, quite suddenly, that he was getting to look more and more like Billy Holt.

I greeted him with, 'Lizzie isn't here. I think she's down at Mrs Molyneux's. How's your father?'

'All right. Better. I'm not here for Lizzie. Can you look at this for me?'

He held out a large manila envelope, addressed in printed capital letters to Teddy at Monksdanes, stamped and franked and torn open clumsily. I put a hand in. Down in the bottom it encountered some unexpectedly small, slippery fragments. Startled, I widened the opening and peered in. Scraps of glossy paper. I tipped a few out: they were pages of a little book, ripped out of their binding and torn roughly into quarters. Each fragment had a lot of white margin and a few words. I read: 'Mr McGregor . . . his hands planting out . . . of him at the . . . neat the go . . . last in' and 'PETER got . . . quietly off the . . .' That was more than enough.

'*Peter Rabbit*,' Teddy said unnecessarily. 'Only . . . what do you think? I haven't seen it for years, and maybe I don't remember it properly?'

I was already delving into the envelope, finding some picture fragments: a white cat on a garden path, a brown rabbit carrying a wicker basket over its arm.

I slid them all back in. 'Was there a note?'

He shook his head.

'I said, 'Well, you haven't forgotten. These are the coloured illustrations – so it's the commercial edition, and it looks like a brand new copy. You can buy them anywhere.'

'Thought so. Then, why?'

'Maybe,' I told him, 'whoever sent this didn't know what the original edition looks like. Or maybe that isn't the point.'

Ted nodded slowly. 'That's what I thought. Well, at least that bastard destroyed his own property this time, not ours.' He turned and went.

Billy? How? 'Where was it posted?' I called after him.

He stopped at the gate and looked at the envelope. 'Postmarked Shepton Mallet,' he threw over his shoulder. 'But everything goes there for sorting.'

I said, 'Well, hang on to it.' He was already outside the gate and didn't seem to hear me. I watched him cut straight across to the end of the chapel and then out of sight.

At the same time, Lizzie called, 'Dido?' and came rushing up from the other direction. 'Was that Teddy? Is something wrong?'

I explained.

She said, 'Somebody's . . . well, taunting him!'

I shrugged. Next time I saw Billy I'd ask about it. Red paint, dead animals, little fires, torn-up books: in normal circumstances it would have looked like a schoolboy feud. Here, I thought, it was one man trying to make another one snap. Just that.

Lizzie worried about it for a moment and then pushed the thought away. 'Dido, Uncle Barnabas sent me to ask if you can go down there. He's finished with Mrs M and me. It's your turn. Honestly, he ought to have been a barrister! Where's Ben? I'll look after him.'

I told her that Ben was in bed and would probably go on sleeping for a while. I explained that if he did wake and fuss, she should comfort his right hand, give him a nice drink, and bring him over to the bungalow.

'He's hurt himself?'

'He was bitten by a rabbit,' I said shortly, and left. I wanted to look at the grand plan and add some information to it. Then maybe I could persuade my father to phone the police in Castle Hinton and try to contact Mr McGregor. The sooner the better. I was beginning to hate Alford.

CHAPTER THIRTY-SIX

The Big Picture

———>•◆•<———

'It's no good,' Barnabas told us quietly. He switched my mobile phone off and handed it back. 'Shall we walk out into the garden? I could use a breath of fresh air.'

Mrs Molyneux opened the French windows, and we stepped out of her dining room on to a patch of smooth green lawn punctuated by a bird bath and flower beds.

'I presume you understood the situation from what I was saying? Mr McGregor is in custody, and will be for the foreseeable future. He is charged with supplying a Class A drug. I understand that means he will *not* be allowed bail.'

I could see that, but . . .

'Perhaps one would be permitted to visit him in prison?' Mrs Molyneux suggested.

My father and I exchanged a speculative look, but neither of us was willing to put money on it.

'Then' – Mrs Molyneux frowned – 'we shall find another way. He will have a solicitor. Perhaps the solicitor would take a message and get a reply? Find out, at least, whether he has his sister's current address? Ask him to confirm that she knows the Warings? No, no, perhaps that might be going too far. But put us in touch with her at least.'

If she was alive, of course.

'It might be possible to find out who is acting for him,' Barnabas was agreeing doubtfully.

'I shall phone a friend,' Mrs Molyneux announced.

I sat down on the grass, leaned back propped on my hands and closed my eyes, and found myself idly considering a lightning raid on Billy's house, next time he went out, for an overdue-books search.

But Barnabas' 'map' kept intruding. His afternoon's work had produced what was basically a chronology of witness statements: an outline of who had said what, about what, and when, and especially which information had been confirmed by another 'witness', also what was hearsay: everything we had heard about the two deaths and the theft of the book. He had linked the details by a network of coloured pencil lines and arrows. It looked very complete, and I knew that in about half an hour I'd be anxious to get into it: the truth was probably there somewhere – the whole picture.

Our hostess came back, looking pleased with herself. 'In hand,' she announced. 'My friend will enquire tactfully and ring back at once. He is always very helpful. Dido knows. Is there nothing we might do in the meantime?'

Barnabas said suddenly, 'I wonder how much of Monksdanes grounds Billy Holt had searched before Teddy fired him? I am speculating whether Teddy insisted on paying him off merely to avoid meeting him, or whether there is something there for someone to find?'

'Joannie's body was hidden *outside* the grounds,' I reminded him. 'If Teddy knew it was there, wouldn't it have been safer to keep Billy busy gardening?'

But Mrs Molyneux was already rushing back indoors. When she returned, she carried an older and more tattered version of the map she had lent me. The two of them unfolded and spread it on the grass, and we leaned over it and found Alford and Monksdanes. Judging by the area of the house, the irregular square of its walled grounds must stretch several hundred yards along each perimeter. The familiar footpath ran from the stile at the lane, along the eastern wall, to where it diverged across open fields to the road which joined the ford and the upper village with the Fosse Way to the west. In theory, Joan Holt's body could have been carried, from a car parked up there, down across the fields to the place where we had found it. It seemed a long way in open countryside for no clear advantage.

'What's that?' Barnabas enquired, pointing delicately at a blob behind the house.

Mrs Molyneux examined it through her spectacles and frowned. 'I'd forgotten about that,' she said. 'There used to be a fish pond. It might have dried up now, and it must certainly be overgrown.'

'A lost pond?' Barnabas mused. 'That would have been a good place for corpses. I wonder whether Holt looked there?'

I wondered tiredly why I found this question obscure. 'But Joan's body wasn't in any pond,' I objected peevishly. 'Why are you interested in a pond?'

'There is still something missing,' Barnabas said gently. 'Where are the possessions of this mysterious body in the library? They could not, I imagine, have been safely hidden in the dustbins, the outbuildings, or the house itself. After all, the police might have chosen to make a search. However, one thing was certainly not concealed in any empty wardrobe – or even, safely, in an outbuilding.'

I cast my mind back and still came up with a blank.

Barnabas shook his head impatiently. 'Mrs Molyneux has recounted your discussion with her neighbour, Major Hitchens. He described Mrs Richards as possessing a car, a large car. I assume that she intended to leave the area in her car.'

'It was quite a big vehicle,' Mrs Molyneux recalled. 'A big old estate car in which she transported antique furniture.'

'Perhaps Lizzie and I should take a walk around Monksdanes in the morning,' I was suggesting when the phone rang in the kitchen.

Mrs Molyneux hurried to answer and returned after a moment looking satisfied. 'A Mrs Alison Jones, of a firm in Wincanton, is the lady in question. I have her telephone number. What shall I ask her to do?'

Barnabas considered. 'She must certainly ask her client why his sister left the area when she did, and whether he has her current address. That seems unlikely, but still, we should make sure of our facts.'

'What about the book? We need to find out whether he knows anything about it. Could his sister have left it with him? That might explain how it seems to have dropped out of sight. Only I can't imagine why he'd admit it.'

'Offer a reward,' Mrs Molyneux suggested promptly. 'I shall say there is an insurance reward offered for its safe return, no questions asked. Would two thousand pounds be enough? If he has it himself, or knows who does have it, he might like to have the money, especially in present circumstances. It's only human nature.'

'But what if he accepts?' Barnabas wondered.

'Then we'll pay him off, on condition that I can deduct the money from the sale proceeds,' I said sharply.

'A sound idea,' Mrs Molyneux agreed briskly and vanished again.

'Not entirely sound,' my father said coldly when she was out of earshot. 'I hesitate to think how many laws you may be contemplating breaking.'

I thought I'd cross that bridge only when it became necessary; because something told me it wouldn't happen.

Mrs Molyneux returned with measured steps to announce, 'I explained. I managed to convince her. I told her about those poor old people at Monksdanes whose lives will be transformed if only their book can be found and sold, and she eventually agreed that there seemed to be no harm in my request. After all, it is entirely unconnected with the charges! She was about to visit Mr McGregor and agreed to ask him our questions. She will ring me later. Well, Dido: you were suggesting a two-pronged attack, with a visit to Monksdanes?'

I pulled myself together. 'It might be interesting to see what Billy was doing at Monksdanes these past months.' My father looked doubtful, and I exploded, 'We have to make sure!'

He said slowly, 'I was intending to work on my plan in the morning.' I caught him looking quizzically at Mrs Molyneux.

'Of course,' she said at once. 'I shall be glad to keep an eye on them. We three can take a stroll in the grounds. They used to be very pretty.'

'We four,' I pointed out, 'assuming Ben has recovered by then.' Mrs Molyneux would be quite an effective back-up if Teddy asked why we were wandering around in his gardens.

'Recovered?' Barnabas thundered. 'What . . . ?'

I was beginning to need one of Lizzie's vodka-tonics: my mind seemed to have slowed down, and I couldn't imagine doing anything useful with it for a while. 'Ben was nipped,' I said, 'by a rabbit. He stuck his fingers through some netting.'

I heard Barnabas remark that he hoped this would be a lesson to us all, but I wasn't paying attention. My attention had hopped, rabbit-like, back to the big picture.

Barnabas had drawn it up in columns to illustrate three crimes: two murders and a theft. The problem I was noticing was that so far nobody had been able to suggest a motive for any of them. Ask why it had all happened, and I came up with a great big blank.

Start with the earliest one, the theft of the book. You'd think that was simple: it was worth a lot of money, everybody knew that; and yet if it had ever been sold it would have arrived at some saleroom or catalogue and Ernie would have traced it by now. If any of our suspects had profited from the theft, he was keeping very quiet and living the simple life. No: it had just vanished.

The death of Joannie Holt: why would anybody want to kill her? If you accepted the story of a firearms accident, that might just work. Well, stranger things have happened. But the moment you thought body-switch, it was no longer an accident, and that left the pregnancy story to provide a motive. However, Lawrence Holt wasn't exactly royalty, or even an archbishop, and Joan had been of legal age long before anything had happened. Nothing suggested a criminal relationship. She had even been ready to accommodate the family's interests. Why would anyone bother to kill her?

Tracy: she was different. Tracy, like her brother, was a drugs dealer: not a safe profession. A criminal, she also dealt in antiques. The Warings had sold off some good furniture. That was probably how she came into the picture in the first place. Had she cheated them? Was that what this was about? Lawrence Waring's fretful question to me had been: 'What have you done with *Peter Rabbit*?' But if Teddy Waring had really asked her to marry him, that confused things. Had she robbed the Warings? Had Teddy killed her in a fit of jealous rage? Women, I reminded myself coldly, are usually killed by husbands or lovers.

Tracy's brother must know something. I could only hope that Mrs Molyneux's initiative would work, and soon. Mr McGregor was out of the way, but Billy and Teddy were still very much around, and that meant trouble. I was starting to believe that the two of them would be glued together like Siamese twins, snarling their mutual loathing, until something terrible happened. That was a nasty possibility that I hadn't even started to think through.

CHAPTER THIRTY-SEVEN

Dry Rust

The tracks of the fire engines passed close under the shuttered windows of the library, curved around the end of the weedy tennis court, and vanished behind a clump of rhododendrons. Following them, we came into sight of the old tennis pavilion. Most of it was still standing, but it was blackened and charred, and the roof had fallen in. Even after thirty hours the area still stank of burning. Perhaps that was why the trees nearby were empty of birds. The three of us advanced as far as what had been a verandah and peered through the gaping doorway at a jumble of implements and charcoal.

'They'll have to get a new lawnmower,' Lizzie observed brightly.

I saw that. But I was looking at a pile of old . . . paint cans? In a corner. They had been burned quite thoroughly.

'Why would anybody set fire to this place?' Lizzie persisted.

Good question. If it was mischief, then I could see why Teddy had assumed Billy Holt was responsible: Billy just didn't like Warings. On the other hand . . . I stared at the paint pots, but it was impossible to see whether any of them had ever held bright red enamel paint. I made noncommittal noises and wondered what proportion of the population of Alford would sympathise with this kind of gesture of disapproval: allowing for a few respectable dissidents like the major and his wife, the vicar, and Mrs Molyneux, say – ninety-eight per cent?

As I thought of her, Mrs Molyneux came striding into sight around the end of the overgrown tennis court. She saw us, waved, and called, 'I'm so sorry! Mrs Jones phoned. I had to stay to explain to Professor Hoare.' Lizzie and I assured her we hadn't started work, and waited.

She shook her head vigorously and then retrieved her glasses. 'Not much luck, I fear. Let me see. He confirmed that his sister had stayed at the Woolpack briefly that year, but they "didn't get on". She packed her bags and "took off", yes, in her car. He does *not* know where she was going. That didn't seem to worry him. Some families are like that, you know.'

I just asked, 'What about the book?'

Mrs Molyneux frowned. 'That was interesting. I do wish I had been able to put the question in person. Mrs Jones's message was that he has never seen the book, but he "believed" his sister had spoken of it.'

I decided that this was the most interesting outcome I could have expected, if not quite the most rewarding from the Warings' standpoint.

'Don't you think that Billy Holt has it?' Lizzie whispered. 'Dido said he knew about the book before she mentioned it to him!'

'He knew *about* it,' Mrs Molyneux emphasised. 'So did I. There has been a story about the village for years of a book that was stolen from Monksdanes, which was supposed to be worth a good deal of money. Some people assume that Joannie stole it. She might have given it to her brother to keep.'

I rubbed my nose. 'He *knew*, yes. But if the whole village did, that doesn't mean anything. Suppose . . .' My mind's eye slipped back to that envelope full of scraps from a modern *Peter Rabbit* and I made a guess at what was happening. 'If Billy knew about it, he'd use it as another way of tormenting Teddy Waring. Basically, Billy wants to make Teddy suffer for everything he did, or didn't do, to Joan.'

'So where is the real book?' Lizzie asked impatiently. 'Is that what we're looking for? Shouldn't we get started?' She made off past the ruin and along the back wall of a stone building that had once been stables, stopping and peering through the first dirty window. 'Should we look through these old sheds?' she suggested over her shoulder. 'There could be absolutely anything in here. I can see an old two-wheeled cart! Ooh, it's lucky this didn't catch – they'd never have got it out!'

Intrigued, Mrs Molyneux and I joined her and found ourselves peering in at a jumble of old things. It was, as Lizzie implied, a place where anything could have been hidden. I located the horse-drawn cart and noticed a spare wheel, some bales of straw so ancient that they seemed to have become welded together, a bicycle . . . Wait a minute, wait a minute . . .

Mrs Molyneux was saying, 'What did you have in mind now, Miss Hoare?'

I didn't answer her. The bicycle that was leaning against the bales was an man's ancient machine with an old-fashioned battery-powered light mounted on the front handlebars, but no rear lamp.

'I could go into the house and get the keys,' Lizzie was suggesting.

Mrs Molyneux said, 'I believe this place is too obvious. Didn't Billy say he searched it while he was employed here? He certainly had access.'

That bicycle was an ancient, upright old machine like thousands of others mouldering in British garden sheds . . . and its tyres were pumped up full and hard. A few things started to make sense.

'Then what *are* we going to do?' Lizzie was asking urgently.

Get away from here, I thought clearly, *before anybody realises what we've just found.* I threw the others a cautious glance, and decided that we were ready for anything in our wellies and old clothes. Even Mrs Molyneux was wearing a tweed skirt which had seen better days and was, probably, thorn-proof.

I tried to pull myself together. 'My idea was that Billy took part-time work here because he thought there was something – his sister's body – waiting to be found in the grounds; and Ted made Helen let him go because . . . well, because he was right. Of course the fire might have destroyed whatever it was. But Billy did say he searched the outbuildings last winter.'

Lizzie shrugged. 'Well, then, what Uncle Barnabas said about the pond.'

'I can guide you there, I believe,' Mrs Molyneux said. 'We used to cut across' – she hesitated and then pointed boldly – 'that way!'

Beyond the lawned areas around the house, a small forest had been growing unchecked. Self-seeding trees, mostly elder and sycamore, had grown into saplings between the gnarled apple trees left from an old orchard. The ground was a tangle of brambles.

'In the old days,' Mrs Molyneux commented, 'they had two or three resident gardeners, I believe. Well.' She plunged into the undergrowth like a jungle guide, stuck at once, dug into the worn leatherette shopping bag that she was carrying, pulled out a pair of gardening gloves and a serious-looking set of pruning shears, and cut her way through. We forced ourselves forward in her wake, first Lizzie, then me carrying Ben, laughing about nothing, high out of harm's way. I tried to ignore the little voice in my head saying that something was coming closer and closer, that if Billy Holt had not set the fire, then maybe Teddy Waring had done it himself. Called the fire brigade. Waited until he knew the fire engines would have wakened people, so that somebody was likely to notice him riding towards the green, pretending to be Billy Holt. Hidden the bike and slipped back on foot? That meant he was trying to incriminate Billy, and why was that so important to him? I tripped over a branch, nearly fell on top of Ben, and pulled myself together.

After ten or fifteen difficult yards, we emerged on to an overgrown bank and looked down into a little sunken oval area.

The flattened space at the bottom was thick with water iris coming into bloom.

'There!' Mrs Molyneux puffed.

I stared at it with less satisfaction. If anybody had hidden something down there we wouldn't find it, not without earth-moving equipment. It was a beautiful nook but impenetrable. A white butterfly was floating above the iris blooms and a bird warbled.

It was Mrs Molyneux who came up with a suggestion. 'Never mind, what we should do is space ourselves out and double back and forth across the whole area, the way the police do when they're looking for missing bodies. If we are lucky, and the ground remains fairly open, we will be able to see . . . What are we looking for, I wonder?'

'Anything unusual.'

'We must hope for minimal undergrowth,' Mrs Molyneux commented. 'Well, shall we start?'

We started. We had five or six acres to cover, and after a quarter of an hour I began to wonder whether we would manage. But somebody had been at work. As we continued we began to find piles of dead branches, and even the occasional signs of a bonfire. On our second crossing, I realised that this was Billy's doing. He seemed to have left a narrow band of the tangle more or less untouched, probably so that his activities wouldn't attract attention at the house. Once past this barrier, he had started clearing a swathe of ground where walking became easier. Beyond that again, the bushes merged into a strip of old woodland where successive seasons of fallen leaves had left a deep mulch, discouraging new growth. No human seemed to have set foot here for years, though we came across a couple of spots where explosions of feathers showed that a predator, bird or fox, had been at work.

When Mrs Molyneux sat down at last on the trunk of a fallen tree, Ben and I joined her and then Lizzie wandered up and completed the row.

'I would say,' Mrs Molyneux puffed, 'that we have covered most of the area. Dear me! How *could* they have let this happen to their land? Lawrence Waring would never have stood for it when he was well.'

'I should have brought a thermos,' Lizzie offered glumly. 'Dido, there's nothing down here.'

I handed Ben over to her, climbed up onto the trunk and balanced there, looking around. It seemed to me that the tree cover grew thinner ahead, and I could see more sky.

'We're nearly at the rear wall. I don't want to give up yet. Look, if you two will hang on to Ben, I'll just go and do it, and we'll be finished.'

I didn't wait for their agreement, but took off. This expedition wasn't looking like a particularly good idea now, and I wanted to get it finished, just get back to the house and think about the hidden bicycle, and what to do about that.

Behind me, Lizzie was starting some kind of clapping game with Ben. Ahead, the boundary wall was still out of sight. I pushed into a line of undergrowth, leaving a wisp of my hair snagged on a branch, did a little cursing and started to get pig-headed, really pig-headed. Then arrived at the north wall: the top courses of stone had fallen, and it was no more than four feet high down at this end.

I turned along it and struggled on. It was so quiet that I could still hear Lizzie clearly. I caught another glimpse of wall straight ahead of me and knew I'd reached the corner of the grounds. I avoided a patch of brambles and slanted left. Last stretch.

Now Mrs Molyneux was talking and Ben was still silent, so he was all right back there. A jay screeched. I stopped to watch the patch of blue, white and grey flutter down into the lower branches of one of the trees ahead. That was where the wall should have been but wasn't: I could see an overgrown hedge marking the edge of the field beyond, which explained why nobody had bothered to rebuild the fallen sections. I moved on and had to climb over a young sapling lying across my route. I had one foot on each side of it when I looked down and saw that its trunk had been snapped. The tree was long dead, half buried in brambles, but the thing was that it hadn't just fallen, because a foot or so at the bottom was still almost upright, rooted in the ground. It had broken – snapped . . .

I looked around. A second dead sapling ten feet away was also broken but held upright, caught in a holly tree. *Wait a minute. Wait a minute . . .*

Lizzie was calling. I shouted, 'I'll be right back!' and drew a mental line between the upright sapling and the one under my feet, extended it towards the wall, and set off along the line. I pushed between two bushes and climbed a low mound of fallen stones under ivy, finding a ditch on the other side and, beyond that, the overgrown field hedge.

The wreck sat sideways in the ditch. It had once been an old Volvo estate car. I recognised it even in its present condition, because I'd once owned this model myself; they held large loads of books – or antiques. This one had been burned out. The bonnet and rear door had sprung up, giving the weird impression that it had tried to fly away to escape the flames. Three side doors were wide open, as though exploded outwards. The interior was a rubble of metal frames and rusted springs. Fire had burned all the paint off the body, leaving rust mixed with smooth, blackened patches. I looked for number plates, but they were both gone. Then I turned and shouted until the others came and stood beside me.

'How did that get here?' Lizzie marvelled.

Mrs Molyneux said, 'I see: it was pushed or driven down that way, wasn't it? And then set alight?'

Lizzie shook her head, and was scrambling down into the ditch. Mrs Molyneux and I both screamed at her. She stopped. 'What?' she asked indignantly.

'Come back,' I said coldly, grabbing Ben who showed signs of following her. 'The police call it "contaminating the evidence". Just come back.'

In the old days, following my instructions had never been Lizzie's major consideration. She held her hands up in the air dramatically to show she wouldn't touch anything and took a step closer. 'I can see something inside, on the back seat.'

Mrs Molyneux breathed, 'Oh dear,' into my ear.

'What?'

'Cloth? No, some of it's a leather coat, I think. I see a sleeve. It's clothing, I guess, but it's in a sort of greyish lump.'

I asked what seemed to me to be the obvious question: 'Then how can you tell it's clothing?'

'Well, it's all wet and mouldy and . . . and gummed together, but I can tell.'

'Lizzie, it's not burned?'

'It's such a mess, I can't really be sure, but it doesn't look much burned. I guess I should come up.'

I grabbed her hand and hauled, and she slid up the muddy bank beside us. I didn't let go. 'Man's, or woman's? There wasn't a handbag?'

She frowned. 'I don't know. I'll . . .'

I still didn't let go and told her that she wouldn't. When Mrs Molyneux repeated my message, Lizzie accepted it grudgingly.

Today, I'd remembered my phone. I pulled it out of my pocket, realised that I even remembered the number I needed, and punched it in. When a voice answered, I gave my name and asked for DS Cole and told him what we had found.

When I switched off, we were left staring at the wreck. I picked Ben up, decided to get him out of it, and pushed him into Lizzie's arms.

'You and Mrs Molyneux go up to the house. Take care of Ben, please; he's getting tired and he'd like a drink. Cole is on his way. When he arrives, can one of you show him where to come?'

'But what are you going to do?'

I said, 'I'm staying here. It looks as though this hasn't been touched since '94, and somebody had better make sure it stays like that.' The way I felt, it could easily vanish in a puff of smoke. That was how these things happened here.

'But Dido!' Lizzie wailed.

'Come along,' Mrs Molyneux said abruptly. 'The sooner this finishes, the better.'

Lizzie looked uncertainly from her to me. I said, 'I'll be all right, and somebody has to watch Ben.' I gave him a wave. Mrs Molyneux nodded grimly; they trudged off.

Then I turned around and looked down at Tracy's car and Tracy's clothing. Probably. But the clothing had not burned when the car had. Somebody had put it there later, maybe when the fire had died down.

I was beginning to hear movement in the undergrowth between me and the house. It wasn't Lizzie or Mrs M, not unless they had got themselves turned around; and it wasn't the police who, with luck, were just about climbing into their cars. I tried keeping very still and not breathing. Despite that, the noises came on. Teddy Waring struggled through the brambles. He was holding a shotgun, its muzzle pointed at the ground.

We exchanged long, cold stares.

I said, 'The police are on their way.'

He thought about it for a moment. Then he just nodded. 'I was coming this way for the pigeons. I saw them coming out – Mrs Molyneux and Lizzie with your baby. I knew you'd found it. Do you mind if I wait with you?'

There was another of the big fallen trees just down the bank. Ted ushered me politely to a seat, and then sat down himself, a few feet away. We listened to the jay's screeches and stared at the wreck.

I thought of something: it was a reasonable guess and this was my chance to air it. '*Peter Rabbit*,' I said to him. 'Did you give it to Tracy, or did she steal it from the house?'

After a moment, he said, 'I gave it to her, and I didn't have the guts to tell Father. This was all my fault. How did you know?'

I said that I hadn't known until now, which silenced him. I listened to the pigeons roo-cooing in the trees at the edge of the field.

He said suddenly, 'Mummy will sell the house. There's nothing left here.' He seemed to be talking to himself. A while later, he spoke again, perhaps to me this time, 'It's all going belly-up now. I shouldn't have come back. I don't know why I did.'

CHAPTER THIRTY-EIGHT

The Rabbit is Dead

———>•◇•<———

Helen and Lizzie had unlocked the drawing room and flung open the shutters and the windows, letting in sunlight and air. We waited, listening to movements indoors and watching the comings and goings at the front of the house. Waiting for it all to work out, or just waiting.

Cole and his people were still in the morning room. At one point, somebody had knocked on the door and asked for Teddy, who left, returned soon, and since then had been sitting in silence at the other end of the room. None of us was saying very much. Mrs Molyneux had gone home and returned with Barnabas; Lizzie had used my mobile to phone Mickey, who was now on his way from Bristol by taxi. At noon Helen had produced a pot of tea and a plate of cucumber sandwiches, then vanished again. We kept listening to the footsteps moving back and forth overhead.

Ben slept on the frayed, eggshell-blue cushions of a sofa, and I sat beside him to make sure he didn't roll off, watching the lawn in front of the house and the gates where a police car was parked. Some people had been gathering in the lane, and at one point I thought I saw Billy there. A farm tractor with a trailer and winch had driven in a little while ago, following the route of the fire engines around the side of the house. When it returned with the rusting wreck on its trailer, under a tarpaulin, that put the finishing touches to the ruin of the lawn.

'Dido, how did you know?' Lizzie asked suddenly. Her voice was subdued.

So it was all up to me again? My first impulse was to scream, '*I don't know anything!*' Then I suddenly saw that Lizzie had given me the chance to get what I really wanted, which was to finish it: to put Ben and Barnabas into the van, yes, and Lizzie too if she wanted that, and drive to London and open the shop and get on with bookselling. And I realised that all I needed to do was lie – lie *really* well. So I was probably going to make a stupendous fool of myself, but it was worth the risk, and a picture had just popped into my head: Hercule Poirot, on Lizzie's television screen, standing up suddenly with his actor's air of unassailable confidence to tell it the way it was and triumph once again over injustice and evil: 'Well, *mes amis* . . .'

I stood up very gently and stepped away from Ben into the middle of the room. The others all looked at me when I moved, but Ben didn't wake. I hooked my thumbs into the pockets of my jeans, threw my shoulders and my head back, looked down my nose at nobody in particular, and started my speech.

'Actually, it was Barnabas: the plan he drew up identified three crimes: two suspicious deaths and one theft. They all happened, all three crimes, without any visible motive, but they *had* to be connected; so I started to look for one motive to connect them all.'

Teddy Waring spoke suddenly from across the room: 'Will you shut up?' He didn't even look at me.

I pushed down a sizzle of rage and said, 'I don't think so.'

Barnabas looked from me to Teddy. I watched his eyes narrow.

'How did you know about the car?' Lizzie demanded again.

I said loftily that it was clear Tracy's car had been disposed of where it wouldn't be found, and there weren't a lot of choices. I had to avoid going into detail, because I still hadn't a clue. Well, literally speaking I had a couple of clues, but I needed a confession. Without a confession, I had nothing certain; with it, we could go home. *Careful* . . .

'Teddy admitted that he gave the *Peter Rabbit* to Tracy, which was what I'd already decided. He thought she'd hidden it in the Barton; that's why he's been making such a fuss about searching the cottage.'

My victim stirred suddenly. 'She told me it was there, or – or anyway she said she'd hidden it nearby.'

'Did she come to Monksdanes to tell you she was going away?' He didn't speak. 'She told her brother she was leaving for good, and then she drove up here. You'd given her the book, and she was going to walk off with it?'

'No! We were going together.'

I focused my mind on the words, *Poor baby!* long enough for my voice to get pitying and contemptuous. Then I said, 'But she was conning you.'

He looked up. 'You don't know anything.'

He was right, but my whole scheme depended on his not being sure of that. I faced him squarely. 'Don't I?' My voice sounded so smug that I wanted to blush. 'Well, tell me!'

Suddenly Mrs Molyneux was on her feet. She crossed the room and sat down beside Ted, putting a hand on his arm. 'It's all right,' she said clearly, 'it's time for plain speaking. You owe those dead girls the truth, don't you think?'

Her voice was . . . motherly? I thought fleetingly, *Good grief, she's going to do a good-cop-bad-cop act with me!* And didn't even want to smile.

'What time did she get here, Teddy?'

He hesitated, but we were all staring at him now. 'After lunch.'

I had an inspiration. 'What did your mother and father say when she turned up?'

'Mummy had gone upstairs for her afternoon nap.'

Barnabas spoke quietly behind me, making me jump: 'How did your father actually kill her?'

It was Lizzie, wild-eyed, who shrieked, '*What?*'

Barnabas said simply, 'Motive. Ted's father hated her, he made it clear to Dido at that homecoming dinner, remember? To him, she was a tramp. The relationship, everything that she was, outraged him. He assumed she had stolen the family's book. You didn't hate her, Mr Waring – I believe you. I'm not sure why you didn't stop your father, though. What happened?'

'I was a fool,' he said heavily. 'Father was right. She was no good, she was a thief and a little tart, and yes she probably *was* conning me, but I wouldn't believe him when he warned me, more fool me.'

'Then,' I said, 'why did she come back? She already had the book. She didn't have to come.'

'I thought she needed me to let her in to the Barton to pick it up. She must have left it hidden there when Father chucked her out.'

'She could have smashed a window,' I said coldly. 'Anyway, it's not in the Barton. You know it isn't. So I'll ask you once more: why did you let your father kill her?'

'*He didn't mean to!*' The room rang with his shout. I threw a quick glance at Ben, who stirred briefly. When I turned back, Ted met my eyes. 'I *always* knew that! No, when she turned up at the door that day, we went into the library to talk. I offered her a drink. She used to drink a lot, we both did. I went into the morning room for the Scotch and a couple of glasses and then the kitchen for some water. Father must have heard us and come down to see who it was. He wasn't as bad then as he is now, but it had started. I just don't know what he thought was happening! He'd picked up the poker from the fireplace . . . But he didn't know what he was doing, I swear this is true! When I came back, she was lying on her face in front of the hearth and he was shouting, "Get up, stop pretending, tell me where you put my *Peter Rabbit*" and she was dead.'

'But you didn't call the police, or a doctor, or anything.' I kept my voice flat.

He repeated more confidently, 'She was dead, it wouldn't have done any good.'

Bastard!

I had one more ace up my sleeve and decided to play it now. I was guessing, but going on what I understood about the Warings I asked him, 'What happened when your mother found out?'

'She said we must protect Father, of course. He was old. It would kill him.'

It almost made sense. Not quite.

'When did Joan Holt appear?'

'Later. I don't remember. She was coming to talk about something, I don't know . . . It wasn't one of her regular days, but she had her own key to the back door. I'd driven Tracy's car around and hidden it in the stables. I was waiting until the small hours so I could drive it . . . her . . . out towards Hinton without being noticed. There's a bridge over the shunting yards just west of the main road. I was going to drive the car over the bridge approach and onto the line, and set the petrol tank alight and hike back across the fields. They would have seen the fire from the road, but by the time anybody got down there, it would be too late to find out what had really happened to Tracy. I was carrying the . . . Tracy to the back door when Joannie Holt walked in. I didn't even know she was due. She started screaming. She wouldn't stop, I couldn't shut her up.'

'But you did shut her up,' I risked, shivering.

He said rapidly, 'She was only a . . .' I saw him glance at my face. He stopped and changed tack. 'Yes . . . of course, you're right. I don't make any excuses. I did it. I told them so. I hadn't meant her any harm, believe me, but she was hysterical. I think I panicked; I believe that I put my hand over her mouth only to shut her up, I can't remember. I was upset.'

Mrs Molyneux removed her hand abruptly from his arm and drew away. She pushed her glasses up her nose and stared. I saw she had only just realised what this was really going to be like.

I was still working it through. 'So there you were, you and

your mother and father, with two bodies now. How funny. Was it funny?' I could hear my voice squeaking with rage, as though I'd been breathing helium, so I stopped and breathed deeply. 'One of them was Joannie Holt, and you all wanted her to be dead because Lawrence had got her pregnant, but her family knew she was coming here to talk to him. And the other body was somebody who had no reason to be here, but everybody in the village knew your father'd had a blazing row with her a little while before. It was beginning to look as though he was in serious trouble. And I'd say it was your mother who worked out what to do. She's the sort of person who takes charge.'

'The backbone of the family,' Mrs Molyneux said faintly.

I suddenly understood how angry I was: how really, blazingly angry. I could only let it carry me. 'So she worked it out? You stripped Joan's body . . .' I stopped because I was actually starting to shake.

I heard him mumble, 'Mummy did.'

I was glad I'd heard that. I breathed in hard.

'And you wrapped her in an old plaid blanket, and when it was dark enough you buried her along the ditch, so that if she was ever found – well, anybody in the village might have put her there, it's a public footpath.' The image of Joan Holt's body – every detail of the eyeless skull with its hank of muddy hair, the ragged blanket, the naked foot – came to me again.

'Then – was it then? – you drove Tracy's car down through the garden, over the broken wall and into the ditch, and set fire to it. Not as good as the railway line, but private enough for the fire not to be noticed at that time of night. I guess you forgot at first that you needed to get rid of Tracy's clothes too, but you came back for them. By the time you went down to the car a second time and threw them inside, the fire was dying down and they weren't destroyed, but I don't suppose you waited to see, and you never had a chance to go back again. You dressed Tracy's body in Joan's clothes and blew her face away with a shotgun – out there in the stables, was it? – and brought her in through the library window wearing your muddy boots, which wasn't too clever because they left traces the police found; and you invented a story about a burglary. And now you had a body that looked pretty much like Joannie, but usefully wasn't pregnant, which turned Joannie into a liar and a crook; and it was the middle of the night, which gave you the chance to invent the story about her breaking in to the library. And then at last Lawrence called the police, and they found you there with the wrong body, and you told them you'd accidentally killed poor little Joan Holt, who was nothing but a sneak thief, and you were crying.' I looked at him, hunched on the settee.

'You served a few years and came home; and everything went wrong, mostly because Billy Holt had guessed part of the truth. You made Helen fire him before you realised he wouldn't stop looking. And you knew there were lots of things at Monksdanes, lies and secrets, for him to find. So you tried to frame him, just as you had his sister, maybe get him arrested, get rid of him, make him back off at least. He played right into your hands with his dead animals on the doorstep. You thought you'd got him. *You* threw that red paint on the cottage and acted as though you blamed Billy, didn't you? I kept seeing you acting a part; I just didn't understand why. *You* set the fire and called the emergency services, and then you tried to frame him again by riding away on a bike like his. It was really too long after the fire had started; but you had to wait for the fire engines to wake a lot of people, so somebody would notice a cyclist like Billy riding towards Billy's house. *You* hid the bike down the track and sneaked home on foot, only I found it. I know where you've hidden it.' I looked at him again. 'You can cry now, if you want to. I've finished.'

The door opened. Helen said, 'They're here. If you want to say goodbye . . .' She stopped and looked from Teddy to Lizzie, and then the rest of us.

Barnabas said, 'We'll wait here. No point getting in the way.'

His tone was so final that Helen, bewildered, closed the door and went away.

I'd had my back to the windows and hadn't noticed the ambulance arrive, but it was parked out front when I turned to look. We listened to them bring the wheelchair down the main staircase, and saw them outside the windows: two men and a woman in uniform, Lawrence dressed in a dark suit, blank-faced and motionless as they manoeuvred his chair into position and hoisted it in. He looked as though he had already left. Helen came into sight, carrying a suitcase and pushing it through the rear door, then stood back, hugging herself in the cool wind; and finally Rose followed her husband, stiffly refusing any help as she climbed into the vehicle, not looking back. The double doors slammed.

'Time he went,' Lizzie said harshly.

Teddy was silent.

'He needs proper nursing,' Mrs Molyneux remarked distantly.

'Now that they've gone,' I suggested to Teddy, 'isn't it time you did something?'

'What's the point?' Mrs Molyneux asked suddenly. 'We must stop now, Miss Hoare. Lawrence obviously can't stand trial, and Teddy has already served his sentence for what he did.'

'Not for everything,' I said, still cold. *Not for his arrogance, not for his cowardice . . .*

It was Barnabas who said quietly, 'There will be other charges, Mrs Molyneux. And there should be an ending. "All the king's horses . . ." '

When somebody knocked on the door, I took it on myself to call out, 'Come in!' because it seemed that nobody else would.

It was Cole. He held a clear plastic bag. He took us all in, frowned, hesitated, then walked across the silent room to me and held it out. 'You're some kind of second-hand bookseller, aren't you? Can you tell me what this is?'

Oh, I could. It was so damaged, I was a little impressed that he had recognised enough to know I was the person to ask. The object in the plastic bag had once been a book in a little slipcase, just the right size for a child's hands; but it was badly burned, and had soaked and soaked again in years of rain.

I said, 'That was in the car?'

'Under the front seat, in a leather handbag that gave it a little protection. It's a book; the pages are stuck together, but I think I can see handwriting. I don't know if it's a diary or notebook. If it is, I'd better get Forensics to pick it apart, but it'll be a long job getting anything out of the mess, and it looks too small for a diary.'

I handed back the plastic bag. 'Don't bother,' I said with authority. 'It's only a children's story book: *The Tale of Peter Rabbit.* Mr Waring can tell you about it.' Ben was stirring. I went and picked him up and told him, 'Come on, we can go home.'

If we hurried to pack and load, I reckoned that we'd be getting in to London in time for the rush hour; and I'd suddenly noticed just how much I was looking forward to relaxing again in an ordinary, cosy traffic jam on the Marylebone Road.